Pelly's Quest.

A Victorian African Adventure.

By

Damian P.O'Connor

For those who might find the tale of a disgraced young Englishman finding redemption among the Tswana people during the imperial expansion in Africa hard to believe, I would respectfully refer the reader to the Colonial Office file CO879/23 African No.31 Bechuanaland Affairs, which is available at the National Archives at Kew, or to an article entitled 'Christopher Bethell and the Securing of the Bechuanaland Frontier 1878-1884' by Andrew Manson which can be found in the Journal of Southern African Studies Vol 24 No 3, 1998.

Chapter 1

Folly and Fall

East Anglia 1873

All I needed was a deuce and it would be all right. I knew the rule about sticking at sixteen but that five card trick would scoop the pool and put me well into the black. I was young then.

It had been a bad day at Newmarket with my thoroughbred certs turning out to be three-legged donkeys and I was in well over my head already when the horse that would have made it all back stumbled at the last and let *Kimberley Diamond* past the post by a nose. I had been borrowing heavily on the strength of my father's credit and now the only way I knew how to redeem it would be at the card table. I thought it lucky at the time that I knew a place where a seat at the tables would be held for me, but it was of course the worst sort of luck. At 19, I, Nicholas Pelly – 'Pelly' to all and sundry - had already been bailed out once by my father and the taps, sharps, toughs and roughs who lived in this *demi-monde* knew that it wouldn't happen many times more and they should make the most of it. The low lit paneled back room at the *Cross Keys* had seen foolish young men on many occasions before and the red boozed out faces and cold watery eyes that frequented it could calculate to a button the length of the shirt that they would take. At the time I was drunk, but I really thought I was more alive, quicker, more able to see the risk, calculate the odds, feel the instinct, than I had ever been before. The sharps had me well measured though and fed me more gin and water, fed me more credit and fed me more cards whenever I asked for them.

All I needed though was a deuce and it would be all right.

Salcombe, the putty faced banker with hair like a haze of cloud, weighed up the cards in the crumpled shoe, and weighed up the hand on the green baize in front of me; Ten of Clubs, Three of Hearts, Three of Diamonds, Three of Spades; total 19. I surveyed the hands of the seven other players; there were three aces, four kings and four queens among them, but no deuces. The odds seemed good and the reward, there in front of me in Bank of England notes, looked infinitely greater than the risk. I was sweating booze, thrumming with the certainty of winning, feeling more alive at that table than anywhere else in the grey world that I seemed to inhabit back then. I was concentrating on the shoe, demanding it yield up that deuce by sheer force of will, my whole world hanging on the turn of a friendly card and believing that I had that same world by the ears because my luck *must* change. It was my turn, my *time*.

Salcombe looked back at me, his pale blue eyes floating in albumen, his corneas yellow with rheum and corruption. He twitched his head, asking me for a decision and I felt the tension.

I needed a deuce and it would all be right.

'Twist,' I said.

'Bust,' replied Salcombe. He said it without emotion, and threw me an Ace. 'That's two hundred you're down, Mr.Pelly. I hope your father's good for it.'

I couldn't believe it but there was the Ace of Spades, the Devil's own card, mocking me.

'Damn.' I gasped in protest. 'That can't be right! I was absolutely sure...I saw the deal! Pull the next one out.'

The other players didn't move, but let their eyes slide from one to the other, avoiding contact with mine and in that moment I knew I had been fleeced. Any appeal would be pointless. Even if there had been foul play, none of the other players would ever come clean about anything ever, *ever*, where Salcombe, cards and money were concerned.

'If you insist,' said Salcombe, with a shrug. 'But it doesn't alter the fact that you're bust, sonny.'

I confess I watched in disbelief as the fat hands of the banker threw out the next card; Ten of Diamonds, then the Eight of Clubs and then, to emphasise my total failure, the Jack of Spades.

I put my head and hands down on the baize momentarily, then threw myself back and breathed out heavily, wondering how I had miscounted the cards. I had been so sure and I did not know where I had made the mistake, but that mistake now sat heavily on my chest mocking me like a clockwork grinning monkey. Trying to master the shock and regain control of my trembling hands, I took a pull at the gin and then made to refill the glass, but the bottle was snatched away.

'Cash only at the bar,' said Salcombe, flatly. 'You know that. And I prefer my notes of hand written legibly, if you please. Carter, over there, will help you.'

I knew Carter, of course. He had heavily muscled forearms scarred with crown and anchor tattoos, a mass of curly black hair and the brow of a battleship bosun and I knew what was coming. I nodded weakly, knowing any excuse was useless, stood wearily and left the table to the other players, who just grunted in disinterested farewell. They had seen young rakes fleeced by their own folly too many times before to be much excited by it and I finally realized why there was a rule about sticking at sixteen. Again, being young, I looked at the door, then at Carter, wondering if I could beat him the five yards to it.

'It's locked, young sir,' said Carter, and I knew it was hopeless. Weariness rose up in me, a bone weary curse at my own cupidity and a black curse at the explanations I would have to give for the second fortune I had lost in an attempt to get rich quick.

'No need for this to be any more unpleasant than it has to be,' said Carter. He had done this so many times before that he spoke quietly, almost cheerfully, but though the words came out by rote, there was no mistaking the force that lay behind them. 'Just send the note to your father. Soonest done, soonest mended and there's worse things happen at sea, I can tell you.'

He placed pen, paper and an ink horn on a plain ebony table against the wall and held the chair out for me to sit.

'Do you want me to give you the words or can you manage yourself?' he asked, as though he were some rough uncle.

I shook my head in refusal of the offer and sat down. I took the pen, dipped it in the ink and let my hand waver over the paper. Just then the tears welled up in my eyes and I beat my hands to my head in shame and rage, spattering ink across my shirt. *How could I have been so wrong! All day! Was it that single magpie that jinxed me? What will I tell Father?*

'Short and sweet is best,' said Carter. *'Dear Father, I have lost money at cards...'*

'I know what to do, damn you,' I hissed.

'As you wish, sir,' said Carter evenly, and then placing a heavy knuckled hand on my shoulder, his voice changed to a low, deep threat. *'Just fucking do it then.'*

I was a strong young man then, a tall six feet with broad shoulders, long thighs and a flat belly to match. My hair was blonde and my skin clear, barring a scatter of freckles across the nose, with a broad leonine forehead crowning a face that tapered down to a strong prow of a chin, marked with a few scrubby red bristles of beard. I was said to be handsome, but there was always a blackness within and I carried a tick when irritated, a quick shake of the head, four movements in one, like a shudder which was as much a dismissal as a warning, people said. The dairy maids and village girls knew it; they had used me in the hayloft at harvest as I had used them, but they did not love me and none would have wanted me as a husband or father whether I was heir to the farm or not. *Nicholas Pelly God forgive you for a whoreson* was their collective wisdom, scratched into the lath and plaster of the top barn at Dines Hall, which all things considered, was fair.

Carter's breath in my ear made my gorge rise. He stank of fish and onions and stale tobacco and looking up over my shoulder, I saw the double chin, broken gums and stained teeth and hated the idea of being made to do the bidding of scum like this. With a sudden snap, I jammed my right elbow back into his groin, leaped out of the chair, shoved another man aside with my left arm and dived for the door as though I could swim to it. I had not gone two paces however before Carter's mate, a wiry old pugilist with a leer like every sin ever committed, stepped into me and slammed a blow under my chin that lifted me so high that my head hit the ground while my feet were still in the air. I had never been hit so hard before and never since; as a big youth accustomed to being accorded a wide berth, I was not used to being hit at all. My head hit with the sound of a coconut striking stone and I can still hear it now. Then, all round me were bigger men, more dangerous than me, their fists full of experience, steel and stamina and when Carter put his boot on my face and ground the skin off it, I wrenched away at the foot in vain.

'Alright Carter, that's enough,' called Salcombe, looking up from the table. 'I want his money not his medical bills.'

Carter stepped back and I looked up at the circle of heads above me. He was breathing heavily, but his mate the pugilist looked cool, relaxed and a glint in his eye told me that there would always be another punch like that on its way and I had no appetite for it. I pulled myself to a sitting position, scuffing shirt and breeches on the brown tiled floor, rubbing my throat and feeling the weight of that monkey on my chest again.

'*Captain* Pelly *will* pay up,' said Salcombe, speaking to Carter but directing his words to me. 'These notes of hand are actionable as contracts in a court of law and his father knows this. But he won't go to law to dispute them because his credit will collapse with every chandler, farrier and factor between here and Essex. He's got two daughters of marryin' age too and won't want it known to their suitors that their dowry could disappear over a weekend here at Newmarket, or down at Chelmsford races where his son and heir pulled a stunt like this two years ago. So write the letter for him, and make it *guineas* rather than pounds for your trouble.'

'Wait!' I cried, outraged. 'I owe you two hundred *pounds* not guineas…'

'Actually,' called Salcombe, pulling a cigar out of his waistcoat pocket, his voice acrid. 'You owe me six hundred since I bought your Newmarket debt off Forsythe before you got here. Clever lad for a bookie, he is. Didn't reckon he had the means to make you pay on those notes.'

He pushed the cigar into the black hole of his mouth, lit up and puffed out tobacco smoke.

'Make no mistake, young Pelly. I *do* have the means to make you pay. And any more pony from you and you'll be signing that horse away too.'

'What? This is…you can't take my horse! I'll find it and put the law on you, you bloody man.'

'The law?' Salcombe coughed. 'Don't make me laugh. *Yes Mr. Peeler my horse has gone missing. Yes Mr. Peeler it was a brown one. In Newmarket, Mr. Peeler, it was.* How many brown horses in Newmarket, Carter?'

'Before or after the Gypsies have gone up to Appleby?' rasped Carter, hacking a laugh out.

There was an answering cackle from around the room as the other gamblers laid down their cards to watch the fish wriggle.

'You bloody yokels think you're clever, don't you?' I shouted. 'Well, I'm *rich* and my family counts for something in these parts, you'll see.'

There was another guffaw from the assembly. Salcombe indicated the gin bottle and bid it go round as he came to stand over me, his shirt scrambling out from under his waistcoat like a line of dirty surf on a grey beach. He tapped his ash over me, with a look of disgust.

'*Rich*, is it?' he said, and big though I was I shrank from the menace in the voice. 'I'll buy and sell you, you little *shit*. And if I let you another hour at my table I'd buy and sell your father and mother too, but that *would* mean involving lawyers and such unsavoury folk.'

I saw red at the mention of my mother and struggled up to go for him, but the pugilist dropped me back onto the floorboards like a sack of turnips before I had got halfway to my feet. Carter grimaced, shook his head, handed me the blank piece of paper and then stamped down hard on my ankle. I squawked in agony as I felt something crack.

Salcombe wasn't finished yet though. He towered over me, tapped ash over me again and then let a glob of white sputum crawl out of his mouth and drip onto my face.

'Aye, and your *fucking* sisters too, if I wanted them.'

Bloodied, bruised, my face scraped raw, the cold grawl sliding down my cheek, my ankle swelling inside my boot and with the revolting picture of the banker and Carter pawing at my sisters floating in front of me, I subsided, all resistance gone. I took the pen and paper and sweeping away the sawdust, tobacco ash and smuts from the fire, cleared a space on the floor and scribbled my name away. I could hardly bear to look at my hand as I did so and instead concentrated on a cockroach peering at me from the underside of the nearby table.

If I had got a deuce, it would have all been right, I cursed.

I was a real piece of work back then.

Riding home in the dark, I let the horse plod. It knew its own way and didn't need me to steer and I had no will left to drive it anyway. Fighting hard to hold back the tears of pain and humiliation, my throat a fist and my stomach a stone, I cursed at my losses and swore to serve out all those who had brought me to this bind, even if I swung for it. My hatred began with the Newmarket stable hand who had claimed to know so much, who had taken my cash so readily and whose tips turned out to be tat; he was smaller than I so I would beat him to a pulp in his own stable yard. Salcombe, I would shoot personally, like a dog in a ditch, anonymously, on a dark night to hide me, while Carter I would leave maimed so that he could rue every day that he lived and starved in pain by the Poorhouse wall. The bookie, Forsythe, I would rob, just as he had robbed his punters with his bent odds and cocky banter, and break his fingers with a bludgeon so he would never write another stub. All this would come to pass just as soon as I got home to the gun cupboards.

I was angry because it was all so *unfair*. Gambling wasn't supposed to work like this, I railed. Sometimes you won, sometimes you lost and that was all in the way of it. Without the occasional disappointment, there could be no triumph or elation when a man's intelligence, wit and daring brought him his due reward and marked him out from the run of the ignorant cattle that made up most of humanity. *Fortune is a woman*, I had read at school, *and if you are to keep her under, she must be beaten and ill-used, for she is a lover of the adventurous, audacious young man.* Where was she today, though, the bitch?

It had always been this way though, I thought gloomily in my self-pity. I had been cheated from the day I was born. I had seen my mother fuss around my younger sisters, always ready to indulge them with a new ribbon or some such treat while I could go hungry or hang. I should have been Rugger captain at school, but that bastard Johnson had got it because he sucked up to the masters so, always willing to fag or bash a blasted book. I should have had that place in the army; how could it be my fault that mother had forgotten to remind me of the appointment with Colonel Pinkerton? Turning off the main road into the driveway up to the family home at Dines Hall, I felt the wind sough through the elms and heard the muttering of the horses in the army stud across the hay field southward. Beyond that, there was a light on in the vicarage, where that stupid bloody Reverend skulked; I had relied on his tuition to get me a place at Cambridge, but he was no bloody good and I had failed the exam because of his inability to teach me properly. I reasoned that I would have to rely on my own wits if I was to make my way in a world that had clearly set its face against me and gambling seemed the fastest way to do it back then.

There was a lamp burning in the quad at Dines Hall too, lighting up the red brick and showing the clock beneath the running fox weather vane. It was a comfortable, prosperous house, the house of a gentleman farmer of the middling sort and although my father did not give himself airs, a proudly respectable house. It was past midnight and there wasn't a glim anywhere, so I let the horse walk past the iron gates and make for the stables, where I dismounted, landing with a gasp on my swollen ankle and, without bothering to unsaddle, tied the horse to a stall ring. The kitchen door was never locked and there was always bread, beer and cheese under a cover on the table for the early risers and the booze had made me hungry. My mouth was dry from the gin and water too and I could still taste Carter's fish breath on my swollen lip, so once I was in, I drew a good measure from the barrel and poured it into me. My mouth smarted where my gums had bled and I touched a loose tooth gingerly with my tongue but still I took another and another long draught. I wanted to be drunk, could not think of anything better than to be drunk and if my mother found me face down in my own puke then it was her fault for not taking better care of me, wasn't it?

I felt the pains all over my body and touched a livid bruise that was tight across my nose and temple. I had a swollen eyebrow, a heavy thumping at the back of my head and a hot stinging across the grazes of my face. My ribs hurt too, from the second blow from the pugilist and although I knew they were not broken, it still hurt to breathe. The sock in my boot was wet and twisted and I could barely put my weight on it, my ankle stiff as a corpse now as I smeared cheddar cheese into my mouth with fingers that were seized and bruised from the struggle. I couldn't remember how I had received that wound, but as I ate in bitterness and empty defiance I knew it hurt now and would hurt worse in the morning. I had been beaten, badly, completely and I was disgusted with a world that could do this to me. Taking my tankard, I went out into the night intending to walk and clear my head, but my ankle would not let me and my head was not strong enough for the liquor I had forced into it, so I ended up just crumpling and passed out on the flags of the kitchen yard.

I was woken a couple of hours later by the voices of Big George and Willie, two farmhands who were always the first in to work, but I preferred to play dead. It was still dark and the stone flags were cold against my cheek and my shirt had stuck to my back, but I realized that here, inside my own head I was at least alone and free to put off the reckoning that was coming. This was the last time that I would be free, for when that letter was delivered sometime today, my father would take stern measures against me. Last time I had been forgiven and made to work off my stupidity with a couple of weeks hard labour, hedging and ditching with the village hands but I knew that I would not be let off so lightly on a second offence.

'Young Master Nicholas has been at it again,' I heard Big George say. I kept my eyes firmly shut but my mind's eye showed the craggy black hair, gap toothed grin and cheerful attitude of the man. Big George the farm foreman had always been a puzzle to me; I couldn't understand how he could exude such contentment when he had so little money and worked so hard for so many long hours.

'Such a waste, when you think of what he might be with all that money and eddication,' answered Willie the groom. As I lay there, I imagined him shaking his head the way that he did whenever there was a problem in the stables. 'Should we get him up or leave him?'

'We can't leave him out here, he'll catch his death,' said Big George. 'Not that he'd be any great loss, mind, but I daresay it would cost money to bury him.'

'We should turn him over and sit him up,' agreed Willie. 'If only to see if the little turd's alive.'

I felt a rough hand on my shoulder, as rough as Carter's, and shook it off. I was not used to being spoken of like this.

'Well, he's alive, at least,' said George, indifferently. 'That settles that. Best call for the Captain – he'll be about soon enough anyway.'

I felt the blackness come over again and pain of the beating and the hangover made me wish I was dead. This life was worthless anyway, I cursed, now that all chance of a career in the army or entry to Cambridge was gone. I *would* not, *could* not, face a life among the dullards who made up my father's farmhands or submit to the absolute hidebound hypocrisy and boredom of village life. I would not waste my life by marrying locally to some stupid brood mare who would demand brats and bangles and all the rest of it, her only thought to live the same old life over and over again. Where was the excitement and adventure in that? It would be no more than a treadmill existence and if pain was the price of a life trusted to that bitch Fortune, then it was a price worth paying; *any price* was worth paying to avoid that bleak and banal future. I think I passed out again then.

The next time I awoke, it was in the comfort of my own bed, on starched, clean sheets that smelled of lavender. The curtains were closed and the heavy velvet gave off its own darkness, allowing only a few bars of light into the prison this room now was. I was still stiff and my mouth was desert dry, and when I lifted my head off the pillow I felt a hammer blow from inside my skull. I gathered only slowly that I had been bathed and bandaged; two fingers of my left hand had been splinted together and when I touched my eyebrow I felt a stitch there. Lifting up the sheets, I saw that my chest had been swaddled and then sank back with a pain that took my breath away, as though I had stepped into unexpectedly hot water. I waited for the wave of agony to pass and then pulled back the sheet to look at my ankle and saw my toes, purple and swollen, bulging out of the tight bandage and feeling hot and tight enough to burst. I tried to remember getting here, but my last recollection was of Big George and Willie and although I had been drunk before, the hangover was usually accompanied by a flood of embarrassment as my memory held me to account for the actions of the night before. This time I had no recollection of being bathed and bandaged; but I remembered well enough Salcombe, Carter and that bone shattering fist.

For that day and the next, I lay alone, never leaving the bed except to limp to the earth closet. I had no desire to look out into the light and was only moved to curiosity when I heard a single gunshot from the direction of the stables. An hour later, I heard the vet and my father in conversation in the hallway downstairs and although I could not make out the words, I could hear the sound of regret clearly. Sometime later, there was a conversation between mother and father in another part of the house; the same indistinct words, the same unmistakable tone. An hour later and my mother and sisters had left the house in the carriage, with trunks packed for a long stay. I guessed that they would be off to my Aunt's in Stowmarket, which they did whenever Father was clearing the decks for action. There were other comings and goings, more than was usual, I thought, but there seemed to be a heavy silence woven in amongst the normal sounds of geese and chickens, the grunting of the pigs that carried all the way from the top field and the usual tapping of the copper beech against the windows. It was as though there had been a death in the family.

The summons for the accounting I must have came on the third day, after the Doctor had pronounced me free of fever, if not, he added significantly, of sickness.

'Get up, you bloody man,' was his parting shot as he closed his black bag. 'Broken bones I can set, but your malady is not curable by my skill.'

'Go back to your poxes, Quack,' I spat back. 'You've been paid, haven't you?'

'The Captain asks that you attend him in his study, Master Nicholas,' chimed Maggie, her head appearing around the door as the Doctor left. 'He was particular that you come as soon as you may, sir.'

I noted the barely concealed delight in her voice as my stomach tightened in nervous anticipation. *How the mighty fall,* she would be prating down among the other servants; and this *was* my fall and I knew it could not be avoided. I pulled on my trousers slowly, painfully and struggled into a shirt, tucking it in with my right hand while I held my left hand aside. I chose a stick that had been placed for my use by the bedside and slid my uninjured foot into a boot before taking a deep breath and heading for the door. Going down the stairs, I tried to marshal the arguments that I had constructed in the last hours but I knew my excuses were thin. They were all I had though and I hoped that they might at least deflect the blow or mitigate its impact. As I came face to face with the closed door of the study, I knew that they would not stand up to much however and as thin as the truth was I decided to stick to a watered down version of it because my old man was too downy a bird to fall for a lie. If I knew my father, he would have all the facts before him and all I would be allowed would be a chance to explain my stupidity but not challenge it. It had been this way since I was a child due a whipping for a broken window or a drowned cat. I put my head down, tapped and pushed open the door.

My father, Captain Pelly, was indeed ready for me. He stood behind his desk, his back to the bookcase, the ship model before him and the clock ticking heavily through wisp of pipe smoke hanging in the still air. As soon as I entered the room I could see the fury in his coal black eyes and the marks of frustration in his ruffled grey hair. I saw the dirty papers with my handwriting on them laid out on the desk in front of him, a desk that was piled with an array of folders and ledgers. It was usually empty, *squared away*; my father was fond of his nautical expressions, picked up when he had served aboard an Indiaman as a youth. The title was an honorific or, as I preferred to think at times like this, just another one of his hypocritical bloody old frauds.

'So, we are here again, but worse,' began my father, announcing the charges loudly and clearly. 'Last time it was two hundred pounds, this time it is six hundred guineas. How do you propose to clear these - *your* - debts?'

'Six hundred *guineas?*' I said in disbelief. 'But it should only be *pounds*, I swear...'

'Guineas or pounds? What difference does it make? What's five percent to a man like you?' he replied. 'Why with your wondrous ability, you'll recoup it in no time. I just want to know how you are going to pay.'

'You know, I can't pay,' I flared. 'So why have at me like this?'

'Why have at you?' My father stopped himself, closed his mouth and turned his head to one side while I took in the profile of the sharp nose and the gritted teeth.

'Look, father,' I said, dissembling. 'I was cheated. It wasn't my fault. Why don't you hire a lawyer to sue them or something? Or just burn the notes – who would know? If it came to court, it would be your word against a bunch of swindlers. No-one would believe *them*. Not over you.'

I waited anxiously as my father took all this in. I could see his mouth working, chewing at his lip in agitation and wondered if I could actually persuade the old man to perjure himself. *It would make perfect sense*, I thought, feeling the urge to gamble rising and seizing on the justification that my creditors were hardly respectable merchants, so perjury would be no great sin. *I wonder what the odds are that he'll burn the notes and face down Salcombe?*

Father stood up and went to the window. He stared out through the leaded panes and shot a weather eye at the late summer sky. There were motes in the dappled light like slowly falling stars.

'Do you know how much six hundred guineas is?'

I realized that he had dismissed my proposal without thinking about it. I suspected that he had not even heard it at the time, although I knew better later. I didn't understand the question though and shrugged my shoulders and slowly shook my head.

'I thought not,' he said coldly, gesturing out of the window. 'But Big George out there does. I pay him fourteen shillings per week. That's thirty five guineas a year, give or take. So twenty years of labour you would owe me, if I was minded to take on your debt.'

'If mother had reminded me in time about the interview will Colonel Pinkerton I could have paid you back easily,' I replied. 'Perhaps he might have another vacancy you could buy for me.'

My father pursed his lips and looked down in despair.

'The purchase of officer rank in the army has been abolished. The arrangement is no longer possible. Now you will have to get in on *merit*. No,' he said. 'I will pay this debt though I cannot do it easily and without pain to people I like and respect. *You* do not fall into that category anymore.' He sighed heavily, slowly, and then gave judgement. 'You will confine yourself to your room and may take your exercise in the rear paddock until arrangements have been made for your removal from this house. Until then, you will do such work as I direct.'

'What?' I cried in outrage. 'What do you mean by *removal from this house*? What does Mother say about it? Where am I to go?'

'Your future has been discussed at length, but I also have to look to the future of your sisters,' replied my father returning to his desk. He turned over some papers and sat down. 'I cannot provide for them while you are under my roof, careless of my property and careless of this family. You will therefore do as you are told or I will hand you over to *your* creditors and you may take your chances with them.'

For two weeks I ate my meals in my room, paced the rear paddock and thought about my predicament. I tried to guess what my father was arranging for me, for I was sure he was arranging *something*, but I had no idea what. I discounted the prospect of being made to labour on the farm as being too ridiculous and racked my brains for a clue, a hint of what my exile would be. Would I be sent to sea to serve as a common seaman before the mast? I found the prospect of being cooped up with the likes of Carter revolting. Perhaps I might be sent as apprentice to a chandler or city merchant, there to scratch away in boredom and frustration among the sacks of dusty corn or the reams of dry paper? Forced down to the garrison at Colchester and condemned to life as a gentleman ranker? I went round and round in circles but with no new intelligence my rage was pointless. I confess that those weeks in limbo were among the worst of my life and that if ever I were to be hanged, I would want it done directly without waiting for leave to appeal, for it is the waiting more than the sentence that is the greater trial.

Looking across at the line of poplars standing guard against the bitter blast of the East Anglian north wind, I saw the new scar in the turf where they had buried my horse. It was in a shallow grave, where it would be best preserved until the Master of Fox Hounds came by with his men to dig it up and put it through the flesh house for the hounds. At that moment, the death of the horse was the only thing in that mess that I really felt sorry for, beyond myself. I recognized that I had made stupid mistakes at Newmarket races, one after the other, but I could not bring myself to feel particularly sorry for them. I knew I had left his father with my debts and wished I hadn't; but I did not regret the *act* of gambling on that deuce, only that I had *lost*. I wished my mother and sisters had not had their social position endangered, but I could not bring myself to feel regret that I had lived recklessly and in the moment, that I had lived *audaciously*. Given the chance, I knew I would do it all over again, and on that reflection, I understood why my father wanted rid of me. I would have done the same in his shoes.

The horse was another matter though. I had always felt a greater respect for animals than for people. I admired the crafty fox started from its covert, the dogged hound that hunted it and the sturdy horse that commanded the chase. I admired the clean fierceness of the pike and the merciless stoat, the stoop of the hawk and the fine senses of the running deer. The only thing that came close to gambling was the hunt, when the dogs worked the copses or the terriers pinned the fox when it went to ground and the horses sweated, champed and snorted. There was no finer moment than when the stag's head came up, looked right back in your eye and knew that you had stalked it, that your craft in the wood was better than his, that your instinct was sharper than his; the moment when you held his eye in yours, placed the foresight on his head and squeezed the trigger; some people preferred the heart shot as easier, but the deer would bolt for half a mile or more before it died and I thought this showed disrespect for the animal. Each of the four times that I stalked the deer, I had chosen the headshot because it killed the animal outright; about the only people I was popular with then were the butchers, who appreciated a carcass not shredded by the shattered shoulder blade resulting from a heart shot. Like the stags, the horse that lay under the paddock had been true to its instinct and its training and it was my own carelessness in not unsaddling, in not rubbing the animal down, in not putting it into the warm stable that had killed it. I had not kept my side of the ancient bargain that in return for the service, meat, hide and milk given to man an animal should be cared for and not abused. For this, I was genuinely sorry.

As the third week of my disgrace began, I noticed an increase in the traffic to and from the house. From my prison window, I saw Carter, delivering a final demand no doubt, and I saw the boy who brought the telegrams in from the Newmarket office more than once, carrying my future with him, folded in a manila envelope. On the day, I saw Maggie trotting across the paddock towards me in her cap and apron, half running and then walking in between, I looked up at the sky and though trembling with anxiety and anticipation, gave a sigh of relief that at least the waiting was over. The noose about my neck would either be tightened or cast off, and I resolved to take whatever was coming; for now, anything was better than this limbo.

'I know, Maggie,' I said. 'I'm coming. To the study?'

'Oh no, Master Nicholas,' she shook her head. Her eyes were red from crying and I saw that she was angry but trying not to show it. 'You are to go with Big George directly. You are wanted at the Yellow house.'

The Yellow house was a good sized cottage surrounded by a hedge full of dog roses on the edge of the estate. It had been home to the Stockwell family for as long as anyone could remember and I had drunk elderflower cordial and eaten sausages there as a child. Judith and Ezekiel farmed the small holding that went with the house and supplemented their income by taking in washing or day labouring on the estate. They had two sons who had gone for work in London and their two daughters were in service. Only Daisy remained at home. She was a black haired spitfire and a particular friend of Maggie's and I had taken a tumble with her last harvest even though I had promised to meet Maggie. I didn't know it for sure, but I suspected it was Maggie's handwriting on the wall of the top barn.

Big George was waiting at the house with a couple of cobs, saddled and ready. I tried to ask him what was up, but he would not answer, simply indicating the horse and then turning in the direction of the Yellow house. It was a mile or more, beyond the top barn to the Stockwell's home but I could see a small crowd and a cart outside it long before we reached it. A little closer and I saw Carter, astride a horse close by my father, and then Daisy Stockwell came out of the house carrying a bundle wrapped up in a sheet and threw it atop an upturned table on the cart. The Stockwells were being evicted and the grinning monkey was suddenly back on my chest; this was how my debts were to be cleared and I revolted at the thought.

I ran the horse forward across the black ash of the burned stubble to confront my father and a murmur of discontent rose up from the villagers at my approach.

'Father, I ask you; don't do this,' I said, my words stumbling out. 'It isn't fair to throw the Stockwells out to pay off the likes of *him*.'

I pointed at Carter and gave him a black look of hatred and defiance. Carter wasn't impressed though and returned my disapprobation with a crooked grin and a casual shrug.

'Oh, *I'm* not doing it,' replied my father, placing a heavy emphasis on the personal pronoun, and I was struck by the look of contempt that came with it. 'But this debt must be redeemed and with American grain in the market driving down prices every week, I must liquidate some capital for the purpose. So, Nicholas Pelly, do not accuse *me* of doing *anything* at all, for this is *your* work. *You* did it and I wanted you to see it. Now on your way.'

'God damn you Nick Pelly!' shouted Daisy Stockwell as she came round the house, brim full of spite and hatred as I turned my horse. 'May the Devil take your black soul!'

Judith Stockwell flew out of the house to silence her, dragging her back by the arm.

'Be silent child.' She was in tears. 'We will need a character from the Captain if we are to find another situation.'

'Damn the character and damn the whole Devil's brood!' blazed Daisy, flinging an accusatory arm straight at me and I felt it jab as hard as a poker into my chest.

'Away with you, boy,' ordered my father, and Big George took my bridle and began to drag the cob away. 'You will find your travelling arrangements ready for you when you get back to the house and I expect you to be gone by the time I return.'

Tears welled up in my eyes as it finally dawned on me that my actions had consequences of a leaden finality for myself, for my family and the blameless Stockwells. The remembered taste of Elderflower was suddenly in my mouth, sweet, intoxicating, guilty. Big George was tugging insistently at my bridle and the horse was beginning to skitter and neigh in protest but I still tried to turn it back, to make another protest, to beg father to burn the note and send Carter on his way. Big George was stronger than me, however, and a huge tug brought me round to look into his face, closed, unforgiving, grim.

'Ezekiel Stockwell is a good man,' said George. 'And now you have hurt him who never hurt you. You are not wanted here, Master Nicholas, and that's plain. So now you must be served out as you have served Ezekiel and Judith and God rot you.'

My head began to swim as though I had been battered by the pugilist again. George's words, words that I never dreamed possible I would hear from a man I never thought would utter them, sank in to my soul stunning me with the enormity of what I had done. They rushed in on me like a black tide and I tried to turn the horse again, to go back, to stop all this, but George would not have it.

'I'm sorry, Daisy! Mrs. Stockwell, I'm sorry!' I shouted over my shoulder.

'We don't want your sorrow, you whoreson,' shouted Daisy back, her voice ringing like a tocsin after me. 'We want nothing from you!'

'Father!' I called once more. 'I'm sorry!'

My father did not turn or acknowledge me and Big George tugged me away.

'You are on your own now, Master Pelly,' said George.

They were the last words that my father and Big George said to me for a very long time; years even. But they were not the last words that I heard from Daisy Stockwell. Not by a long chalk.

Chapter 2

Baptism at the Hands of Adamastor

Nowadays, I always make a point of looking around at the *lolwapa* and take the time to understand and appreciate what real happiness is. Ragwasi – *Ja, Ja*, I will come to him in good time - and I have built our homestead at the foot of a semi-circle of low olive green kopjes which have enough brush, camel thorn and blond grass to support the goats we graze there and still allow a share for the springbok and giraffes that come through from time to time and in which we delight. He has built his hut and the separate huts that each of his wives demand in the traditional shape of the horned buffalo, with his main house in the centre, Boitumela's in the place of honour due to a first wife on the right, with those of her relatives following on; on the left are the huts of his Left-hand wives, each in due precedence, while behind the centre are the cooking and storage huts and huts for children, yellow ochre, gold and sienna sat under their silver thatch, each door a nose and each window an eye, like the face of some ancient, quiet person long gone. Our families are all mixed up together now and when my wife and his wives, our children and grandchildren gather in the cleared area in front to gossip, it is a rare and fine sight to see. The ladies put bright beads of turquoise and red and white in the braids of their hair, show off new dresses and hats, scold children and prepare mealies and the boys play rugby football and make a nuisance of themselves. Those whose job it is to look after the pumpkins and gem squash that day can be seen raking and hoeing in the gardens beyond the scrub thicket fence while up on the hill the fine brown cows, russet against the red earth, graze under the watchful eyes of young men under wide-awake hats and everywhere the sound of squealing children playing chase, catch-me, tig and scattering the troops of blue guinea fowl fit perfectly with the chitter and chatter of the bright weaver birds and iridescent, long beaked bee-eaters that flit about the feathery flame trees and purple jacarandas.

My own house is more of a four square construction with walls and roof of green thickly painted corrugated iron, surrounded by a wide veranda for summer and containing a large sandstone chimney breast for when the winter nights demand a roaring fire; the stoep is my favourite place and I have bought two strong wicker chairs and a table for the purpose of sitting and talking with Ragwasi while the moon rises and the million stars of the clear Karoo glitter out of the luminous sky. Down before us is a good river of sweet water that runs all year and which we have dammed into a small lake around which gathered willow, fir, bluegum and date palms like village elders come to discuss a weighty problem. Up above, the cotton wool clouds in the azure blue of the sky proceed one after the other like great flat bottomed barges under sail on the open sea. The dam we have stocked with Cape trout too and it has been my pride and pleasure to have taught all the children of this desert to fish in it and swim as each came to the age suitable to the learning. In the high summer of the Karoo when the heat hums and whirrs that water is a blessing I can tell you. We have even sunk a well and put a wind pump over it; Tepo – she is my wife - is there now, supervising my son Joseph as he draws up water for cooking.

I savour these moments of peace and happiness because they have been hard earned and a long time coming and too often disturbed by troops of flying horsemen and the crack of guns. I am telling you about them because it is an important thing for a young man to learn – not that he will ever listen long enough to an old man to actually learn the lesson – that the path you take in life may seem very stony at the time but if you persist then luck will come your way eventually. But of course it is also true that troubles will always come and go and when you have solved one problem, another one will come along to get under your feet like an irritating dog. This is life. At this moment in 1910 we are all thinking very hard about this Act of Union and wondering what it will mean for our beautiful country for we fear that it will divide the black man from the white; what this means for my children, who are a bit of both, is anyone's guess. Anyway, this story is really about how I got from being a wastrel boy from Dines Hall to where I am today and of what happened to Daisy Stockwell and what happened to Ragwasi and how I found a wife and how I tried to make things right and what happened to my country. Well, some of it. If I told you all about everything you would be sitting on my stoep until the stripes drained off the zebra and the *mampoer* barrel was empty and you would be in trouble with Boitumela then, which is not something I would recommend. *Eesh!*

*

A casual observer aboard the *African Star*, an ordinary 3000 ton, three-mast, two funneled, iron hulled steamer, a little rusted, but proudly headed for Cape Town and Durban by way of the Azores and the Gambia river, would have noted little unusual among the passengers. There were perhaps more soldiers than usual because Sir Garnet Wolseley was campaigning on the Gold Coast, but the hopeful Cornish, Irish or German colonist was there too, as expected, off to make his fortune on the diamond fields at Kimberley. They were the ones peering over the bow and anxiously discounting the tales of failure that had seeped back to Europe from those who had seen the diggings at first hand. There were a few established colonists returning from visits to relatives in London or Amsterdam where they had extolled the virtues of South Africa, perhaps too loudly in the opinion of their distant cousins, and were now watching the water run past the ship taking them back to the hard toil of a poor colony permanently on the brink of collapse. There was a Boer farmer from the interior, big, bearded and rangy, unhappy to have had to spend so much time in London, trying to sell his Transvaal wool to the English heathens who had forgotten their Bible. There was a new secretary for the Governor and a shipping agent touting for business along the coast, but they were all supercargo on a ship carrying the commodity that South Africans depended on above everything else; guns and ammunition. Without guns and ammunition there was no meat from game, cattle could not be protected from the lion or the leopard, the blue fox would take the chickens and no farmer anywhere could feel safe from the bandit, the ruffian or the predator. Guns were the sign of status for the young Basuto, amaXhosa, Tswana, amaHlubi, Zulu or Soshangane warrior and he would labour long in field or mine for the chance to acquire one. They were also the guarantee of the Boer's dominion over his black slaves to the north and, because the British government at the Cape controlled the supply, the hated *Rooinek* hand on their collar restraining them when they went too far.

All who lined the rail looked out towards the present landfall, the sweating settlement at the mouth of the Gambia River, an old slave state lying long and low among the choking mangroves and each laboured to breathe the hot, grey, thick, heavy air that weighed on the coast like a pillow on a dying man's face. Their hearts beat with the same slow, torpid beat of the slack kettle drums that came over the water from the funeral of another man who had met his maker among the clouds of marsh insects. A small, desultory party trudging along the scar of a track beneath the limp palms carried a body on a makeshift stretcher to a patch of land a little higher than the rest where the inundations of the rainy season did not open the graves so quickly. To the left, anchored in midstream, was an old coaster rotting at a rusty anchor chain, its sails limp like dirty shrouds below the yellow jack quarantine flag. There was no movement to be seen aboard her, except the roll of a neglected upturned pot hacked and screeched at by a lone gull; there had been talk of scuttling her, the crew, the cargo, the fittings in the hope that salt water would scour her clean of the fever. Even the Corporal's guard slowly roasting in a boat anchored upwind of her would venture no nearer than half a mile. The town itself was low, dirty, squalid under the lowering clouds, its whitewashed compounds crumbling faster than the half-hearted repairs could be made. Where there was brick, it was badly laid and bleeding mortar as the sweating black timbers warped and shifted in the damp heat. Over all, there was a silence so profound that it seemed tangible, swamping the kettle drum until it was barely a muffled grunt. When the First Mate, the only man authorized by the Captain to go ashore, being salted and so considered partially immune to the plagues, smallpox and dengue, was sighted putting off from the crippled jetty in a small sailboat a murmur of fear passed from lip to lip among the first voyagers, as though he was the Yellow Jack personified.

'Wait and watch,' came the reassuring voice of the Captain from the bridge. 'Ladies may wish to retire.'

As the sailboat approached, a hosepipe was rousted out and a powerful jet of sea water directed on to it. The First Mate rounded to and washed himself in the cascade then stripped off his shirt and breeches and dropped them over board. A line was passed and a cask of vinegar dropped down to him as he came alongside – but never touching - which he opened and washed with once more. When his beard and dark hair had been thoroughly doused and rubbed and then rinsed once more all over with seawater, he took a marlin spike and stove in the bottom of the sailboat. As the water gurgled up, he tossed the marlin spike down, hung a canvas parcel around his neck and dived into the sea, crossing the ten yards of open water separating the two vessels as easily as if he were swimming the Serpentine. A rope ladder was let down and he swarmed up it, naked, grinning and handing over the double waxed and oiled, turpentine and disinfected packet. He was greeted with congratulations, a towel and a round of grateful applause from the passengers.

The casual observer would probably not have noticed, however, the unhappy young man who kept himself to himself all the way down the London River, out by the Downs, through the grey curtains of rain off white Brighton and the sunshine off green Falmouth where the telegraph cables came ashore. Moving from cabin to rail and back, sitting silent at meals and drinking as much as his purser controlled allowance would buy, he seemed to be each night and day imprisoned in his own solitude. Across rolling Biscay, his absence caused no remark for there were many who found the bucketing too much to bear and by the time the ship had raised the kind Azores, he had been forgotten entirely. As the ship left the oily swell of the Gambia River after picking up rice and groundnuts from bumboats certified clean by the Port Admiral and depositing the mail and most of the soldiers, he could be seen at the stern rail blank faced. He paid no attention to the ablutions of the First Mate, but instead watched the children bailing out the muddy water from the sinking huts along the dock and wrinkled his nose at the fetid smell of the dun mangrove. He could be seen drinking from a case bottle, lighting a cheroot, smoking it slowly, drawing the hot vapour deep into his lungs, holding it and then exhaling slowly, evenly, as smoothly as the glide of a black swan. If by chance he had drawn attention, then the observer would have seen him finish, flick the butt into the flat water, so heavy the screw hardly churned it, and then, pushing a hand through his fair hair, drop lightly over the rail, like a rag doll.

'Man overboard! Hard a starboard! Get the propeller away from him!' roared a parade ground voice, before its owner kicked off his boots and went over the side in a racing dive.

'Get a line on him!' cried a deckhand throwing a lifebelt out. A rush of feet came aft. 'Lower a boat!'

The ship curved around and came to a halt as the boat crew rowed hard towards me, Nicholas Pelly, lying limply in the arms of my rescuer, all volition gone, caring little whether I lived or died. I didn't struggle as I was hauled aboard the boat, nor protest when hoisted back onto the *African Star*, nor care much when the ship's surgeon had me hung upside down to get the seawater out of me. Coughing and choking, swinging by my heels as the acrid vomit cleared the gin out of my system, I was indifferent to being pronounced alive and I experienced all these things as if I was at a distance, watching someone else being raised from the dead. I was simply empty as I was carried to my cabin and tossed into my bunk like unwanted flotsam. All I could really see was Daisy Stockwell's face and the black hatred blazing out of her eyes at me.

'Tom G. Cole, Lieutenant, Royal Engineers, at your service,' he said beaming. 'No questions now, just stay there while I get your boots off and then you must get out of those wet clothes. The sailors say that you belong to me now, seeing as how I rescued you, so no arguing either.'

Tom Cole was a scrubbed young officer in his early twenties, stocky rather than tall, and everything about him declared him to be pleased to be alive. His hair was auburn with a touch of red in it, a little unruly now it was wet, and I could see that if he grew a beard it would be mostly rusty rather than brown. His face was pale with the sort of skin that the sun would punish, but there were two blue eyes above a smile that took delight as its natural shape. Cole's attitude towards me in that moment was of appraisal not condemnation and for that I was very grateful indeed. I had had an unremitting diet of that bleakness of judgment all the way from the Yellow house to the Pool of London and when I boarded the *African Star* I half expected the Captain and Purser to have publicly announced my disgrace to the passengers and crew. They hadn't, of course; my own guilt and surliness had done that.

I wanted to lay back in defeat and stare at the ceiling, but Cole was having none of it and hectored me out of my clothes, over to the wash stand handed me a towel. I also watched as he opened the porthole and tossed two empty gin bottles and a half full one straight out and into the sea.

'Rule One,' said Cole with a grin, handing me my brush and comb. 'No drinking alone. Bad for the spirits, if you get my drift.'

I was captivated by Cole's certainty and meekly nodded, as if being instructed by the Games Captain on the first day of a new school.

'Rule Two,' continued Cole, handing me a dry shirt. 'No moping about. Up and out and plenty of exercise. That's the ticket. From now on, we'll do ten laps of the deck before breakfast, another ten before lunch and again before dinner – that's at the double, what d'you say?'

I did not know why I was accepting orders like this, but Cole's personality would not be denied. I submitted.

'Rule Three,' said Cole holding up a corresponding number of fingers. 'Join in with company. Time spent with people who have seen a few things and been a few places is never wasted and the fact that you are on a ship means that you have been supplied with an embarrassment of riches in this respect. So make the most of them.'

There was something impishly compelling in Cole's happy visage and, however reluctant I was to leave the comfort of my misery, I felt the lead in my stomach being lifted for the first time since I had left Dines Hall.

'Right,' Cole declared. 'That's that. Now *I'm* off to get dried and changed.'

He paused by the door and looked straight at me. There was steel in his voice that the merriment did not conceal.

'I'll give you what's left of today and tonight to get over whatever it is you need to get over, but I'll be back in the morning, when you'll be ready for our first ten laps. Understand?'

I understood that it was not a question and the next morning, I was indeed pounding round the deck, with Tom G. Cole pushing me, barking at me like a happy dog and chafing me when I slackened.

I was truly reborn then. I am not a religious man and never have been but that dip in the Atlantic was as much of a baptism as I have ever needed. When he roused me out in the silver and purple dawn the next day, I felt the blood pounding round a soul that had been dead since Salcombe had spat on me. The Bushmen of the Kalahari have the same trick for pulling a man out of a brown study; they will make a man walk and walk for days if necessary, believing that movement clears the mind and I cannot disagree with them.

'There,' cried Cole, panting, as I threw up over the side. 'Now you know it's doing you good. Too many cheroots! Bad for the wind!'

I tried to say something but my guts heaved again.

'I bet you feel better for that!' cried Tom Cole, laughing, the spindrift lighting up his eyes and ruffling his hair, as I retched again. 'Come on. Let's have some breakfast. Strong tea and fried eggs and devilled kidneys will sort you out.'

I looked down at the grey water as it slid alongside the ship and for the first time since leaving London river I saw more than its grey monotony, for just underneath the surface a pod of dolphins sped along side. The leader broke surface with a great smile and then three, four, then six sleek animals leaped in unison, arching and diving and knifing through the water like scissors through silk. In a flash, panting and retching though I was, I made sense of why I had turned to gambling, why I had led such a wastrel existence, why I had failed at everything and ultimately, why I was on this boat. It was the fear of the grey that had haunted me, the fear of the monotony of doing the same thing, with the same people, in the same way that my father had done, knowing that every day would be the same and that there would be no distinguishing the previous day from the next. I would not study at my books for fear they led me to the clerk's desk, there to write an obituary stretching away over a lifetime. I had missed that appointment with Colonel Pinkerton because I feared a deadening uniformity of drill and barrack life. I had trusted to Fortune because I thought that she would bring me riches without the drudgery that I so dreaded.

Watching the dolphins leap clear and spray silver crystals in a wake of clarity, I also understood that I could not blame my ruin on gambling and fickle Fortune but that my absence of a clear direction was at the heart of my troubles. Seeing the instant shifts and intricate weave of the dolphin's play, I realised that my folly had not been the result of any particular decision I had made, but the absence of *any* decision. Calling 'twist' on 19 was not a decision, I realised, but a thoughtless act of wantonness. As the dolphins turned and turned again, spinning a silver threaded rope in the water, I understood that my father's eviction of the Stockwells was what really constituted a *decision*; a direction chosen, a choice made for the longer good, or perhaps the selection of the least worse option, by someone who accepted the responsibility and the blame for failure if necessary. I saw in another flash of bright water spattered from speckled dorsals that my father would not be reviled by the villagers, but gain in respect for taking the decision that caused the least pain for the estate and for everyone who made their livings by it. I knew the Stockwell boys were earning good wages in London, so Ezekiel and Judith were more insulated than most against the relentless mathematics of business, and that though there was no concealing the distress, my father had the steel to know that one family cast adrift on the roads was better than ten. If he had not paid off Salcombe immediately, perhaps the pain would have been merely delayed, only to be the greater as the lawyers' fees piled up, credit and confidence evaporated and the estate must lay off more workers and evict more families to survive in business. All these things I saw, but seeing them did not give much comfort for though my understanding gained, my sin was not, nor could not be, forgiven by it.

As the dolphins shot out of the grey sea once more, scattering bright water that turned salt tears into gems, the revelation came to me that if I were atone for my sins, I too must make a decision and choose a direction. I remember putting on a wry smile as the thought struck me that perhaps my father had been wiser than I gave him credit for, in putting me aboard a ship where the choice of a direction had already been half made for me. He had set me on my quest for redemption, but how this might be achieved and how restitution might be made to the Stockwells, he had left up to me.

I looked up from the dolphins as a packet of green sea detached itself from an unexpected wave and slapped me in the face. I nodded, gasping and shaking the salt out of my eyes, followed Tom Cole to the wardroom where an urn had been produced and breakfast laid out on a buffet. We filled plates and mugs and sat at the mess table, where I shook off my biliousness. I was hungry, for I had not eaten much over the past days. Finding company too difficult, I had avoided the mess before now.

'Cape Town or Durban?' asked Cole. 'Where are you headed?'

'Cape Town,' I answered. 'My father has a business contact there. I am to be given a position, but I don't know what it entails.'

'I'm off to join the Ordinance Survey,' replied Cole, wolfing a second egg and laughing. 'We are to make a new map of Cape Colony and all points northwards according to *scientific* principles. Soon there will be no more vague directions, best guesses and the expensive guides that we must rely upon now. The Colonial Office has finally decided that it wants to know exactly *where* Kimberley is according to proper measurement now that it has been annexed as British territory.'

'Kimberley is it?' interjected Bramson, sitting down beside us. He was a shipping agent who had the look of someone who understood how to turn a profit and was lucky enough to know not to buy a pig in a poke. Right then he was in shirt sleeves, mutton-faced with white woolly hair, and unbuttoning a waistcoat that he had regretted putting on against a morning chill that we had left behind in Biscay. I suppose he must have been about forty years of age, and he reminded me a little of the landlord of the Kings Head at home but then at that age all middle aged men seemed to me to look alike. What I found novel was his easy manner, unfamiliar to one who had been brought up to pay at least nominal respect to my elders; he didn't seem conscious of my age at all. 'Why, the diamonds that come out of there might save our colony yet, if only the supply was managed. They are pulling them out of the ground so quickly – too quickly - that the price is bound to collapse any day now. It's a dangerous place too, from all accounts, and getting worse by the day. Every tough nut in Africa is up there and in possession of a gun and a bottle of Cape Smoke brandy; Germans, Fenians, Zulus, the lot.'

'I thought Africa was a sort of El Dorado,' I said, remembering some of the racetrack talk. 'I mean, isn't it supposed to be another India in the making?'

'Stuff and nonsense, if you don't mind me saying so,' replied Bramson with a friendly smile. 'If it was possible to get rich in Africa, believe me, the Boers, us English and the Africans themselves would already be rich. Don't be deceived because Kimberley is turning out to be a second Golconda. I've heard stories of African gold, diamonds – aye and unicorns – all my life and none have ever turned out to be real.'

'But the newspapers are full of Kimberley,' objected Tom Cole. 'And why else would the government want Kimberley if it wasn't for the diamonds?'

'The government don't let me in on its secrets,' replied Bramson, shaking his head. 'There might be untold wealth in the Mountains of the Moon, along with King Solomon's mines and Prester John too, but unless you have a railway you'll never get it out. Stick hard by the coast, would be my advice.'

'What's wrong with a horse and cart?' I asked, innocently. 'And in East Anglia, we still move the geese down to London by walking them.'

Bramson smiled again, a good natured smile, pleased to be amused by the innocence of young men. He opened the marmalade jar, peered at the contents, raised his eyebrows, then closed it shut.

'Tsetse fly will kill most horses unless they've been *salted* and rinderpest will kill off the oxen you'll need for your wagon – that's after the lions have had their share,' he said, in a matter of fact sort of way. 'You'll have to pay tribute to every chief along the way – and there will be more than you can imagine - and the young warriors will steal your guns and your food whether their chiefs forbid it or not. Then malaria will kill off your drivers and you'll have to borrow at exorbitant rates to survive and replace your losses and by the time you get what's left of your gold, jewels, precious stones and unicorns down to the Cape, you'll find a glut will have robbed you of any hope of profit and you'll be selling your boots for a pound of *biltong*. And that's *if* you find King Solomon's mines in the first place, which might be a thousand trackless miles north of Mzilikazi's country, which is a thousand miles from the Cape already and *if* he's still alive and hasn't been chased off it by his Shona enemies.'

He offered us cheroots, but both I and Cole refused them, mindful of our new physical regimen.

'And as your friend here can tell you,' he added, indicating Cole. 'There ain't no maps and no one really knows where any place is unless they've been there and can find it a second time.' He took a piece of bread from the plate between us and buttered it. 'As to what the government wants,' he continued, returning to Cole's previous question about Kimberley. 'That's anybody's guess; vacillation is the history of this country as far as old Lady Whitehall is concerned. They don't want the colonists massacred by the Africans, they don't want the Africans enslaved by the Boers, they don't really want the expense of the Colony at all, but they won't give it away to anyone who does want it because it's the only decent stopping point for a ship on the way to India; and they don't want to spend a penny to achieve any of this. It's not like Gambia River which they keep trying to give to the French, but which the French keep refusing. If they offered them the Cape we'd be sailing aboard *L'Etoile Africaine* in two minutes flat.' He lit up his cheroot and blew a long thoughtful stream of blue smoke into the air. 'No,' he said, giving judgement. 'In my opinion South Africa is a dangerous place worth nothing outside a twenty mile radius of Cape Town docks. Like I say – stick to the coast.'

'But what an adventure it would be,' declared Cole, undeterred. 'Think of it! Paving a way for civilisation by laying the maps for the railways to follow.'

I was out of my depth. In one sense I was flattered that Bramson addressed me as an equal, as an independent adult rather than an adjunct of my father's pocketbook, yet in another sense I was overwhelmed by the fearless enthusiasm of Tom Cole. I kicked myself for missing that appointment with Colonel Pinkerton, for I now realized that the army life might have been just the ticket, but then resolved that I could have no more regrets and could not look backwards. I must look forwards, to acquire and maintain forward motion, breasting the obstacles thrown in front of me, just as the steamer pushed through the waves. Should I choose the caution urged by the experienced Bramson and look for a life close to the coast in Cape Town or choose to live life audaciously, like Tom Cole, and head for the blank spaces of the interior?

'What would you advise a man in my circumstances to do?' I ventured, trying to keep the uncertainty and insecurity out of my voice.

'I do not know your particular circumstances, young fellow,' replied Bramson, holding up his hand to still my attempted explanation. 'And nor do I wish to. From the look of you, and from your, ahem, decision to take a swim earlier, I'd say you were no different than a lot of other men who have found themselves alone and with their way to make in the world.'

He waved to the steward, who brought more tea. I flushed with embarrassment at being reminded of my ducking. My attempted suicide already seemed to belong to a foolish past that was already a lifetime away.

'I have found it wisest not to give nor listen to advice that was not backed by money or personal and long acquaintance,' continued Bramson. 'But I will say that I have found more disaster to emanate from prevarication and procrastination than by even the most foolish of courses chosen.'

I mulled this over for a moment.

'So any decision is better than no decision at all?' I queried.

'That's about it,' replied Bramson.

Tom Cole nodded in agreement: 'It's the unofficial motto of the army, you know.'

*

If we were an unlikely troika, ours was no stranger than a thousand other shipboard companionships struck up on a long voyage. In the week that was left to us, Bramson answered our questions about South Africa with his cheery cynicism, while Tom Cole happily challenged him, seeing only adventure and opportunity where the trader saw danger and bankruptcy. Cole and I became firm friends and our three times daily races around the deck gave everyone something to smile about, while Bramson put up a chalkboard in the saloon to keep score. I was glad to have such guides as I slewed off guilt I could not assuage, put away sins that I could not be absolved of, and concentrated on filling in some of the blank spaces on the new leaf I had resolved to turn over. For I had decided that my future was South Africa; my direction was South Africa; my fortune was South Africa and when I glimpsed my first sight of Table Bay, I swore that the trader was right. I would stick to the coast; I would stick to Cape Town.

It was mid-afternoon and I had never seen a sky of such azure nor a sea of such calm French blue. On my left I marveled at the long sweep of Bloubergstrand and Losperd's bay, curving like a wing in flight to curl under Cape Town itself. To the right, I saw the Lion's Head rising up like a Sphinx and in front the great Table Mountain itself, like the broad forehead of a giant, its shoulders swathed in blue-gray limestone scars like the scales of a dragon, its encompassing arms spreading wide while the clouds streaking back from its summit gave it a head of purest, gleaming cotton white hair. It was breath taking in its magnificence and having only ever been used to the flats and fens of East Anglia, I was overwhelmed.

'The Portuguese say that the last Titan lies under that mountain,' said Bramson, catching my awed gaze as the *African Star* waited for the pilot boat to take us in to Table Bay. '*Adamastor*, who was appointed to keep them out of the Indian

Ocean by whipping up the seas that gave it its original name; the *Cape of Storms*. The name was changed to *Good Hope* to put heart into the Portuguese mariners.'

'It's easy to see why,' I replied, looking about with wonder. 'I have never seen a mountain before and if I never see another I shall be satisfied.'

'The Devil's Peak – three thousand, three hundred and seventy six feet high exactly,' chimed in Cole, delightedly pointing at the mountain. 'Surveyed by Her Majesty's Royal Engineers and as accurate as a chain, theodolite and Pythagoras can make it. Ain't it a sight though?'

'I like to think that old Adamastor stands guard over the interior these days, now that the Indian Ocean is a well-travelled highway,' continued Bramson, who had grown more thoughtful in the last few days. 'Hopefully he will keep us from the temptations of legends and the follies of dreamers and protect us from whatever evil the Gods send in this direction.'

I watched as the pilot boat skimmed across the clean water towards us, its sail close hauled and its crew clearly enjoying the spectacle of speed and grace that only skill, seamanship and a leading wind off the top of Table Mountain could present. I was in love with Africa before I had even set foot on it.

'Over there is Robben island,' said Bramson, pointing to a flat pancake surrounded by chalk white surf off to starboard. 'They used to put the bad lads there. An inhospitable place in the winter.'

'I can't believe that winter could ever come to this place,' I answered delightedly. 'Why it's October and I swear today is warmer than yesterday.'

Cole and the trader looked at each other in amused disbelief.

'Neptune and Badger Bag never did come aboard when we crossed the line,' said Bramson, laughing and turning to Cole. 'But make sure he has a big, thick winter coat for Christmas, eh?'

I was an ignorant little bugger in those days.

I saw my first black men later that day and I was surprised to find that they were not all alike as I had imagined. There were Cape Malays with skins that were only a little darker than the labourers at home after a hot harvest working on the dock alongside men who were so dark that I thought they were almost blue, while there were others who I thought were Chinamen but – I learned later – they were really descendants of the Bushmen, the *San*, the people who had lived in the Cape when the Dutch had first settled here two hundred years ago. As I say, I had never seen a black man, and neither had anyone in Dines Hall apart from my father who had encountered them in India and although I found them strange – I had to catch myself from staring too obviously sometimes - I soon got used to them. I'm telling you this because later on South Africa became a different place where black and white were not treated equally. It was not like that when I arrived at the Cape. Everything was in flux then and there was no way anyone could have guessed that sensible people would come to believe that black men were less than white men – *different*, yes, well that was obvious and no bad thing. When I arrived at the Cape the only people who thought like that were people who had never met a black man – or Boers.

*

Some people you see again, others never. Some, you want to see soon and some, like house guests, you will be happy to see after a respectable time has gone by between meetings. Others it has to be admitted, however much Christian charity you possess, you dread seeing again but know in your heart of hearts that such a meeting is unavoidable, fated even. Sometimes, when the partings are upon you, it is also sometimes hard to know into which category different people fall, which is in itself very unsettling.

Bramson was bound for Durban, by way of Port Elizabeth, obeying his own rule about sticking to the coast and I shook his hand wondering if we would ever meet again. If we did not, I counted myself lucky enough that chance had brought us together anyway. He had taught me a lot about Africa in a short time and if I wasn't an old hand, I felt that I was at least not entirely green. Tom Cole was met at the dock by a carriage, for he was to report to Simonstown on the other side of the Cape Peninsular, and was gone with not much more than a handshake and a cheery wave but somehow, in my heart, I knew that we would meet again somewhere up in the mountains or the plains beyond Table Mountain, sometime, perhaps sooner than later.

I resolved to put Daisy Stockwell out of my mind until such time as I could actually do something to make the situation better. What else could I do? It was either that or mope about like a penitent, and a young man is by nature unable to wear sackcloth and ashes for very long. I wished Daisy and Judith and Ezekiel well, promised that I would make amends when I could, and decided that I would make forward motion in my life. When the time came to disembark and part company I felt that I was almost as good as new and would be better if I could just shake the dread of seeing Daisy Stockwell again and I consoled myself with the thought that she was at least, a long way behind me back in England. Aye, the folly of youth.

So almost as soon as I landed, there I was, left alone on the tip of Africa, equipped only with a letter of introduction and a tin trunk that seemed to have been unduly battered in the hold. I picked it up, put it on my shoulder and, ducking under a derrick landing the rice we had loaded at the Gambia, threaded my way off the dock. Cape Town wasn't a crowded place and the *African Star* was the only ship in that day so it took no time at all to find my way past the Somerset Hospital, pass between the magazine and the Amsterdam Battery and go into the town proper. It was a lovely spring day and there were flowers in bloom that I had never seen before; bougainvillea in all shades of pink, cerise, purple, white and yellow ran like confetti across white walls, honey coloured stone and corrugated iron roofs, while every window box seemed to be exploding with daffodils, tulips, hibiscus, pink roses and blue agapanthus. There was a smell of orange blossom in the air and a heady smell of spice on the cool sea breeze which could not fail to invigorate me as I walked tall and eager for adventure through the dusty streets. It was like champagne or a cleansing bath under a waterfall. What struck me most that day was the brightness of the light. I was used to the big skies of East Anglia, but somehow, here the light was a little clearer, the sky a little higher and the sun a little brighter. Looking at the oaks and pines that every house seemed to be sleeping under, I guessed that the summer sun would be hotter and harsher than I was used to in England but also that winter would be kinder than at home.

The town itself, I had expected to be bigger, perhaps as big as Norwich, but really it was only a small place and a little tatty to be honest. Government House on Adderley Street was the centre but like everything in this country then, the title was more impressive than the reality. It was just a long low bungalow and Dines Hall could probably have given it a run for its money. The Castle was more impressive to my inexperienced eye for it was a real Dutch star fort with a parade ground in front and nothing but the railway between it and the shining sea. If a knight in shining armour had ridden out of it, I would not have been surprised, for the banners of the Governor, the Colony and the garrison all floated above it like a picture in a book of legends.

Crossing a wide boulevard, I heard the crack of a *voorlooper's* whip and I saw my first ox wagon, with no less than fourteen tan oxen inspanned. They were long-horned Brahmins with sagging necks, a hump behind their shoulders where the yoke went over and a low call rising to a pitch just short of panic when the whip snapped above them. Behind them the wagon was smaller and narrower than the haywains of home but it seemed to be of rugged construction and the rattle and creak of the traces and the ironwork holding all together carried the sound of long experience. It was an impressive sight and I wondered at the skill required to manage so many animals, but in loyalty to my homeland, I thought them not to be compared to the Shire horses that the teamsters and draymen back home used. The Transvaal wool trader who had been aboard the African Star was on the box beside the voorlooper and as the cattle loped along the broad straight street heading for the road that led up to Sir Lowry Coles Pass and on into the interior, he touched his hat. His companion with the whip gave me nothing more than a scowl from within a bushy beard and I remembered what Bramsom had told me about the Boer hatred for the English. Watching him go, I confess, I missed my horse, for I would have ridden over the Kloof straight away and if I had seen the broad strand of Monkey Bay or the homely peace of Hout bay on that day I would probably never have returned, so beautiful are they.

My father's correspondent was a lawyer by the name of Cronjie and when I presented myself at his house on Langstraat, which was also his place of business, he welcomed me in and did his best to make me feel at home. He was a beanpole of a man, taller even than I was, and slightly severe of face, no doubt from all the meanness and lying he had dealt with in his business over the years. He tried to be jolly through his wrinkles, I think, to disguise the fact that he dealt in unhappiness for most of his days and he probably did not relish the prospect of telling me the terms of my father's trust that he was required to execute. I am so glad that I never became a lawyer; there never seemed much satisfaction to be had in dealing in bad news, quarrelling relatives greedy for a bigger slice of a will or arbitrating between swindlers. Besides, I have seen many honest men go into a lawyer's office, but never a single one come out; it seems that the lawyers make liars of us all; it is a necessary skill if you expect to win in court more than once. Mijnheer Cronjie might have been an exception though. He never swindled me, I should say. Perhaps I have a prejudice against lawyers.

Mijnheer Cronjie's wife laid a meal for us in the yellow wood *voorkammer*, a big chamber for dining, business and entertainment, which led straight off the *stoep*. It was a rather grand room, having a long, dark polished table running its wide length upon which lay embroidered lace runners, some curious silver candlesticks which I took to be of Indian origin, and blue Delft crockery spread. Against the walls were dressers and cupboards of the same bright yellow wood, containing glasses, more blue china and the miniatures, gewgaws and souvenirs that scatter themselves across the shelves of all homes, but in this one they were attended by a young woman servant in a good blue pinafore, her hair tucked into a white linen cap and her hands folded demurely before her. She had polished bronze skin, high cheek bones and narrow eyes and was made in such a delicate fashion that I found myself gulping at her good looks. She looked back at me quickly and then dropped her eyes as Frau Cronjie bustled in with a spray of flowers for the table and I took a deep breath to control myself. The voyage *had* been a long one.

'So what are your plans, Mister Pelly?' asked Mijnheer Cronjie, showing me to a place at the table and plucking at his turkey neck. The accent was strange to me the first time I heard it, although I suppose I have picked up the twang myself after all these years. I do talk out of a thin mouth these days, and pronounce my 'e' nearer to an 'i' – 'niver' rather than the 'never' I was born with - but I still can't roll my 'r's or make those Dutch vowels that sound like Big George grawling up after a night on the beer and cheroots.

'I rather thought that you would tell me that, sir,' I answered as politely and humble as I could. 'I understood that you had a position for me. I will do my best at it, I can assure you, sir.'

Cronjie looked over his spectacles at me then scratched at his pinched nose as a great platter of pork knuckle, pickled cabbage, sausages, a strange yellow porridge and what I thought were several small pumpkins was laid down before us. My father often said that it was not possible to live in another country if you could not take the food to your heart and he would sometimes have an Indian curry made, even though none of us children would dare share it with him as we thought the spices might burn our tongues off. After the food on the ship which, if plentiful and familiar was also monotonous, I was looking forward to a change but was apprehensive about what the colonists, foreigners and natives ate. I was used to good beef, bacon, bread and cheese of course, and I had tried rice before but I had no idea how meat was dressed in Africa and with the scent of spice still in my nostrils from the docks, I feared that curry would be only the first of many assaults of the unfamiliar on my palate. Still, even before I had made my introduction, the aromas of grilled lamb, beef and pork too, toasted over charcoal, were making my mouth water, but I confess I regarded that yellow porridge and those small pumpkins with great suspicion.

'Your father has asked me to act as the disburser of an allowance,' he replied apologetically, spooning a pumpkin onto my plate. 'But he did not ask me to provide you with a position.'

The single shilling that was all that I had left suddenly shifted in my pocket and for a moment I felt as lonely as only a man cast adrift on a strange continent can. I was excited though and not afraid to be alone. Indeed, in that moment I was so filled with possibility that if you had asked me to walk from the Cape to Cairo, I would have accepted with no more thought than I would have given to a trip to the top barn.

'And I should say from the outset that I am not empowered to advance you more than fourteen shillings a month for a period not to exceed a twelve month.'

Fourteen shillings; the weekly wage my father paid to Big George.

Mijnheer Cronjie stopped talking and watched me like a hawk.

'Don't look so disappointed, Mister Pelly,' he said after a pause, passing a second plate piled high with lamb chops. 'Fourteen shillings will go a lot further here than you might think and there is always work available for a fit young man in this colony.'

'Do you mean I should go to Kimberley to dig for diamonds?' I asked, taking two of the charcoal flavoured chops. I bit into one of them. It was delicious, and I found the taste of the tingling spices which had been added to them very exciting.

He shook his head and smiled.

'No need for anything as drastic as that, young man. Just beyond the Table Mountain you will find hundreds of miles of the best farmland in the world, full of farmers short of an intelligent young man with experience like yours.' He passed over the dish of yellow porridge. '*Mealiepap*,' he said, smiling. 'Indian corn beaten up with water and salt. It is what the Africans take as their bread.'

I tasted it and found it as bland as a mashed potato. This was a little disappointing after the lamb chops.

'Or if you can read and write, you could be a travelling teacher,' he continued. 'There is demand for that, I can tell you, even if the pay is poor – or perhaps, if you know your bible, you could be a *Predikant*, a preacher. Or you could stay in Cape Town and become a clerk, if you wished.'

Preacher, teacher, clerk or farmer? The choice was all mine and for the first time no one would or could help me in choosing the direction of my life. I had made the decision to make South Africa my home already and so I must now make a second decision. Sitting in the voorkammer with Mijnheer Cronjie watching me, I dismissed the first option as comical, the second two with horror and although being a farm labourer had been no part of my plan, the advice of Bramston and Tom Cole rang in my head: *any decision was better than no decision at all*. So I became a farm labourer and that's how I met Ragwasi.

Chapter 3

Ragwasi

I have admitted to being an ignorant young man back then; my friend Ragwasi says I still am, forty years on. He thinks it is very well to write down what we remember so that our children might know what a mighty warrior, hunter and hero *he* was, but he does not think it will change anything. He says that fate and great men make the world and the little people like us must just do the best we can in it. He might be right, but I should also say that it does not stop him sitting on my *stoep* and drinking my Cape Smoke or eating up all my good beef and biltong while he makes helpful suggestions. He also does not think that writing down my story will do any good in stopping what is coming here in our beautiful country when the Act of Union goes through and white men divide themselves from black men. In this, I think he is right too.

Anyway, where was I? Of course, Cape Town, back in 1873.

Mijnheer Cronjie agreed to let me take my allowance for three months in advance when I told him that I would seek work on the farms, so with nothing but two guineas, a change of shirt and linen and a straw hat donated by Fraue Cronjie I set out on my new direction. And what a direction it was! I shall never forget the happiness I felt as I went from farm to farm in those two summers of 1873 and 1874, for work was plentiful and I came and went almost as I pleased. It was a beautiful country and I did not feel disloyal to my native East Anglia in admitting it. The oaks of Stellenbosch were so golden in the summer that I was sure that they must have been polished, while the blue-grey mountains of Franschoek formed the prettiest valley I was ever in and gave up a wine so sweet I thought they must have laced it with sugar. They named the town of Ceres for the goddess of plenty and she would have been honoured by it for I had never seen such good corn land as I saw stretching from that town eighty miles south as the crow flies down to Bredasdorp and for a hundred miles eastwards from Cape Town to Swellendam.

I met Ragwasi when I was working on a farm called Schalkenbosch near Tulbagh, a prosperous and attractive place under the Groetwinterhoek mountains in one of the flat bottomed valleys that go up like a staircase from Cape Town until they reach the top of the escarpment. There we grew fruit and raised wheat, beef, sheep and pigs too. There was good water from streams and bore holes channeled into a dam and the snow melt that came off the silver tops of the mountains in July allowed the farmer to irrigate six thousand acres or more. It was a big farm by English standards but there was never enough labour to work it all and I could not help but wonder how happy the Stockwells would have been to swap their two acres for a corner of a farm like this. They could probably have had one for a song too because many of the farmers here were always nearly broke from paying too much for wages and not getting good prices in a market that was always glutted. My master was no different in that although he could wholesale fresh food to the ship's chandlers at the Cape, as well as more than satisfy his own needs and more, he still felt himself hampered. He complained often that he could not find more labourers to help him put more land under the plough or journeymen with the skills to extend the neat, white-washed and ornately gabled house that he had built in the Dutch style. He particularly wished to replace the thatched roof with a tiled one so that he could point to it and prove that he was every bit as good as any Dutchman back in Holland.

My own house was rather more humble than I was used to, it being only a white washed adobe shack a few yards square and indeed, smaller than my room at Dines Hall. That did not matter to me very much because although I had been accustomed to modest comforts in England, here I was learning to be a different sort of man and I found a more Spartan existence very much to my taste. There was good shade under an oak, a charpoy for me to put my bedroll on, a fireplace inside for the winter and at the back, two conveniently spaced trees which served for my washing line and sometimes as anchors for a hammock. Wood was plentiful and I honed up my muscles by splitting logs and drawing water up from the communal trough for washing and making *rooibos* tea in the morning. I learned to keep my clothes clean by steeping them overnight in the soap that we made from sheep fat, potash and sweet herbs and then rubbing and rinsing them in clean, fresh water. I also learned the use of a smoothing iron, although I decided early on that life was too short to waste on this task and, apart from very special occasions, resolved to go about crumpled. The one thing that I found hard to get used to was using the communal facilities, especially when it was hot and the flies proliferated. The master was very strict in insisting on the use of the privy and chamber pot though and would tolerate no deviation from the proper disposal of bodily waste, but it was difficult to persuade everyone of the importance of keeping the facilities clean. I knew then that disease comes from insanitary practices and disease is to be feared more the further one goes away from the doctor. Our nearest physician was fifty miles away in Cape Town.

I was happy with the hard work and though it took a little while for my hands to stop blistering and my wrists to thicken a little, the beef, *boerwors, mealiepap* and a glass of Cape Smoke brandy in the evening with the other workers was reward in itself. Being cut off by distance from the possibility of neighbours, we made up our own little world there under the china blue skies or the golden shade of the willows and oaks, toasting our meat and baking our gem squash on the open fire, while the women mixed our mealies with a little sugar or spice. The master was an Afrikander, a Dutchman who had chosen to stay in the English colony rather than go up to the Transvaal with the Boers, and most of the workers were descendants of mixed marriages between settlers and the natives who were called the Cape Coloured and who had no tribe. We shared our pipes and stories and songs, stretching out our legs under the stars without regard for race or nationality or station for there was no entertainment or sport here that was not homespun and a man who insisted on fine distinctions would find himself alone very quickly. It was only in the matter of business or religion that we deferred to the master, for it was his farm and he held the deeds from his father and his father before him. Each Sunday, he would read to us from the only book in the valley, the only one anyone on the farm had seen, sticking to the Old Testament and even then, sticking mainly to the familiar stories of the Temptation of Eve, Noah's Ark, David and Goliath and Exodus which we lonely farmers on the edge of the world found comfort in.

Just like a lot of other places before though, my idyll came to an end just as soon as the master found out that I could read and write. This happened on one

Sunday when just before our small service under the main oak, he swallowed a wasp, which set him choking fit to burst and then cursing at the sting that it left behind. We gave him water and honey to soothe him, but he insisted that the beast had been sent by Satan to test him and he would not give up the sermon. His tongue swelled so much however that we were compelled to put an onion vinegar poultice on it and tie his jaw up in a rabbit-eared bandage and I was moved to such pity that foolishly I volunteered to read the lesson for him. He agreed reluctantly and handed over the ancient book, which was heavy being eighteen inches tall, four thick and bound in tooled boot leather, and I took his place at the front of our gathering. I placed it on the small table that we used as an altar, looked at the expectant faces before me and opened it at the point indicated by the thick red bookmark; Luke 15, 11-32. The Prodigal Son.

The next day, I was taken away from the physical work and from then on given clerk's work or made to act as schoolmaster to the children. Despite the choice I had made in Mijnheer Cronjie's voorkammer, it seemed that God intended to mock me for my misdeeds not just by reminding me of them in his book but by making me into a teacher, preacher and clerk rather than a farmer also. I resolved to take to the roads once more in the hope that I could show him a clean pair of heels.

Ragwasi was a regular visitor to the farm in the months that I worked there. He was a transport rider who we always recognized from afar because of his broad brimmed leather wide awake hat, long stout boots, plaid shirt and blue denim trousers which he wore to show off that he was not a homespun yokel like the rest of us. We welcomed him when he turned up in his ox wagon to carry away goods for the Cape because we knew he would return with the tobacco, cotton cloth and metal goods that the master could not provide for himself or us and always brought with him a bottle of something different for us to try in the hope that we would order more of it from him. A full black man with a round face, big flat nose and a short beard and moustache which he kept trimmed close, I was fascinated by him from the outset because he was a real, proper African from the interior beyond the mountains and the Karoo. Not as tall as me but broader, he was ten years older than me and getting a little stout around the midriff, but he wasn't bothered by this. Indeed, he seemed a cheerful companion to me, always with a sort of upside down smile and sideways smiling eyes. The way he spoke, with a wide mouth and careful enunciation of his words, was also interesting to me because it seemed that his voice was ever on the edge of telling a joke.

'There is no better life for a young man than as a transport rider,' he told me one evening. 'For you get to see so many places, be your own boss, solve your own problems, have plenty of fresh air and have the satisfaction of knowing that everyone is pleased to see you. This is because you are bringing mail, presents or long awaited goods and even if you are late they are nice to you because they need you.'

'If that is so Ragwasi,' said Joe, one of the farm workers, laughing as he passed the bottle. 'Why is it that you are alone and without an assistant again?'

'It is because they do not appreciate the true wealth of freedom and an understanding master,' he replied, the firelight glittering across his big smile.

'You mean that you have not paid them again?' Joe took the bottle back. 'Just what is this thing you have brought us to drink?'

'It is an Indian drink,' replied Ragwasi. 'And I pay all my workers from time to time when my cash flow allows it. Just because a man might be impatient to get to the diggings at Kimberley does not mean that my cash flow will allow me to instantly disburse large and liberal sums into his hand.'

Joe passed me the bottle and I drank the fiery liquid. It tasted like turpentine.

'You say this came from India?' I choked. 'God preserve us.'

'Of course,' he said. 'Do you not know that many good things come from over the sea in India?'

'My father made two voyages there,' I replied. 'But he never came back with anything like this.'

'Your father was a travelling man, I see,' said Ragwasi, suddenly interested. 'It is in the blood then. I am sure that you must also have the desire to see all the world and India too. Perhaps you should consider the life of a transport rider. I may even have a vacancy for an assistant.'

Joe burst out laughing. 'That is an offer that a sensible man I will refuse,' he cried. 'I have seen many wonders in my life, Ragwasi, but the inside of your wallet is not one of them. Not even Pelly would be so foolish as to work for you and he is almost fresh off the boat.'

'Do you want me to teach your children to read and write?' I asked, flippantly.

'No,' Ragwasi replied, surprised. 'Whatever for?'

'I'll take the job,' I said. 'When are we going?'

*

'We are going to the Drosty at Swellendam first,' said Ragwasi as I joined him on the box. It was mid-morning and I had just taken my leave from the master. He was resigned to my going but said he would not stand in the way of a young man with his fortune to make and promised to forward the balance of my wages to Mijnheer Cronjie next time he went to market.

'Indian tea, Indian coffee, Indian cloth, Indian pepper and Indian tobacco for the Afrikanders,' he continued, stretching out his long vowels and jabbing a thumb over his shoulder at a jumble of packages in the covered wagon. 'I do not know why they cannot be content with African things but I am glad they are not because it is good for my business. There is also a good blacksmith at Swellendam and I need a new wheel. After that I do not know where we will go, but sometimes they send me on to Mossel Bay to pick up more things from India.'

I learned quickly that Ragwasi called anything imported 'Indian' but I was content with all things African then and I looked forward to this unexpected journey. Mossel Bay was about a hundred miles away and further than I had been before and as we rattled down the dusty roads with the green mountains to left and right, folded like the toes of a giant, the corn lands started to give way to moorland and the streams started to cut deeper valleys. There were zebra and kudu to be seen here and I was minded to shoot one for the pot, but Ragwasi wouldn't lend me his gun because he had no salt with him, nor any place to make biltong and he said he was damned if even a greedy young man like me could eat a full kudu before it went bad. He also said he had no time, but this was something I did not believe for in an ox wagon all you have is time and you can do a lot of talking. I told him about England and Dines Hall while he told me about Basutoland, the land in the Drakensberg mountains where his family had lived. There had been some hard times of war and famine when he was a child, the *mfecane*, he called it, or sometimes the *difaquane* and he had lost his lands in war to the Boers about fifteen years ago. This reminded me of the Stockwells but I did not tell him of my shame. He had come south to work on the farms when he was my age and that was how he got the money together to become a transport rider.

'So your tribe is Basuto, then?' I asked.

'My father was probably a Zulu, but they called him a Matabele,' he replied. 'So I grew up speaking Zulu but then when the Boers came we became Basuto because the old Chief Mosheshwe was fighting them. And then when Mosheshwe died and his sons started fighting over his lands – that's when my father and mother were killed – I became a Tswana for a while. When I got my first cow, a beautiful red-brown with white socks and a white star on her forehead, the Chief took away my first calf and that is when I realized that I did not need a Chief at all and went to the Cape. Now I am just *uBuntu* – a person.'

He had a team of twelve oxen which was small by most standards but he had ambitions to build up and hoped that he could buy another pair soon. After a couple of days of travelling, I said he should sell them all and buy a couple of horses because an ox wagon was so slow. We would start the day by inspanning the oxen as soon as the sun came up, which entailed rounding them up first because they would wander off in the night even though we hobbled them. Once the harness was on – and the beasts were not like horses in this respect, because they would give you no help at all – Ragwasi would whip up and with a great lowing of protest the wagon would jerk into motion, creaking like an old man's knees. At first I rode on the box, but then I discovered why the assistant riders that I had seen before chose to walk; it was quicker and less hard on the buttocks.

'Jesus, Ragwasi,' I complained after the first few hours. 'You must have an arse of steel. Now I know why Africans have big, round ones.'

'What is the matter? Did you leave yours in Cape Town?' He grinned that upside down smile. 'I would say that white men have no arses, but I have seen the Boers and they have very big ones.'

We would travel for maybe six hours and cover no more than a dozen miles before we had to outspan the animals again to allow them to graze. This could take all afternoon, especially if the troublesome beasts decided to go to sleep in the shade of a big tree like Ragwasi did most days, and then we would inspan them again and go on for another couple of hours. After that, we would outspan them again where there was water and let the animals drink. We would hobble them as the evening drew in and let them go off to graze again while we built a fire and made our own meal. If we made fifteen or sixteen miles in a day, Ragwasi was pleased and he laughed at my impatience.

'Where are you going that will not be there when you arrive, uPelly?' he scoffed. He often put 'u' in front of the names of things because that is how Zulu is spoken. 'And the cattle will not go faster because you are hungry for a woman because they have been castrated and are jealous of you.'

He was right. The oxen could not be driven and would just drop dead in their traces if they were. The advantage of using them was that they were cheap, needed much less care than a horse and you could turn them into biltong when they were past it. This was important because it was a fact of life that you would lose some of them sometime to the leopard down here on the Lowveld or to the lion up on the Highveld.

I learned this lesson when we were a day short of Swellendam and had just let the oxen loose for the night. Ragwasi and I had both missed the spoor of a dead zebra concealed in the long grass and brushwood not fifty yards from our camp and we were well into our second glass of Cape Smoke and a tall story when the leopard came straight at us out of the dark.

Oh My Lord! That thing came without even a warning growl and it hit Ragwasi full in the chest as he stood up to reach for the bottle. A snarling hundred and twenty pounds of solid muscle, bone and sinew wrapped around hide-slashing claws and skull crunching teeth and if ever there was such a thing as nature red in tooth and claw, the deep chested leopard was it. Ragwasi went backwards over the traces and the beast was on him and ready to bite when I grabbed hold of its tail and hauled it back. I must have been crazy but in those situations you don't stop to think of the consequences and just act. The thing whipped around in mid-air and came at me this time, ears back, eyes golden and snarling, bowling me over and slashing at my shins with the claws on its hind legs. I was thrashing around and trying to punch it off but then it caught me in its eyes and I went limp with terror for I found I was looking into the eyes of the devil himself. No other animal has such terrible eyes as the leopard for they seem to be on fire with hatred and savagery, as though their owner wanted to finish you in hot pain and agony. This is what our ancestors in the caves must have faced, I remember thinking, and the paralyzing terror subsided and a strange calmness came over me as I accepted my death. It was not like when I tried to drown myself, for that was a horrible blackness on me, but instead it was a peaceful acceptance of the inevitable, as though time had slowed down and was just going to put me off to sleep. I have never been afraid of death since then, for I know now that it is just like going through a door into another room. Don't get me wrong – I like being alive, but when the time comes I hope it will be quick like with the leopard and not a long drawn out painful death by disease or some other thing.

I did not die that night because Ragwasi hit that terrible animal with the cooking pot and scalded it with hot water from the billy can and the next instant it was gone. The whole fight cannot have lasted more than thirty seconds or a minute but Ragwasi's plaid shirt was clawed up and I could see some really deep gashes diagonally across his chest. My own trousers had been ripped open and my left forearm ploughed up too and we were both holding ourselves stiffly and trembling from the shock and stinging pain. Somewhere in the darkness the leopard was growling but the cattle had all gone completely still and silent and Ragwasi was beside himself with worry that it would take one. We did not know about the dead zebra then but Ragwasi guessed that the leopard must have attacked us because we were close to a kill. A leopard will not normally attack two big men near a fire, which is a good job because it is strong enough to kill you and carry your carcass up a tree.

I was about to go into the wagon to look for some cloth to use as a bandage but Ragwasi stopped me.

'We must take off our clothes now, uPelly,' he said. 'All of them are tainted with blood and that is the one thing that attracts all predators. A lion may follow this leopard and that will be even bigger trouble.'

'But these are just about the only things I have,' I protested, climbing down from the wagon stiffly.

'We must build up the fire, pour water on our clothes and leave them until the morning,' he insisted. 'And we must sleep inside the wagon with the flaps closed tightly.'

'A bit of canvas won't stop that beast from getting in,' I said in disbelief. My wounds were stinging, my hands were shaking and I was dripping blood. I was also feeling the anger that comes on after a big shock. 'Let's get the gun out and shoot it if it comes back.'

'If the leopard has made a kill it will attract other predators looking for a share,' he said, pulling off his torn shirt. 'If not the lion then certainly the hyenas, which are the most dishonourable of creatures and dangerous because they never give up. You cannot shoot them all and unless you do shoot them all, they will beat you.'

I did as I was told because it was clear he knew things that I did not and I was coming to understand that I should listen more than talk if I was to prosper in South Africa but I still did not understand how the wagon would protect us.

'Animals cannot recognize the shape of a wagon,' Ragwasi explained, as he laid out our clothes and poured water on them to get the scent of blood off them. 'They have no instinct for it and so do not know how to react. If the flaps are open, then it may think it is a cave and come in but if the flaps are closed they think it is just a big rock and will ignore it.'

'You hope,' I said, slapping at the insects that were now descending on me, biting and stinging and buzzing at my wounds. 'Can I keep my boots?'

'Place them by the fire. The flames might keep a scavenger off,' he replied, shaking his head and picking up the Cape Smoke bottle. 'Rub this over you too, it will take away the scent of your blood.'

He took a rag, soaked it in Cape Smoke and began to dab at his wounds and indicated I should do the same. Man! It hurt, but then he pulled out his *muti* box and we smeared comfrey in lard along our cuts and gashes which he said would make them heal better. He was right too and I was glad that it was too dark to see how bad the wounds really were with only the flickering of the firelight to show us. He did take a length of the Indian cloth though and we tore it into strips and tied ourselves up as best we could. I remember the clean smell of that cloth against the wood smoke, my own stink of cattle, sweat and brandy and the burning meat of our wasted stew which had gone into the fire when Ragwasi struck the leopard. I remember it so clearly because it was then that I first realised that in Africa you live with danger all around you all the time, and when you are good and properly lulled by the beauty of the land and the sky and the cinnamon scent of it, that will be the time when the devil will leap out at you in the form of a leopard or worse.

Once we were in the wagon and wrapped in our blankets, Ragwasi pulled out a small horn full of more *muti* which he put into a pipe and lit. We didn't normally smoke inside the wagon, but there were so many insects in there that some fumigation was needed and besides, he said, *dagga* would take away the pain and stop my hands from trembling so. It worked too even though the smoke was too hot and dry for me, but I slept only fitfully and with bad dream that night because Ragwasi snored fit to wake the dead and we did not venture out of our refuge until the sun was a hand's breadth over the horizon.

I suppose I must have had some sleep because I did not hear whatever did come into our camp maul around at our clothes and carry off my trousers. Ragwasi also had the cheek to complain about me snoring away all night and seeing me still thick headed from the fug under the canvas, he gave me some more *dagga* which we used as snuff to clear our heads. That worked too and I felt that I was now well on my way to becoming a proper African.

I sorted and salvaged what clothes I could so that we would not have to ride into Swellendam naked, then put water in a can over the fire so that we might drink some tea to get some warmth into us. The clothes could be mended for the most part but I was dismayed to find that the scavenger had been brave enough to make off with one of my boots and both of Ragwasi's so I would have to travel in my socks alone. Ragwasi just slipped on some sandals he had and wandered off to inspan the oxen, as naked as Adam in Eden, not counting the bandages of course, and I realized that I could not become a proper African fully because I could never wander around so unselfconsciously naked. He found the zebra kill and came back singing because all the oxen were accounted for and so the only permanent loss was our boots, which he said could be replaced in Swellendam when we got there. After that we inspected our wounds and Ragwasi showed me how to put a stitch in myself with a strong thorn and grass for a suture; this was useful knowledge but also proves the rule that pain is a very good teacher. Actually, it is not that different from the sewing we did to mend our clothes except that I noticed that it is much harder to push a needle through your skin from the inside than it is from the outside. So with our bodies and our clothes stitched together, we inspanned for the last leg into Swellendam, happy to be alive and chewing on our biltong, even though we were limping a bit.

The town was just two parallel streets on the southern side of a shallow stream that ran through lush willows and dappled meadows. The mountains were still close, of course, forming the steep barrier of the Zuurberg which had always been on our left as we came down through the glorious fruit farms of Worcester, Robertson and Bonnievale. Here, the sleepy houses were solid, steady constructions of white-washed stone and thatch, just like the master's at Tulbagh, with kitchen gardens and pretty orchards, and breathed an air of safety and security. There was a cooperage, a smithy, a couple of general stores and although they could not properly be called restaurants, places where the farmer's wife would cook up a braai or give you something from the potjies pot for a few pennies. It was an important town too, because this was where the magistrate for the district had his residence and so it was the place for legal and government business, the payment of taxes and, of course, the storage of guns and ammunition. People were always coming to and fro, whether from nearby or far away to do business, trade and hear the news, and so two barefoot ragamuffins with an undersized ox train towing a squeaky wheeled wagon did not excite much comment.

We dropped off the Indian things at the Magistrate's Drosty, a big Dutch-gabled house, nicely thatched and white washed in a courtyard full of roses as our first task and then took the wagon around to the smithy to mend the wheel. Next we went to the general store and I got my first pair of *veldtschoen*, which are ankle boots made of untanned leather that can be brushed clean and do not need to be polished and which are lighter and more comfortable than the stouter variety I was used to from England. Ragwasi said that *this* was my first step in becoming an African; he was fond of poor jokes. We also bought new shirts and strong homespun trousers so we could put off mending our ripped up clothes until later. After that we treated ourselves to a big feed of chops and baked bread and coffee in the kitchen of a farmhouse, before going back to the smithy to collect the wheel.

'Did you receive your wages from the farmer at Tulbagh?' asked Ragwasi as we walked along the street in our new shirts and boots.

I nodded.

'This is a good and fortunate thing uPelly,' he said, patting me on the back. 'Because I must borrow some from you to pay this man who mends the wheel because I have a cash flow problem.'

'What is a cash flow problem?' I asked.

'It is a business word which means you can't pay someone right now,' he replied. 'But I will pay you later, of course.'

'Of course,' I said, taking out my wallet and counting out some money into his hand. 'Will you pay me back at the same time that you pay me my wages?'

'Of course, of course,' replied Ragwasi, tucking the money away into a special bag that he carried inside his shirt. 'Wages. Yes, definitely.'

The smithy was at the end of the street, his forge glowing hot and red inside his iron roofed shack and the ringing sound of the hammer clinked clearly up the street, carried on the wind like a silver bell. He had done a good job in putting a strong new iron rim onto our wheel and while I took it outside to replace on the wagon, Ragwasi stayed behind to pay. When I came back ten minutes later, he was still negotiating the price.

'But I have a cash flow problem,' he said, holding out his wide hands. 'Surely you can give such a good and regular customer as myself a discount?'

'You still owe me from last time,' replied the blacksmith. 'So pay up or I'll take the wheel back – and the other two that I see are still doing good service for you.'

Ragwasi saw me as I came into the smithy.

'Very well,' he said, turning away and reaching for his money. 'I shall give you something on account. But I shall expect a big discount next time.'

'As I will, on the bar iron you said you would bring last time,' replied the Smith with a gruff laugh.

Ragwasi counted out half of what I had given him into the big sweaty hand of the Smith and then hurried me out as though he were embarrassed. Once outside in the clear sunshine, he patted me on the back.

'That was good business,' he said. 'Now I can pay you from the profits of hard bargaining.'

He handed me a pound note. *My* pound note.

'There,' he said. 'Now you have your wages paid in full.'

We picked up some sacks of wool as our load which I was happy about because I could ride in comfort by sitting on one, but we also picked up some big wooden crates with rifles in them and some boxes of bullets to deliver to the army up at Beaufort West.

'Brand new Martini-Henrys,' said the Magistrate, as I signed a receipt for them. 'The latest breech loaders, accurate out to four hundred yards or so and quick to load. If you miss with your first shot, you've still time for another. The bullet is big too. It'll drop anything that it hits first time and no mistake.'

'And they are needed quickly?' asked Ragwasi. 'You know I will need to be paid in advance for this vital work?'

'Well, I don't know,' replied the Magistrate, looking rather serious. 'It's common for government to take a month's credit at least, you know. All to do with cash flow.'

'What is 'cash flow'?' replied Ragwasi. 'Cash in advance, please.'

We could not resist opening the crates to admire the weapons once we were clear of Swellendam. We were both used to guns but we had always used flintlocks and these were objects of great wonder to us. They were beautifully made, with shaped and polished wooden stocks, good gun metal and when we worked the locks up and down, it made a solid, reliable sound. I wanted my own horse and I knew that with the money I had earned I could probably afford one now. I added this rifle to my list because every young man wants to own a horse and a gun and I asked Ragwasi how much money a rifle like this cost to buy and where I could buy one.

'You must go to Kimberley,' he replied, hammering down the crate lid and sliding it further down the wagon. 'If you have money you can buy it there and if you do not have money then you can work for it there. But I do not advise you to go, you understand uPelly? I have seen Kimberley and it is not a place for you.'

*

Up until that point I had seen nothing but beauty in South Africa but at Kimberley I saw nothing but ugliness and worse. This has always been a troubled land and there has always been war and strife between the peoples who live here, but that is nothing different from anywhere else in the world. Looking at the world from my *stoep,* here in 1911 though, I can trace all the misery that followed from that accursed place, for it was there that I first saw the division between white men and black men emerge. Of course there had always been division but the sources of the strife were not *because* men had different colours of skin. Before Kimberley, they fought over land or cattle or grazing rights or water, not over the colour of their skin, but after Kimberley, the black man always feared that he would not get justice and the white man always expected special or better treatment. Mr.Bramson had told me on the boat that the greatest hatred in South Africa was held by the Afrikaner Boer for us English because we had stopped him from keeping black men as slaves. I had no experience of this at the time because I had only met Afrikander like Mijnheer Cronjie and I looked at the Cape Coloured people as a result of the harmonious union of different people, for were they not the product of love between white people and black people? For myself I had not been brought up to have feelings of race hesitation for any man. At Dines Hall the only people we did not like were the Gypsies, but that was because they kept no law and did not respect our fields or fences rather than because they came mostly from Ireland.

'Kimberley, is it?' said Mijnheer Cronjie. 'There is trouble brewing there and I would advise you to stay away if you want to be clear of it.'

We were talking in the voorkammer of his house in Langstraat where I had gone to collect the monies that he held for me in safekeeping for I had never yet spent all my allowance and had sent him my savings from time to time. I was still working for Ragwasi but we had parted company temporarily, arranging to meet up at Tulbagh before heading for Beaufort West.

'I respect your opinion, Mijnheer,' I replied, honestly. 'But I must raise my capital and I do not know another place where I can do this quickly.'

'You know that that General Cunynghame is marching there because there is so much trouble with the diggers? He will be there in June or July, I think.'

I could tell that he was alarmed by my intention but I was determined to continue my forward motion and for this I needed a horse and a gun. The horse, a good salted tan mare stood outside but I could not bear to think of the time it would take me to save up for a Martini-Henry when I had heard it was possible to get enough to buy one in a month in the Kimberley Hole. It seemed a fortuitous coincidence that Ragwasi and I would get work from the army to carry their things for them from Beaufort West to Kimberley, if that was where they were going. I can tell you now that there was nothing fortuitous about it at all though.

We arrived at Kimberley just after the army arrived, which was good going because we set out three weeks before them. They had mule wagons, you see, and they did three miles to our one and Ragwasi would not meet my eye whenever one went past us on the road, but just sniffed and said I should try eating mule before I made a judgement. He had not wanted to take this job but after he had heard what the prices were like in Kimberley for every necessity, his pocket book persuaded him. As well as the load he carried for the army, there were extra barrels and cases loaded that he called 'supercargo', but which I knew was Cape Smoke. Miners are thirsty people and will pay a lot of money for a drink. We found this out straight away when we sold that brandy at a profit that would make you stare: those men had got used to paying *five shillings for one bottle of beer!* So then, with my share I reckoned I had enough in my pocket book to buy a Martini-Henry without having to become a digger.

Kimberley was famous because it had a big hole in the middle where the diamonds were mined but the rest of it was a dirty scar of infamy, a smear of filth and shanties housing the worst of humanity scraped together from the pits of the world. There were four hundred thousand lost souls here, which was equal to the population of the rest of the Colony put together, sweating and toiling to build an inverted tower of Babel. This is what the Big Hole looked like when you stared down into it because when the shafts were shored up, they looked like Martello towers but square, not round, or houses with flat roofs. Each man had his own claim and dug straight down, putting the scooped out earth into a bucket which his mates at the top would pull up and hope there was a diamond in it. This needed a lot of hope and a lot of rope – the hole looked like a handloom there were so many - and a lot of mates and this was the reason why all those good farms were short of honest labour. There were Griquas, Bathlapings, amaNgwane, Xhosa, Prussians, mPondo, Soshangane, Irish, English and everything else that you could think of and in less than an hour I heard more languages than God had cursed that Biblical Babel with. In fact, cursing was mostly what I heard, along with the smashing of Square Face bottles and the discharge of firearms as customers tried out the wares of the gunrunners. You were supposed to have a permit to buy a gun, but as far as I saw, cash was the only permit you needed.

Ragwasi would not go into the town and insisted that he would stay in the wagon lines with the rest of the transport riders, again advising me not to go, or at least to leave my money and horse with him if I must see it. I agreed that leaving the horse behind was a good idea, but I needed the roll of bank notes in my pocket if I was to buy a Martini-Henry. He said I was a fool but as I was determined to kill myself, I should put my money in my underpants where they would be safe from everyone but a woman. I did as he asked in this respect, but it did me no good in the end.

I understood what everyone meant about trouble from the minute I walked into the town. Squelching through the mud from the mine pumps, you could feel the tension and the hatred in the air as each nationality or company formed its own district for self-preservation. There were hard times here and the causes of them were laid out in the booths of the interloper diamond merchants. The bigger companies had got together to try to regulate the price of diamonds, but the interlopers bought anything stolen or pilfered and undercut them, which meant there were too many diamonds on the market and the price had collapsed. White men were unemployed and did not have the means to return either to the Cape or to their countries and black men were unemployed and turned to Square Face gin and soon the gutters were awash with Africans that had only tasted weak millet beer before and that rarely, or at festivals spaced apart. The drunk Dutch or Irish or English said the Africans were inferior because they could not hold their spirits and white men both drunk and sober, employed and unemployed, started to say that as the black men *could* go home, they *should* go home and leave the jobs to them.

I heard this from an Irishman who was stood on a box waving a black flag and haranguing a crowd of adventurers, speculators, jobbers and rowdies of every class and description of white men. Next to him was a placard declaring that he was a member of 'The Committee of Public Safety'.

'This is our *cunthry*,' he was a small, dark man with a strong accent like the Gypsies from home and his face was brick red, but I guessed it was more from gin and getting worked up than from hard work under a hot sun. 'We made it and we have a right to it! This was empty land before we came here and the *Kaffir* has no right to it! And who are the English government to command us? We have guns here in plenty! We Fenians know how to fight the *verdammtestenglishers*, by God.'

Verdammtestenglishers. He said it as one word, a mixture of Afrikaans, Dutch, Prussian I think too and the crowd loved it and he had them forming lines and marching about in no time, as if they were an army. For myself, although I had chosen to be an African, I was still enough of an Englishman not to like this talk or give it much credit, for I knew that it would dissolve into wind at the first appearance of the soldiers.

Moving on to where the gun runners had their stalls in search of my Martini-Henry, I saw that Kimberley was an armed camp indeed. Inside the Morton Brothers *Diamant Koopers* store, a green painted corrugated iron shack with a couple of Boers making the most of the shade on the stoep and a couple of tough looking Irishmen behind the counter in top hats, I saw the unholy trinity of Kimberley under one roof; diamonds, Square Face gin and guns. There were all sorts of ancient firelocks, Brown Bess and Tower muskets, double-barreled shotguns, and the long barreled pieces that the Boers favoured. A lot of the African young men had been sent here by their chiefs to work so they could buy guns and they mainly bought these as being the cheapest. The Sniders and Prussian needle guns were in the middle range but the Martini-Henrys were new and so the most expensive. How Morton's had them, I don't know, because by law they were only supposed to be bought and sold by the government but, as I say, there was no law and very little government in Kimberley.

I had just finished paying for my treasured rifle - which I am pleased to say I got at a knock down price because the Morton Brothers did not want to be found holding such things with General Cunynghame waiting outside the town - when the commotion began. Two young Griquas, they were like Cape Coloured people but they lived further out, had come to buy guns but the Boers did not want this so they started to abuse them. I heard the shouting and then the sound of blows and one of the Boers burst through the door aiming to get hold of one of the guns. I looked around for a way to escape because when bullets fly from heated men they do not care who they hit and those Griqua men had friends with them. At that moment, the Fenian with his newly formed militia came marching down the street and seeing black men with guns, started haranguing again about *schwartzers, kaffirs* and his *cunthry*. His mob went straight for them, swinging pick helves and shovels and someone fired a shot and every loafer, mobster, miner or man with a grudge, black, white, coloured or whatever appeared from nowhere and piled in. It seemed that the only people who did not want to trade a blow or an insult were me and the Morton Brothers, who quickly shut up shop, pulled out pistols and bludgeons which they handed to their three Xhosa clerks, and took up positions behind the counter as if it were a barricade. I thought of joining them, but this was not my fight and I decided I would take my chances out the back door.

Taking my rifle and bullets with what was left of my bankroll in my crotch, I pulled open the door and headed out. I could hear the sound of jostling and fighting from the front of the store so I doubled back around in the hope that I would come out at the rear of Paddy McGinty's Fenian fusiliers. This was not a good idea as at that moment the Griquas and their pals were getting the better of them and I ended up being trapped in an alleyway, hard up against another corrugated iron store with a mob of Irishmen and Prussians baying for my blood. They had been beaten by the Griquas and like the worst sort of bullies, they wanted revenge and there I was a *verdammtestenglisher* caught like a rat in a trap. I pulled the rifle off my shoulder and threatened them with it, but this just made them madder and the Black Irishman, who had been doing the haranguing just stepped forward, punched me in the face and snatched the Martini-Henry out of my hands.

'You bloody English!' He spat at me and hit me again. '*Pogue mahone!* If it's not my cunthry yer after, it's someone else's. And I'll thrash ye for the sake of it.'

There was a murmur of approval from his mates and his face went a furnace red as he drew back to hit me again. I put my hands up but I knew I was in for a beating, because the other bastards were about to join in and no-one, not Achilles himself, can fight ten to one. How I wished for Big George by my side at that moment because he had a fist that could lay out a Gypsy.

At that moment the side door of the store flew open and a man appeared, dressed like a banker in a waistcoat, shirt, collar and tie. He was of middling height, tanned, like everyone else in this country, and had an air of command about him even though he was only my age. I could see he was not a habitual manual worker because although his hands were callused, his wrists were thin.

'Sean Logan, what the devil are you doing kicking up a bloody fuss on a working day?' he said in an English accent, and then looking past the Irishman he addressed the Prussians directly. 'Hans Gaiser? You too? And Pieter Brucke? Don't you have work to do?'

He looked at me and I saw that there was absolutely no fear in his eyes, but that they were lidded, slightly bulging and fronted a brain that was calculating, weighing up everything it took in. It was written plain on his face that he was a man who went through the world making deals and did not like anything that got in the way of making those deals, especially if it made a devil of a noise and scared customers away.

'I'm going to thrash this English bastard within an inch of his life and then further,' replied Logan. 'And I'm doing it because you English bastards are giving our jobs to the Kaffirs and you're bringing the soldiers to drive us out of our cunthry.'

'Oh don't talk wet, Logan,' replied the young banker, speaking with an authority well beyond his years and stepping out into the alley. 'You're out of work because you got caught nicking diamonds from Waterboers' claim and you've pissed your wages against a gin shop wall.'

'That's a black lie, Mr. Rhodes!' Logan spat back. 'It was the Kaffirs that did the stealing and I got the blame because they ganged up on me.'

Cecil Rhodes. Everyone knows that name now, but then he was just making his way like me, seeking a life less ordinary, trying to live life audaciously. Well, he did it, but so did I and although he ended richer – he was making a hundred pounds a week even then - and more famous and more powerful than me, I can look myself in the mirror when I shave. So can he probably, because he had that *amoral* quality that powerful men have. He was a big man in Kimberley then and later on he got so big he was able steal the whole of Lobengula's country and re-name it Rhodesia. Imagine stealing someone's country and naming it after yourself! Most pirates keep their crimes to themselves.

Anyway, Rhodes never moved when Logan shouted at him. He just pushed his tongue up in front of his teeth and then picked at them with a finger. Then he looked at me again and asked simply.

'What do you want here? You don't look like a miner but you don't look like you're fresh off the boat either.'

'I want my Martini-Henry and I want to get out of here,' I replied.

'Got any money?' he asked.

'A bit,' I confirmed, warily.

He thought for a moment, sized up Logan and the Prussians and then made his judgment, as if he were a Magistrate.

'Right, Logan – give him his rifle back.'

Logan hesitated, and then threw it at me.

'Good, now whatever-your-name-is, give Logan a pound and ten bob each to Hans and Pieter here so they can go and buy Square Face and celebrate avoiding the noose when Cunynghame gets here and starts asking too many questions about The Committee of Public Safety.'

Logan looked defiant still, but Rhodes knew he had crushed his rebellion. Rhodes held out a hand for my wallet and I rooted it out of my crotch. He sorted through the coins and notes.

'Don't worry, Logan,' he said, slapping a pound note in his hand, and pouring coins into the outstretched hands of the Prussians. 'I'll tell the authorities it was just piss and wind as usual. Now on your way.'

The Prussians took the money and ran, but I could see Logan was seething still and it took Rhodes another moment before he imposed his will.

'Alright, Logan,' he said. 'I'll tell them all about your black flags and your plans to run all the blacks off the diamond fields. Then you can take your chances as a Fenian trouble maker with an English government or with the mine owners who need black workers. It's your choice – but choose now.'

Logan spat, put the note in his pocket and disappeared.

'There is always a reasonable compromise if people would just approach things calmly,' said Rhodes, absent mindedly taking five bob for himself then handing me my wallet back. 'The days of the independent digger are coming to an end, you know. If they had any sense they would look at the prices in the market and go into business selling meat and salt to mine owners like me, Mr....what did you say your name was?'

'Pelly,' I said, holding out my hand to shake his.

'Pelly? Where do you hale from then, Mr. Pelly?'

'Dines Hall in Suffolk,' I replied. 'Do you know it?'

He thought for a moment.

'No, not really,' he replied. 'Do you know the Stockwells though? They come from Dines Hall. A sister and two brothers? The boys used to work for me.'

My heart leaped straight into my mouth and the blood began to roar in my temples. The Stockwells! Here in Kimberley! I confess I felt terrified at the prospect for though my opportunity had come to make amends, I dreaded the prospect of meeting Daisy again. I could not imagine that it would be a pleasant interview under any circumstances at all.

'Where are they now?' I stammered.

'No idea,' he replied, very off-the-cuff. 'You don't expect me to keep track of every man, woman and dog who wanders in an out of Kimberley, do you? Now, Good Day, to you Mr.Pelly, but I'm sure you have business to attend to just as I do.'

He was about to turn away, when there was rumble of hooves and who should come round the corner at the head of a troop of Cape Coloured horseman, but Lieutenant Tom G. Cole all done up in pith helmets and blues. He pulled up, drew a pistol, gave that bright smile and boomed.

'Cecil John Rhodes – you're nicked.'

I got nicked too, and for the record, it's the only time in my life that I have seen the inside of a police cell. Actually, it wasn't a police cell, but the Morton Brother's store because the Magistrates were improvising. I wasn't in there for long either, because Tom Cole stood up for my character and they needed the space for the real ruffians, which Cunynghame's 24th Regiment redcoats were rounding up.

'Well this is a welcome surprise,' he said happily, as we rode back to the transport lines on his troop horses. 'I have often wondered on what became of you and I've always hoped to bump into you again.'

I filled him in on what I had been up to but he seemed to have had the more exciting time.

'I started work on the Survey,' he said, brushing a fly away from his face. 'But then we had orders from London to inspect the Colonial forces so I've been out to Grahamstown and as far as Durban and then back to the Cape. Then we heard about the Fenians setting themselves up as a Digger republic and when we'd stopped laughing, I was told to recruit a troop of native soldiers and come up here to arrest them.'

'Who are your soldiers, then?'

'Cape Mounted Rifles mainly, re-enlisted from before they were disbanded a few years ago,' chuckled Cole. 'That's one in the eye for Gladstone, eh? Always trying to pare back the army and always failing. My CO reckons that there's been a weather change with Lord Carnarvon at the Colonial Office now. He says he's never known London to take the Colonies so seriously before. Apparently there's some big plan to make South Africa one country, like Canada.'

'Well whatever the plan is, you can count me out,' I retorted. 'If it means me having to live in the same country as Kimberley, you can keep it.'

We parted company with all good farewells and wishes at the edge of Kimberley and I was certain that it was not the last time that I would see Tom Cole. Something also told me that I would see Daisy Stockwell again, although under what circumstances was anyone's guess.

*

Chapter 4

Tepo Boapile

I went into Kimberley only rarely and reluctantly from that first visit onwards, for the truth was that I did not want to bump into Daisy Stockwell unless I was fully prepared and both of us warned well in advance. Once or twice, I made enquiries after her, but never with any satisfactory reply, and I should confess to being secretly glad with this state of affairs; it seemed to me that my uneasiness was a price worth paying to avoid meeting my shame head on and when I thought about it, I knew I was a long way from facing up to the things necessary to achieve the redemption that I sought.

I took Rhodes' advice though and Ragwasi and I went into business supplying meat and salt to the mines there. You will say I am a hypocrite for helping to keep Kimberley supplied when I hated it and see it as the source of all evil in South Africa. You would be right too, but everyone is a hypocrite when his wallet or his family are concerned and the profits to be made were so steady and good that we could not argue against these facts. With my horse and my Martini-Henry every springbok, kudu, blesbok, hartebeest, wildebeest, eland, zebra or ostrich for a hundred and fifty miles north and west of Kimberley was a free meal, and biltong and hides to sell.

Back then the game was plentiful. Indeed it was so plentiful that on first seeing it I could hardly believe my eyes. Down in the farming areas of the Cape the game had been mostly shot out and it was only in the wilder mountain areas that there were still leopards and zebra and buck. That and baboons, of course, which are a trial sent by God to anyone who wishes to farm fruit because they always turn up at harvest time and are both greedy and quiet. They are also clever and aggressive too and you must keep your wits about you when they are around. This is because they are not like the monkeys you sometimes see in cages or sitting on a barrel organ in a silly hat. They are big, so big that they are not afraid of a man. Once I was walking through a farm near Stellenbosch when I heard the sound of two ponies running towards me from behind. Only when I turned around I saw that they were not ponies, but baboons and they passed either side of me running like the wind. It gave me a fright, I can tell you.

In many ways the Cape was like Suffolk – apart from the baboons, of course – in that there was game about but it had been pushed to the side to make way for civilized agriculture. Cows and sheep and pigs were grazed over areas that had once been the range of elephants and hippopotamus and the buck that did remain kept as much to the woods and forests as the deer at home did. There was always ground game, of course, and plenty to keep the fisherman occupied but by then the landscape had been tamed for many miles about. Hedges had been planted, woods felled, roads laid, bridges thrown across the wide and deep fissures cut by the streams that cascaded down the escarpment and now, even the railway was coming. About Kimberley, however, the opposite was true. Although I had seen sizeable runs of fallow deer in the rolling hills along the Essex border, nothing had prepared me for the vast herds that lay before me now. The zebra ran like drifts of snow in moorland hollows while there were absolute sandstorms of springbok. On one occasion I counted three thousand before I gave up. Thousands upon thousands of the docile wildebeest could be seen making their slow, steady progress across the veldt, lowing stupidly when they lost their calves, which they did often, and raising the dust in the midday so that it lay like mist. The red hartebeest was a favourite quarry because it reminded me of the stags of home; they were also very profitable because one bullet would provide the makings of a lot of biltong. All we had to do was drop it, skin it, slice it up, rub it with salt and hang it up in Ragwasi's wagon and it would cure on the way into Kimberley.

Actually that makes it sound a lot easier than it was. Just like a stag or deer at home, a hartebeest or kudu or any kind of buck for that matter has to be bled straight away when you kill it or the meat goes foul very quickly. For this reason, I would usually take the shot and then Ragwasi would drive the wagon up and we would quickly get a block and tackle over a tree branch or onto a special frame that I invented if there were no trees handy. Then we would take the rear legs and hoist them up high so that we could cut the animal's throat and drain the blood out. At home, we would use this to make Black puddings but out here on the veldt it was too hot to really bother with this luxury because we had to concentrate on getting to the meat quickly. Again, at home we would skin and butcher the animal in a cool shed that faced north away from the sun and was sunk into the earth a little so as to keep it cool, but here we must do it in the full glare of the light and heat and amid clouds of flies that appeared from nowhere and got everywhere. They would crawl into your mouth and eyes and ears and drive you mad but there was nothing that could be done. We tried to light fires sometimes in the hope that the smoke would drive them away but when this did work, it was at the cost of nearly choking us. Finally, we would slice the meat into long, thick chunks, rub it with plenty of salt and, if we had them, herbs and spices, and hang it on frames to dry in the sun. Back in Suffolk it would be usual to hang up beef and game in the cool house for a week or two so that the meat would be tender but this was another luxury we could not afford in the heat of a veldt summer. In winter, it was not so bad and we would supply more fresh meat to the hungry miners, but in the main it was biltong, biltong and more biltong for them.

Most of the buck we killed tasted like venison but I was surprised to find that ostrich does not taste like a big chicken as you would imagine, but is much more like beef. The leather was highly prized and if you have ever been to a show at a certain type of musical hall, you might have seen ladies fluttering big fans made of ostrich feathers in front of them. The men who supplied these essentials had big farms down at Oudtshorn and made a lot of money by farming them. You can ride them too if you have a mind to, but only if you are very stupid because they are horrible smelly birds and bad tempered. If they give you a kick then you will know about it; I once saw a dog disemboweled by an ostrich with a single kick from its big, clawed toes.

Our main competition came from the sheep farmers who drove their flocks in to Kimberley from time to time so that the miners might not go completely mad from eating just our biltong. Actually, I think our biltong was better than their sheep. As you know, sheep breed only once a year and so if you don't eat spring lamb, then what you get is mutton or hogget which in South Africa is no great shakes. Sheep need to be kept in a very rainy climate like Wales or the north of England if it is not to be too tough. The farmers here make a big noise about Karoo lamb and sing its praises a lot; but it is a lot of noise only because you cannot raise sheep in a desert and expect it to be as tender and lush as a well-watered hillside in England or Wales.

The best game is warthog, which is a wild pig that looks a little like a wild boar. I say this not having seen a wild boar properly, except in pictures. My father had an old boar spear in his study but England has not seen a wild boar since the wolves were hunted down. Anyway, this warthog is an ugly grey critter with tusks and trots about with its tail very high and very straight up in the air and has a mane and fringe on its head too. They are not very big either, being about half the size of the pigs that go to market and Ragwasi was unwilling at first to use the Martini-Henry to kill them because he said the bullets were so expensive as not to justify wasting one on such a small animal. I let him try to hunt them with a spear, which he soon gave up on, and once I had tasted the meat resolved never to eat anything else ever again. It is like pork but smokey and has a delicate texture like lamb. Oh how I do love roast warthog! It can be salted too and makes very good bacon, although it could do with a bit more fat in this respect. Ragwasi can eat nearly four pounds of meat at one go when he decides he is hungry and when we had shot any other sort of animal I would let him have first go. Not with the warthog though, for he can be very greedy, and I always made sure that I had the chops and the ribs and the shoulder while he had to be content with the leg. I don't think he minded though, but he did use to tut-tut at the supposed waste of the bullet. I did not listen to him and counted every warthog a boon and a success.

This is not to say that we did not have our disasters, like the time I tried to make *boerewors* out of zebra, but for two years we were ahead of the field and we coined it hand over fist and bought horses, guns and more oxen whenever we chose. The salt too was free because Ragwasi knew how to find it in the Kalahari, so we just dug it up and loaded that on the wagon too. Salt was expensive then because they had to make it at the Cape from the sea and then cart it up. The only other place was in the north of the Transvaal at the Soutspansberg, but you needed salted horses up there and it was a long way.

The only thing that I did miss from my chop during this time was butter and cheese. I do not know why the Boers did not make butter because they had enough cows but really they preferred to spread the fat from a sheep's tail onto their bread. It was a bit like bread and dripping but cold and greasy. I always tried to toast mine a bit. Cheese was just unknown outside of the Cape and sometimes I used to lie awake at night dreaming of big truckle cheddars, Lincolnshire poacher and Stilton. The Tswana had a sort of salty sour milk which they made in baskets inside their huts and although I got to quite like it, it could never replace the cheese, cream and butter of old England. Once I managed to buy some from the soldiers who had brought it with them as part of their rations but I think it must have been first issued during Queen Anne's reign and so I could not eat it. It was dry, hard and as tasteless as plaster.

Actually, now cheese is easier to get these days I eat it a lot. I have even been able to introduce Ragwasi to Stilton. He did not like it, being conservative in his tastes, and watched me with an undisguised fascination as I shoveled it down with a packet of Crawford's biscuits that came all the way from England too.

'uPelly,' he said, when he first tried it. 'I have eaten some very odd things in my life, but this is something very strange indeed. It tastes like a spear.'

Being out on the open veldt was a very new experience for me too and I should say here that it made me very homesick sometimes even though it was very beautiful and majestic. In England I was used to a landscape of woods and hedges, green fields and long low hillsides where the vistas were pretty in a manicured sort of way, but not often very long. Out on the veldt you can sometimes see so far into the distance that you can almost see the curvature of the Earth. The mountains too are more dramatic, even than those of the Lake District that I have seen pictures of. The Drakensberg is a very spectacular range and it does indeed resembled the spines on the back of a dragon; the Zulus call it the 'Hedge of Spears' and they are not wrong either. Right out in the east towards Lourenco Marques there is a place on the escarpment called 'God's Window' and it is so high above the plain below that I have seen a signal rocket fired upwards towards me and yet looked down on top of it as it exploded. Imagine that: seeing fireworks from above.

Anyway, I could not help thinking of my family back in Dines Hall and wondering how they were getting on. Each time I went into Kimberley to check the Post Office for messages from Mijnheer Cronjie, the thought would always go through my mind that perhaps a letter from home would be waiting for me. I was always disappointed and each time vowed not to be disappointed again, but it never worked. Hope springs eternal, it is said, but as the months and years went by without a word, hope began to dry up in me just as the Kuruman River dries up in the summer. Of course, irregularity in the post was normal back then and even Cape Town was not connected to England by the telegraph. It did not help that sometimes the mail cart got robbed and letters were lost or that the drivers sometimes got drunk and did not deliver anywhere near the time that they should have done. Mail was sometimes handed on to casual travelers for forwarding to some of the remoter settlements in the far flung places that Europeans got to in those years. Nowadays we have telegraphs and regular mail services that bring the newspapers from England every Thursday come rain or shine aboard Mr. Currie's lavender line Union-Castle ships. One day men will go to the Moon perhaps and then they will know just how isolated Africa was back then.

Mijnheer Cronjie heard no more than I did. After the first year, he received only a note from my father's solicitors to cease paying my allowance and that was the end of it. I thought about writing a letter to him, to say sorry and to express to him my regret but though I started that letter many times, I did not finish it. Each time I wrote the salutation, I had a vision of my mother standing in the doorway at Dines Hall, always with her fingers to her mouth, her brow anxious. She was looking down across the fields to the Yellow House, watching the eviction of the Stockwells. I would screw up the paper then, replace the pen in its holder, thank Mijnheer Cronjie and then get up from his broad table and take to the road. As time went by, I gradually put away my thoughts of home, suppressed the grief that sat in my stomach like lead and concentrated on becoming an African.

*

You will say I am doubly a hypocrite when I tell you that I also bought diamonds from Kimberley but when you are reading this you will maybe also have a diamond on your finger or perhaps your wife has one on hers. When you look at it properly, like you did when it first slipped onto a finger, you will see how it can seduce you away from every good intention. At first it just looks like an ordinary piece of glass but then you look a little closer and you can see clear points of starlight within it and you wonder how something so pure and bright could ever come out of a hole and you will think that maybe it is a piece of a star fallen to earth. You hold it up to the light and suddenly there are points of blue and pink and fire and a whiter light than even before and you twirl it and there are forty legions of angels dancing in there. You can see their wings and flaming swords flash, and their hot silver shields shine the light of God straight out into your eye. Now you are properly interested and you will try to see how the diamond has been cut and polished and try to count the facets, but you can't because each time you move it another thousand are revealed or burnt up in the thousand new prisms you have just created. In a moment you will look at the clock and realize that you have been lost in that light for much longer than you expected and you will understand me better when I say that a diamond will seduce anyone. It is a great pity that such a thing of beauty can turn men into devils. This lesson was brought home to me at the end of those two good years of selling game to Kimberley when Ragwasi got a message from his kin up near a place called Kuruman, that their cattle had been stolen.

I knew from the outset that Ragwasi had children for it had been a condition of my employment with him that I would not have to teach them. When we came up to Kimberley with the army, he was able to see them more often than before and sometimes he would take my horse and go visit while I looked after the wagon and the biltong. After a while, he invited me to go with him and I met his wife – actually I met all three of them – and his nine children, who shared a *lolwapa* or kraal happily together.

'Look at this, uPelly,' he said, sweeping his arm along the line of beehive huts laid out in a horseshoe shape around a central space. 'Is this not what makes a man, a man? Is this not what makes life living. Here I am my own chief and master and can do as I wish.'

I looked at the well-made huts, the thatch silver grey like the finer feathers on an ostrich and as tightly woven as good broadcloth. Each one was neatly kept and the ground around it freshly swept while just beyond were small vegetable gardens where the children tended to gem squash and pumpkins. Around the whole lolwapa was a rough fence of thorn bush to keep out the lions and the leopards, while standing tall above it were fine bluegums and yellow woods to give shade from the hot sun. From the far side of the fence where the wide fields of mealies stood up high, I could hear the sound of women singing and the accompanying hollow beat of the sturdy sticks they used to pound the corn into flour. Two small boys peeked at me from around the corner of a hut, their eyes wide and I guessed that they had not seen a white man before.

'Three wives, Ragwasi?' I asked. I had not been near a woman in several years now and I admit I thought that having three might be very pleasant if greedy.

He gave me one of his tired looks as we walked over to look at the cattle coming in from the veldt.

'It is expected, uPelly,' he said, scooping up a snotty child chewing a corn cob. 'But, believe me, it is not always a blessing. You should stick to the white man's ways and have only one wife. Women are very noisy and they talk a lot.'

'It looks comfortable to me,' I retorted, and thought some impure thoughts that made me blush. It was a long way from the Dines Hall hayloft, I can tell you.

'It is good sometimes, I admit,' he teased, looking sideways at me and giving me his upside down smile. 'But you should not be deceived. If you do not treat them strictly according to rules that they make up and keep secret from you, you will be in trouble. I am in trouble a lot. That is why I am a transport rider.'

The boys were herding the cattle into the centre of the kraal and it was a fine sight to see such good brown beasts lowing and jostling in the copper light of the evening. The Tswana talk about cattle the same way we talk about horses and they have many more words to describe the different shades of brown or the different pattern of markings on them than we have. They remember their cattle with the same fondness as we remember a first pony, a favourite dog or a horse.

'How did you tell your first wife that you wanted a second one?' I replied, teasing back. 'It must have been a difficult interview.'

'It was her idea,' he grinned, as he put the child down on the red earth. 'I was too much of a man for her and she needed help.'

'You mean you gave her *dagga*,' I laughed, and dodged his cuff.

'That is it!' he declared, in a high tone of mock indignation. 'I see I shall have to find you a woman, uPelly. Then you can find these things out for yourself and not importune me with your rude questions.'

I thought he was joking, but he was not and that evening as we drank millet beer, I was introduced to Tepo Boapile who became my wife. I do not know *when* she actually became my wife, because Tswana marriages can take place long after you have been sharing a hut and have children, so I count the time from that first meeting. She is still beautiful to me today, but then *Het!* she was a picture. When Ragwasi's wives brought her up to sit with us by the fire, I could only stare like a calf. Her skin was the colour of milky coffee and copper combined and she had perfect collar bones and high cheek bones and a big smile, modest - but still full of fun. Her hair was braided close to her head with thin plaits that came down to her shoulders and ended in blue, green and red beads and she was wearing a tunic and kilt of softest springbok. She was slim and graceful and if Ragwasi's wives had demanded I be married then and there I swear I would have agreed. I could see that she liked me too because she had the same look in her eye that the girls of Dines Hall had at harvest when they had been at the cider.

This, of course, was a very big thing for I knew at once that if I married in Africa then all my links with England would fade away and come to an end for it is a rule of life that a man must live where his wife lives or there will be no peace. A woman always wants to be near her mother and if she is not then you will always be visiting and trekking about until you give up and go to live nearby. And it is worse if there are children, because then her mother will always be visiting you and telling you off about how the children are not being brought up properly. Many married men say this happens anyway, but it is worse if a woman is not near her mother because eventually her mother will turn her against you and as you cannot turn them out of the house, you will end up turning yourself out of your own house if you ever want to have some peace. It is a big reason why Englishmen like their gardens. No, it is better for a man to let his wife live near her mother or he will never hear the end of it.

When we rode away the next morning I had a lot to think about therefore. Ragwasi did not help but kept smiling and slapping me on the back and making lewd comments about skinny girls and how they make poor wives. I did not care because my heart was as high as the sky. Tepo was the daughter of one of the wives of an important chief called Montshiwa who had come to live in Ragwasi's lolwapa because her mother had fallen out with Montshiwa. I am not sure that Montshiwa knew this because he had many wives and probably did not miss one more or less. This sort of problem is quite common, Ragwasi tells me, but I should like to see the look on the face of the curate at Dines Hall if I told him. Actually, he would be scandalized at a lot of things that go on in Tswana families because they have very different customs as I have said. One of them is that the whole village gets involved in bringing up the children which I have come to accept as a good thing. What did that poet Tennyson say? 'The old order changes making way for the new, lest one good custom corrupts another,' or something like that. Anyway, I think it is wisdom. Tepo and I understood each other very well despite the differences in our background and nationalities and as I was willing to do things in an African way and learn what she could teach me, things worked out just fine. Over the next few months I thought up many good business reasons to hunt near Kuruman, which Ragwasi snorted at, but which led to a growing feeling between Tepo and myself. Finally, he said I should buy a cow and send it into Montshiwa's lolwapa as a sign of good will and as a down payment on the *mokwele* I would have to pay to marry Tepo.

'*Mokwele*?' I said, as we rode up to a lolwapa said to possess many fine cows for sale.

'It is the custom to buy your wife with a cow,' he said. 'And you must take your time in choosing the right cow too, because this is what you will be judged on for the rest of your life, believe me. If you choose a poor specimen, then your father-in-law will not respect you and your wife will have a long face forever.'

'How am I to choose?' I replied. 'The cattle here are so different from the beasts I was used to at home.'

'Look for a beast with clear markings and good, long horns,' he replied. 'She must have sweet breath, firm hooves and a good tail.'

We rode into the lolwapa calling out our greetings and holding our hands in the air to show we had come in peace. This was not really necessary as the lolwapa belonged to an acquaintance of Ragwasi's called Kelebogile, but it is always well to have good manners and while I went to look at the cattle, Ragwasi sat down to negotiate with his friend. I did not take part in the haggling over price for this Ragwasi forbade on the grounds of Tswana custom. That was a new one to me, but I had grown used to Ragwasi inventing things when money was involved and the only thing I heard from a distance was his repeated use of the word 'cash-flow'.

There were eight cows for sale, each one different in shade but all of them good red-brown, solid beasts, well cared for and likely to make good breeding stock. Their eyes were bright, their coats shiny and none limped or shied when I pushed them around to see how they moved. The ninth one, however, caught my eye for being white, a little smaller, with a distinctive spatter of black markings down its back and sides. When I turned it about, I saw that the markings were identical on each side and this I thought to be both remarkable and lucky. I was a white man and so I thought that a white cow would be suitable mokwele and so I settled on this beast.

'Ragwasi,' I called, standing by the white cow. 'I have made my choice. Come and tell me that I have made a good choice.'

'uPelly,' he said, coming over. 'You are a bigger fool than even I would take you for. Why cannot you be content with a good Tswana cow? That is an Nguni cow. It is a royal cow and you will not believe what it will do to my cash flow.'

I did not care. I had chosen and as Tepo was a chief's daughter, I thought the mokwele would be doubly acceptable if it was indeed a royal cow. I insisted that he pay a just price for it and he went back to a smiling Kelebogile with a very long face. While he haggled and haggled and bargained and wheedled, I sat down in the shade and drank beer thinking of how many slapped faces would be received by applying this custom in Dines Hall but when in Africa you must do as the Africans do. When all was done and the price agreed, Ragwasi put the halter around the cow's neck and handed it to me.

'This will make Tepo's father very happy,' he said, miserably.

'It's only money,' I said, slapping him on the back.

*

The news that cattle had been stolen from Ragwasi's kin affected me too because I was now as interested in Ragwasi's clan as he was and I wasted no time in taking my gun and mounting up to help Ragwasi bring back the cows. I could only guess that the rustlers were rascals out of Kimberley, hoping to live by theft. This was not a new idea of course for cattle lifting was a fact of life in all Africa. The grass here is not as sweet as in England so it is often not possible to keep more than one or two cows on an acre at any one time and so the herd boys must disperse them over wide distances. No one liked it when they had a cow stolen by a Bushman or taken by lions but this was life. Stealing the whole herd though was as serious as an act of war and when it happened your kith and kin would be called out to take them back. You could not appeal to the Magistrate out here because the gun and the assegai were the only Magistrates with authority, so you armed yourself and went after the thieves.

Six of us set out to hunt the rustlers, and there would have been more, but Ragwasi and I insisted that only those with horses and good rifles should go because it was speed, stealth and firepower that was required, not numbers. He did allow his son, Seretse, a lad of about fifteen or sixteen to come because he said it was time he saw these things for himself as they were new things. It was easy enough to pick up the spoor because the rustlers had made such a hash of rounding up the cattle. Whatever they had been before, it was obvious they had not been stockmen because they did not know that you must move cattle from water to water and although there is water in this arid part of South Africa it is sometimes difficult to find. They did not know where to find it so the spoor was marked by cattle that had wandered off from the herd and collapsed from thirst and this made us angry at the waste. We also saw another one lost to the tawny lions that are always present but our blood boiled when we came across little Sipo, one of the herd boys from Ragwasi's lolwapa. He had been beaten with a *sjambok*, a stiff rhino hide crop that the Boers were fond of, so that his buttocks were cut deep and he had been hit in the face with a rifle butt so that one eye was swollen up and closed. I thought that his skull had been broken and so I bandaged it as best I could while Ragwasi put comfrey on his cuts; it was not enough though, and Sipo was never right in the head afterwards.

'This is the work of inexperienced white men, uPelly,' Ragwasi said, wiping the tears away. 'Tswana do not make war on children or lose their way with cattle in their own country and Boers do not turn children away when they can take them as slaves. What is wrong with you white people? What devil is in you that makes you do such things?'

I had no wish to answer this question. Every man has the devil in him whether white or black.

We caught our first sight of the stolen cattle a day later as the last rays of sunset showed them as a smear of ochre dust against the pale straw of the grass and the red of the earth. We had been tracking them for three days and they would have got clean away by now if the gang had not been so greedy and kept trying to sweep up the strays from other herds. So the next morning we began our stalking, counting the cattle, counting the numbers of thieves and guns and seeing what sort of men they were. We were not impressed. There were a dozen of them and I cannot say I was very surprised when I recognized their leader as Sean Logan, for being loud, lazy, cowardly and unhandy, he was made to be a thief. I had him in my sights first at 400 yards and it was clear he had no idea that he was being hunted. I have seen more alertness in rhinoceros, which are nearly blind and as content as donkeys. I did not kill him then because I wanted to be sure and 400 yards is a long shot even for a professional hunter like myself so I let him live and we moved in closer, watching them the whole day.

They were the worst sort of townie robbers it was clear, because all twelve of them drank late and slept late and started in the darkness at noises that would never disturb an honest countryman in Africa or East Anglia. We proved this when Ragwasi and one of the other Tswana went in close after midnight and threw a bullet into their fire, which cooked off and sent them into a real panic, blazing away in all directions. This trick I thought was undisciplined behaviour, but Ragwasi had a cold fury on him and said he wanted them to know they were being hunted because he wanted them to feel Sipo's fear before he killed them.

Killed them? You will think me stupid, but until that moment I had not actually thought of them as *men* who would be killed for the sake of justice or revenge, just as another kind of animal to be hunted and even though I had put my sights on Logan already, there was no hate in my heart. It was then that I remembered that Ragwasi had seen men killed before and perhaps had actually killed men back when he was a young man. I had never asked him and he had never volunteered this information but when he said this I decided I must ask.

'Twice,' he revealed, tightly. 'One Boer, one Basuto. They were both bastards and I do not regret it, but I wish I had not. Tomorrow I will add perhaps a miner.'

He would only meet my eye fleetingly and it was clear he had made up his mind to shoot to kill when the chance came. I think he was cursing me a little too, for I could see that he saw me as white man and was therefore in some way responsible. I was not responsible but I could not blame him for feeling this way. I think he also knew that he was cursing me unjustly because I had told him many times that white people belonged to as many different nations as did Africans. At that moment, I felt that I was both an Englishman and a Tswana because I also thought of Tepo and I resolved to prove it tomorrow by killing Logan, for whom I had no feeling at all.

So the second time I had my foresight on Logan's head was towards noon the next day, a clear shot, no wind and only the cicadas in the thorn trees going quiet whenever I moved to give me away, not that he noticed. A man does have a sixth sense though and even if it has lain dormant while he boozed away in a gin shop, or whored away in the bright lights of a big city all his life, it is still there. As I evened out my breathing, pulled in the last breath, kept both my eyes on him while my right eye looked down the barrel and my thumb pushed the safety catch forward, I began the slow squeeze on the trigger that would dispatch him. I had become the hunter again, one with the smooth wood of the rifle, conscious of the little notch on the stock that I had scratched in to give the perfect position for my left hand, conscious of the slight tension in my right breast ready for the recoil, conscious as I pumped the blood slowly, evenly into my trigger finger, resisting the temptation to snatch the shot. I had already imagined the flight of the bullet and I knew Logan was dead from the moment I had put the Martini-Henry in my shoulder. I felt the trigger began to move…and then Logan leaped up like a jack-in-the-box, his red face redder than ever and his hat off, pulled out a revolving pistol from a pocket in his tan check suit and began to shoot wildly in all directions. Something had startled the game, so I lowered my rifle to watch for it. I did not have long to wait because a lioness loped past a hundred yards in front of me, a big creamy tan cat that I had not spotted and had no inkling was there. So much for the professional hunter! It had been warned off by the noise of Logan's pistol but I was still enough of a hunter to know that lions hunt together and that some big puss might right now be licking its chops and thinking I might make a tasty meal. This was a more pressing issue so Logan could wait, I thought.

This was a mistake because a little later in the day, we came across two more pieces of his handiwork that stopped me thinking of him as game, put hate in my heart and started me thinking of him as an ugly bastard who it would be a pleasure to kill.

Logan's gang had divided into two and while he did his best to drive the herd on, four of the others had gone off to investigate some beehive huts which looked deserted because the outer fence was broken in several places. Ragwasi had divided us into two teams as well and while I and two of the Tswana shadowed Logan, he followed the freebooters heading for the huts. They were jumpy now and you could see that they knew they were being followed and pushing the herd on faster than they should, but a hundred cattle are hard to manage if you don't know how and they kept slipping through their fingers like mealies out of a sack. Logan tried to move them faster by firing his pistol to scare them into urgency, but a cow is never urgent and all he did was wing one of the beasts which set up a fine lowing and screaming. He tried to silence it by shooting it some more, but he was obviously the sort of man who had only ever eaten meat from a butcher's because all he did was waste bullets before he got bored and rode off to catch the scattering herd.

My division was following the herd concealed by the dust and dead ground and acacia trees and we three exchanged disapproving glances at the cavalier attitude of these scoundrels to animals which were both pride and property. When I came across the beast that he had shot but not killed I saw red because that was the very Nguni cow that I had bought as *mokwele* for Tepo. Now we had to leave it to die because we could not risk being discovered by the sound it would make if we cut its throat – believe me, cows make a hell of a din when you try to kill them this way – and we could not shoot it for the same reason. I felt personally aggrieved by this, because it was my love token to Tepo and I felt like Logan had soiled it.

We were discussing in whispers what we might do when we heard the sounds of more gunshots from the direction of the huts, but these were different in quality. I have come to believe that guns speak with different voices when they do different things, which you will say is foolish, but it is what I believe nevertheless and I have heard them speak often. *These* guns spoke murder, deliberate murder, because the shots came two together and then two more after a reload. My instincts were confirmed when we saw Logan's men galloping down from the beehives, laughing out loud, waving their shotguns and calling to each other, with two herd boys slung across their saddle bows like sacks.

Ragwasi and his men joined us in the late afternoon again and told us that Logan's men had killed two elderly ladies when they tried to protect the boys. He was in tears again and his son wanted to attack them immediately but Ragwasi refused. We agreed that they must attacked but he said we must do it properly, like warriors, not ruffians. We would waste no more time in stalking these men, but would hit them hard in the morning, killing as many as we could and then hunt the rest of them down in the long daylight that would follow. When they were all dead, we would go back for the cattle and go home. This was a plan that we all accepted and I looked at Ragwasi in a new light then because he had grown; he had acquired the power of command and had temporarily put aside being a transport rider and had become a chief.

We were in position early, before dawn, overlooking their campsite. As we were only six, we could not surround them so we formed a sort of curved line running from 3 o'clock to six o'clock so that we would have the light behind us to shoot by. Logan's gang had tethered their horses to a pegged out line and had gathered the cattle in a rough compound made of brushwood and surrounded by long ropes tied together, before building a fire and laying out their bedrolls by it. Two sentries had been posted, but I saw straight away that they were asleep. As the dawn came up, a line of ochre first, like a dust storm in the distance, then silver pushing away the purple night, I looked down into their ragged encampment and felt contempt for them. Their fire was glowing, but they had not kept their *potjies* pot over it on its tripod so they would be eating a cold breakfast and they had no water, so there would be no coffee or tea either. One of them was up already, huffing and grumping as he tried to rub the stiffness out his arms and then he relieved himself not three yards from the fire, which was a foul thing to do and showed he was no countryman. These may seem small things to you, but a man needs breakfast if he is to do a day's work on the veldt and there is a good reason for the saying that you should not piss where you eat. As the shadows began to slide back towards the sun, I counted only ten men and signaled a question to Ragwasi. He noted it and we scanned the bush to see if the two others were anywhere to be seen; I guessed they had deserted and we never did find them.

Logan was still there, rolling out of his blankets in his tan check suit, a red kerchief tied below his red face and pushing a hand back through his rumpled black hair. That's when I put the foresight on him for the third time and looked over, waiting for Ragwasi to give the word to fire. I had killed many animals before but this would be my first man and it did make me feel different; it made me feel like I was wasting a bullet because I could not skin the bastard or make biltong out of him. It was not the fact that he had given me a beating and taken my money in Kimberley that made me hate him. Sipo's broken head and the waste of my *mokwele* were not enough good reasons either, although they were serious reasons, you understand, but it was the fact that Ragwasi had cursed me for being a white man that made me hate Logan, for before that we had no such thoughts. This is what I mean when I say that Kimberley poisoned everything in South Africa because if there were no diamonds there would be no Logan. I pondered for a second the idea that if there were no Logans then there would be no diamonds, but this I recognised to be foolish and I looked over again at Ragwasi for permission to make the kill.

This was going to be a difficult shoot because although Ragwasi and I had Martini-Henrys, the other men had only firelocks so they would not have time to reload before fire would be returned. I was impatient to fire and I thought

Ragwasi was waiting too long for soon the light would reveal our smoke when we fired and put us in danger. He was looking for the captured herd boys who we could not see yet and who he did not want to be caught up in the firing. It was a hard decision to make but I raised my eyebrows to him and motioned towards the rising sun and he resigned himself to the risk. He gave the nod.

I squeezed the trigger, but before I could blow Logan's head off – we were only forty yards away from his camp – Seretse let fly and Logan jumped like a cat so my bullet went through his right collar bone rather than through his head. I thumbed another round into the chamber and looked to make another kill, chose a blonde haired fat man – he looked like a Boer – and hit him in the stomach, which I knew would kill him because a Martini-Henry bullet has a flat, soft nose so when it hits, it flattens out and will punch a fist sized hole as it goes all the way through you. After that second bullet though, I could not get a clear shot because of the gun smoke and I knew I had to change my position because that same smoke had given me away. Logan's men were blazing away now and they made a lot of noise with their pistols which scared Seretse into lying down among the rocks and hoping he would be safe. Ragwasi and I knew how hard it is to hit anything with a pistol at anything longer than eight yards range so were more concerned about strays and ricochets as we moved to get another shot in. In fact I made two more kills in quick succession before the cattle started moving and Logan's horses tore up their pickets.

I saw him make for a horse, throw himself over it and give it a crack with a sjambok and I put my foresight on him again, but the horse jinked, a ricochet made me duck and then he was gone into the bush. I was not so bothered because Logan had a big hole in him and I could track him once I had dealt with the rest of the band, who by now seemed minded to surrender. There were only four left now and two of them were badly wounded, so Ragwasi ordered them to throw down their guns and we went in and took them. We looked at the wounded and knew they had not long to live so we turned our attention to the two survivors. Their names were Jake Smith and Barnaby Pike, and they were trembling with fear as well they might for our little *impi* was still full of spunk and anger.

'Where are the boys?' was Ragwasi's first question, directed to the younger of them, Jake, who had arched eyebrows and a gap in his teeth. To me, he did not look very bright and his answer confirmed my first impression.

'Dunno,' he said, directing his words to me. 'Hey Mijnheer, you will tell your boy not to kill me, won't you?'

This is what I mean by the bad influence of Kimberley. Here was a youth fresh out from England, who could not have been in the country more than five minutes and he was assuming that *I* was in charge because I was *white*. Anyone with any sense could see that Ragwasi was our leader, by his age, his commanding bearing and his Martini Henry.

'Answer his question,' I replied sharply. 'And show your respect – he is my boss, my *bru*, not my *boy*.'

Ragwasi cuffed him and repeated his question.

'I dunno,' he spluttered. 'They never came into the camp. I think they must have gone with Tom and Luke last night.'

'Tell me truthfully,' ordered Ragwasi. There was power and coldness in his voice and I confess I felt a chill. 'And I will spare your lives.'

They both dropped to their knees and protested they didn't know anything and I believed them. They were just two stupid, frightened boys who had been seduced out of their depths by diamonds and Logan and I stood ready to argue if Ragwasi went ahead with his threat. Ragwasi did not appear to be in a forgiving mood, however, and the other Tswana looked ready for murder, so I caught his eye and my expression let him know that he should not do this thing. For a moment we looked deep into each others' souls, like we were connected spiritually – I cannot explain it fully or properly – but it was a real feeling nonetheless, as though we had pushed into each other and touched steel that we did not know was there. At that moment the herd boys came calling and scampering across the veldt and the tension went out of the air as Ragwasi gave a huge sigh of relief and I loosened my grip on the stock of my gun. I was surprised at how my hand had tightened around it.

We looked at each other again then and we felt a new respect for each other because we realized that we had won a battle together and we had not had to fall out over the prisoners. He knew I would not let him kill them in cold blood and I knew that he would not have tried. I know it is complicated to explain because the friendships that men strike up are not simple and go deeper than they have words for because they are not like women when it comes to talking.

What Ragwasi did do though was to bend down and pinch up three fingers worth of red earth and place it in my palm.

'The earth is red because too much blood has been spilled on it,' he said. 'But you have earned this earth now and you are part of it and will always be part of it uPelly.'

In that moment he did become my *bru* and I took pride and comfort in being his.

Ragwasi had not finished with our captives yet though. He turned to the other boy, a scrawny, pale youth with thin blonde hair.

'Where did you get these horses and these guns from?' he demanded. 'I do not think you are such men of wealth as to afford these things.'

'Mr. Logan gave them to us and said we would be able to keep them when we brought the cattle to the *Regt Dopper*,' replied Barnaby Pike.

'*Regt Dopper*?' inquired Ragwasi, as though he had heard a name from a long time ago.

'He was a Boer - the one who hired Mr. Logan,' Barnaby stammered. 'I don't think he liked us.'

'Mr. Logan didn't like us either,' interjected Jake. 'He always gave us the bad jobs and we were to get a smaller share than the others too. Luke and Tom were promised much more than us because they were his friends.'

Ragwasi looked over at me. *Regt Dopper* - that gave me a start at the time because I can tell you there were not many *Regt Doppers* in Kimberley. They were the kind of Boers who *hated* the English and would get in their wagons and head north, east or west – anywhere – to get away from English government.

'I know these *Regt Doppers*,' said Ragwasi, quietly. 'Their leader is Om Paul Kruger and it was one of his *Kommandos* that stole my land, uPelly.'

Paul Kruger; he was the President of the Transvaal Boer Republic and a man much, much worse than even Rhodes. I have told you my impression of Rhodes as an amoral deal maker. Well, Kruger was an immoral, cowardly thief who had nothing in his heart but black hate for black men and Englishmen alike. He had read his bible and understood nothing because he took it too literally. Apart from thinking that it was God's will that the Boer could take any black man as a slave, he thought a giraffe was a camel because there were no giraffes mentioned in the bible. He thought that he was Moses going into the Promised Land and that he had a right to kill, enslave or steal whatever belonged to the people who were already living there. And he hated the English even more because they would not let him do as he pleased. Actually, I do not think he was very bright – intelligent and cunning, true – but he had no mental flexibility because he had never been educated even in a village school. I am getting ahead of myself though.

I went off to track Logan, but I never did find him, but again I wasn't trying really hard enough because I knew he had a big hole in him and would probably not survive long. We had the cattle to round up and there was still the question of what to do with our prisoners, Jake, Barnaby and the two fat men who were badly wounded. Ragwasi said that the two boys must lose their boots, guns, water and blankets and be put to work rounding up the cattle and then released if they behaved well. This meant they could not simply gallop away, as I made clear to them, because the veldt would kill them if I did not catch them first. They were glad enough of the reprieve and as I got to know them over the next couple of days, I realized that they were indeed stupid but cheerful boys, rather than animals like Logan and the rest of them. One of them had been put ashore by a ship's captain for some misdemeanor that I was not interested in, while the other was a clerk from Bristol. When we got the cattle back to Ragwasi's lolwapa, I let them keep their horses, gave them biltong and mealies each and directed them to Mijnheer Cronjie, with a character and a letter asking that he would find them a farm where they could do honest work. I don't know because I never saw either of them again, although they did go and see Mijnheer Cronjie. Maybe they went to America? A lot of people went to America in those days, full of hope, just like those poor people who were drowned on that *Titanic* last year. The two fat men died of their wounds within a couple of hours of each other and at the time I guessed Logan went the same way. Like I say, a Martini Henry bullet makes a big hole.

What a homecoming it was though! With us driving the cattle in across that good red earth under that bright blue sky, re-uniting little Sipo with his mother while the two new herd boys were welcomed into a new lolwapa by Ragwasi's aunt – I think it was an aunt, but it is hard to tell when there are several wives in a family. A cow was slaughtered and roasted, millet beer was brewed amid the smell of honest wood smoke and I shared my mealiepap with Tepo, which was the best thing about coming home as a conquering hero. The girls did a lot of singing and dancing, which was a fine sight and a sound so high and happy that there is nothing to beat it. Jake and Barnaby had never seen African girls with bare breasts before and they stared with such open mouthed hunger that I had to remind them that they were still in disgrace and were not to importune the girls in any way. That did not stop those girls swaying their hips and fluttering their eyelashes and importuning them though, I can tell you. Anyway, Africans seem to be born with a musical talent for singing and dancing and when they start swaying and clapping and stamping their feet in the firelight, I can also tell you, you will be enchanted. Ragwasi had a good baritone voice when he sang, but I do not think my singing of *The Recruiting Sergeant of Rochester* raised any fears of Africa being overtaken by England in the musical stakes. Tepo damned me with faint praise too when she said I danced very well – *for a white man*.

A proper Tswana celebration goes on for three days or until the cow is all eaten up and the beer is all drunk or the people have tired of dancing, and this was a right royal one and one to remember especially because Tepo and I started to share a hut then. Like I say, I might have been married then, but I am not sure and do not care if I was not because I was in my heart. I think my firstborn was conceived then, in that month we spent up at Kuruman, so I was well on the way to being married at least. It was 1877, I was 24 years old, fit and healthy, with money in my pocket, a good boss and now respected as a warrior as well as a hunter, I had the whole veldt to ride across and I intended seeing all of it. I had forward motion and I was living my life audaciously, which you will have gathered by now, was important to me. That was such a golden time and these days when Tepo gives me a ragged ear for drinking too much or snoring, I give her a pinch on her broad bottom and she knows what I mean, even if I get a slap in return.

The only note of discord in all this marvelous music was the intelligence that two of Logan's accomplices were called Luke and Tom; Daisy's brothers were called Luke and Tom, but neither Jake Smith nor Barnaby Pike could say if their second name was Stockwell and nor did they know of a sister who went by the name of Daisy. I prayed that this was a just a coincidence but, really, I knew that it was not. Your fate walks behind you wherever you go. Fortunately for me, the arrival of Tom Cole put off that appointment for a long while, for he had a job for Ragwasi and I that would lead us away from Kimberley and the Stockwells for the foreseeable future.

*

Chapter 5

A Mission of Secrets

You know, when I sit on my stoep here in 1911, chewing my biltong and sipping my Cape Smoke, I think about this Act of Union that will soon go through the Cape Parliament and I am glad of it but not glad if you get my drift. Now that everyone in South Africa is officially British we might go back to the situation where all men are free and treated the same. I know I am seeing things through rose tinted spectacles, but I would advise everyone to do this because the world really does look better that way.   Before Kimberley, there was a chance that injustices and problems could be ironed out because there was a sense of fair play in the British government.   Mr. Bramson had told me that the hatred between Boer and Briton was because the British would not let the Boer keep slaves and this hatred never went way among the *Regt Dopper*. They had left the colony in 1837 in a great *trek* so that they could get new slaves and live that life but the British had pursued them to stop them causing trouble. Africa is too big not to be able to escape into though and so the British government had to be content with keeping Piet Retief, Kruger – he was just a boy then - and the rest of them from gaining a port where they could buy their own guns and be properly independent.   The *Regt Doppers* formed two countries, the Transvaal Republic and the Orange Free State but also thought that they should own Kimberley, even though it was called Griqualand and belonged to the Griqua, and when the British government took it over the Boers claimed that it was *they* who had been cheated, not the Griquas. Actually, I am not sure how this happened and it is contradictory to say that the British government always played fair - but it is not contradictory to say that the Boers *never* played fair. Actually some of them, like Mijnheer Cronjie did, but I am getting confused now. I am also sorry if this is beginning to sound like a history lesson because history is usually about kings and queens and important people. Sometimes, however, it explodes into ordinary people's lives and that is what has happened here in South Africa in my lifetime. This Act of Union might make it possible for the black man to get back something of what he has lost but I also think that the Boers already have been given too much. Here on my farm I will be fine for whatever days are left to me whatever happens, and I might see 1920 yet. You never know. But my sons and daughters are now coloured and although I cannot see them as being anything but a mix of

English and Tswana, that word *kaffir* is used too often for my liking when people think I am not listening.

I say *this* Act of Union because there was another one before it but which was killed stone dead thirty years ago. It was the events surrounding this one that Ragwasi and I played a part in and I think that if that one had worked then we would have had a better balance and harmony between the people. Tom Cole told me about it that day he arrived at Kuruman, while Tepo gave him millet beer and slapped her sister for making eyes at him. He was as cheerful and chippy as ever and swigged at the beer like an elephant in a drift on a hot day.

'What's up, Tom?' I asked, after he had seen to his horses. There was a young white man with him, but he seemed to be keeping him away from us and did not introduce him. 'Come to return my five bob from that Rhodes fellow?'

'I think I might have blotted my copybook there,' he laughed and shrugged. 'Perhaps *You're Nicked* will be my epitaph, all carved up in gothic letters on a tombstone in the churchyard at Chew Magna. Wouldn't that be splendid?'

'It would,' I agreed, handing him more beer and making space on the bench for Ragwasi. 'But what about my five bob?'

'I'll do better than that,' he replied, laying out his stall. 'There's a new governor at the Cape and they say he's got big ideas about getting all the different people of South Africa to join together in one big confederation.'

'This is a very big idea,' muttered Ragwasi, sceptically.

Cole ignored him and frowned at three small, very cheeky herd boys who were poking their heads out from around a hut and singing *Old King Cole was a Merry Old Soul*. To my shame, it was me that taught them that and there was no hiding place.

'As a first step to ending strife and bringing peace, he intends to stop the gun trade at Kimberley, issue new permits and confiscate firearms from troublemakers and bad hats.'

'This is a very big job,' muttered Ragwasi again. 'You will have to take every gun out of every house, wagon and farm in the Transvaal and Orange Free State to achieve this.'

'Well that's the thing,' said Tom excitedly. 'Have you heard about the Transvaal's war against Sekhukhune and the Pedi? No? It's over on the other coast, north of Zululand. Well, Sekhukhune got his hands on breechloaders and thrashed the Boers, so they have asked to be annexed by Britain so that they may save their skins! Isn't that the best news! With the Transvaal under British rule, we can have gun control, confederation and bring law and order to the whole of South Africa.'

Ragwasi let out a tremendous fart at this – he did this from time to time and I did not mind as long as he did not do it in the wagon when we were sleeping in it. This time I did mind because I was embarrassed in front of Tom. I did not want him to think my friends were uncouth, even when they could be from time to time.

'Cole uLootant,' he clucked. 'This marvel will never come to fruition. The Boers will never accept British rule, *ever*. It is just a trick they are playing on you and you should be wary of it. We must *all* be wary of it.'

He gave me that sideways look of his and then took the beer pot from Cole.

'And also tell me, Cole uLootant,' he asked slyly. 'Where did this Sekhukhune get his breechloaders from when he is not supposed to have them?'

'There's the rub,' answered Tom. 'We think he got them through Lorenco Marques in Mozambique – that's Portuguese territory, so the Foreign Office will have to deal with them. But we also think that the Boers are smuggling them in across the Namib desert for their own uses. Have you ever heard the name of Einwald?'

We shook our heads.

'Lüderitz?' Cole proffered.

'Well, Einwald and Lüderitz are Germans known to be sympathetic to the Boers, well in with Kruger and they've been sniffing around Zululand, Pondoland and up and down the guano islands on the west coast. The Governor wants to know if it is possible to smuggle arms across the Namib and my job is to find a couple of likely types to answer the question for him. Likely types who can keep a secret, I mean. What do you say?'

I was about to ask some questions, but Ragwasi beat me to it.

'We'll do it,' he announced. 'How much will he pay? And it must be in advance. I have a cash flow problem.'

I should tell you that ever since Ragwasi had lost his first calf to a chief, he had taken a dim view of taxes. Later on, when the hut tax came in, he would go to great lengths to avoid paying it and when the assessor came he would wear ragged clothes and pinch his children so that they would cry loudly. This never worked, but he still tried it year after year and blood from a stone does not begin to describe the difficulties the assessor had making him pay. However, when he heard that the government was to spend money he would start slavering because he held the firm view that if a man was not spending his own money, he could be easily persuaded to spend more of it. Last week, I told him about Mr. Lloyd George's plan to give pensions to old people in England who had not saved up and he almost set out for London on the spot. Luckily he was drunk so he did not get further than the end of my stoep and two of his wives had to take him home. They told me off too as if it was my fault.

We settled on a price after Ragwasi had been haggled down from his original outrageous demands to something more reasonable, with only half in advance, but I was a little puzzled at why he had been so keen to take on this job. Money talked very loudly in Ragwasi's ear, but I had known him long enough to know that there was something more, something that he was keeping to himself. Even while he was scratching his head and complaining to Tom Cole that he would be left destitute by this price, I could see that he was excited by something more than a long trip into the Namib and he was almost hopping with excitement.

Tom Cole was up to something too and at the last minute, just before the deal was closed, insisted that he must send someone with us to make sure that government funds were being spent properly and brought forward the white man that he had been keeping secret from us.

'I'd like you to meet Constable Nathan Walker,' he said, with a smile that was concealing a straight face.

Nathan Walker was another youth who did not look to be much of a big gain to the population of South Africa. He had grey eyes, a button nose and thin, fair hair, and a chin that had not yet got a beard, but had managed to acquire two large ears that stuck out at right angles from his peanut shaped head. I thought that at some time in the future he might make a well-proportioned man, but Ragwasi and I both agreed that this could be a *long* time in the future.

'What is *that?*' snorted Ragwasi, his eyes bulging with impatience and frustration, his finger pointing at *Constable* Nathan Walker. 'This *boy* cannot have been circumcised yet and he is a *Constable*? And I am expected to take him into the Namib? Do I look like a nursemaid, Cole uLootant?''

'He is our newest recruit to a constabulary that we hope to form for the protection of the law abiding subjects of Her Majesty, the Queen Empress Victoria in her South African dominions,' replied Cole grandly. 'I am sure he will do very well too.'

Ragwasi got up, went over and looked poor Nathan Walker up and down, taking in his baggy serge uniform, his unpolished buttons and the boots that were too large for him. He then took a turn around him, as though he were inspecting a cart.

'How old are you, boy?' he asked, exasperated.

'Eighteen,' replied Walker, confidently shoring up a baby face.

Ragwasi looked at me and then Cole and then back at Walker. He walked around Nathan Walker once more and I could see he was making calculations of the financial variety.

'Very well, I will take him,' he decided, finally. 'Even though he is a very bad liar. He can help the herd boys and sweep out the wagon and make up our mealipap and he is not to eat too much either. And this will cost you an extra fee of five shillings a day, Cole uLootant.'

'When can you leave?' replied Cole closing the deal with a handshake.

'We can leave right away,' said Ragwasi. 'We must be away as soon as we possibly can.'

My ears pricked up at this. Ragwasi never did anything right away. He was a great believer in the virtue of Africa Time which is not the same as Greenwich Time and moves at a much slower pace than the hand that goes around on any watch I have ever owned.

'Right away?' I said. 'You mean in a week or so?'

'No uPelly,' he replied. 'We go tomorrow. As soon as we have thrown some biltong and some mealies and this Nathan Walker into the wagon we will be away for the Namib.'

'Ragwasi, this is not possible,' I protested. 'We must make proper preparations. Why the mad hurry?'

'Are you not a white man who is ruled by the clock and your measuring sticks?' he replied. 'Are you not always urging me to go faster and to replace my oxen with mules so that we can get to where we are going before we have set off from where we are starting from? Are you not the one who loves speed and hurry so much?'

'If it makes you happy then I am for it,' I said. 'But we cannot go without adequate supplies and these will take at least a week to gather. We must buy coffee and sugar at least.'

'Very well, uPelly,' he said. 'If you cannot stand a little hardship and must live your life in luxury then we must wait a day or two. But there is no time to lose.'

I was at a loss as to why he was so eager to be away but I humoured him and set out that day for the store at Kuruman where supplies were to be had. This took a day longer than I expected because they had run out of Cape Smoke and I was absolutely certain that Ragwasi would not be pleased to set off into the desert without a few essential comforts. It meant that I had to go on to a place where a friend of ours made his own brandy. He also had tobacco to sell, so that was fortunate too. When I got back though, Ragwasi was hopping with impatience.

Nor did things improve much when Boitumelo, his first wife, announced that she would come on this journey too and took an age to pack up all the many things that a woman needs to travel in a wagon with. Ragwasi almost tore his hair out. Actually, this was not something that I was very happy about either because she was always nagging Ragwasi and made him bad tempered. She was a strong woman and a good cook, with a stately figure but unfortunately the high cheek bones, narrow nose and high colour of her pleasant face was often clouded with an aggrieved and dogged look. This was most noticeable when she put one hand on her hips, pursed her lips and raised one eyebrow, which she did very often. When Tepo announced that she was coming too and everything had to be unloaded and re-packed he was positively boiling and when we finally whipped up the oxen, he almost made them gallop like horses.

We were a regular cavalcade by the time we set off. Ragwasi had his team of eighteen oxen now and the two herd boys, Dikeledi and Kagisso, the same ones that we had rescued from Logan to look after them, while Tepo and Boitumelo walked along side or rearranged things in the wagon. I tell you they drove Ragwasi to distraction doing that, for reasons that I will tell you in a while. Nathan Walker and I rode our horses and led four more as remounts so that we could all be mounted if necessary. I had insisted on bringing remounts – we had to wait another day for them - because I was not willing to place Tepo at any risk at all and I was really haunted by what Logan's gang had done to Sipo and those two elderly ladies. It was true that Logan was probably dead by now, but Kimberley was full of things a lot worse than Jake Smith and Barnaby Pike and many of them were to be found wandering as desperadoes.

Nathan Walker I got to know a little more as we went along but I was aware that he had a secret that he did not want to share almost from the outset. That is because when I called his name to wake him one morning he answered 'Who?' and then covered his tracks with some bluster. I wondered what a boy so young could have done to have to change his name and hide himself inside a constable's uniform in Africa, but then I remembered with a jolt what I had done. I felt sympathy for him and it is true that for the first time in nearly five years I felt homesick for Dines Hall and my family. This was made worse when he told me that he was Suffolk born and had been to Newmarket races several times. I was eager for news but all he could tell me that was that the problems that American grain had caused my father's farm were common and getting worse and that there was precious little paying work in the countryside these days. Ragwasi warmed to him too, especially after he had taken advantage of his inexperience to send him to look for an elbow grease tree and then told him that a Cape buffalo was only like a big cow and he could pat one on the head easily. He was about to walk over and do it before I stopped him from meeting his certain death, because it is a bad tempered and unpredictable animal. We were all glad to have him with us after a while because he was like having a large, clumsy, sad but good natured dog for company.

The reason for Ragwasi's impatience to get away became clear a few days into the journey when Boitumelo was rearranging the things in the wagon for about the ninetieth time and laying into Ragwasi with a shrill insistence. It was breakfast time and the worse time to hear sounds like this and Nathan Walker and I were finishing our coffee prior to saddling up when her head appeared from the rear of the wagon. She was holding up an old wooden powder horn, elaborately carved and inlaid with silver filigree, and she had that pinched look on her face.

'Ragwasi, what are you doing with this ancient thing when you have spent all our money on a modern gun?'

This was a very good question and Ragwasi caught me looking at it and then looked away shiftily, fiddling unconvincingly with the harness on one of the oxen.

'Is it for keeping *muti* in? Or are you bringing that horrible *dagga* along with us after you promised not to smoke it anymore?'

'This is not anything for you to be concerned about, woman,' he replied, testily.

'Come on, Ragwasi,' I chaffed. 'What *are* you doing with such an old thing like that?'

'Do not talk about my dear, right hand wife like that,' he clucked. 'She deserves respect from young men who have not been circumcised or have not got children of their own.'

'*She* deserves to know why you will not answer her question,' scolded Boitumela, shooting me a look that hit like a stone on my brow.

'Have I not given you an answer?' barked Ragwasi.

She looked at him.

'Alright I will tell you!' he bellowed. 'Then perhaps I can get a little peace in my life!'

He went round to the back of the wagon while Boitumela scrambled through it, and from under a canvas sheet he drew out the thick, stubby octagonal barrel and massive stock of an ancient smooth-bore firelock. The muzzle gaped open like a drain pipe, nearly an inch and a half across and there were iron reinforcing bands wrapped around it. It was Zanzibar made I guessed. Walker, Tepo and I came closer to look while he produced an equally ancient wooden box, copper banded and marked with Arabic script. He took out a bullet from the box and dropped one into my outstretched hand and I was amazed to feel the weight of half a pound of lead in my palm.

'I am going to shoot an elephant with this Indian gun finally,' he declared excitedly. 'And in the Namib, the elephants are *giants!*'

'What!' roared Boitumela, each word coming out staccato, like a series of punches. 'Have.You.Taken.Leave.Of.Your.Senses?'

'What!' cried Tepo, echoing indignantly. 'Ragwasi you will not take my husband and get him killed by an elephant!'

'Ragwasi we have argued this over and over again,' I protested. 'Elephants are not good business.'

Ever since we had started hunting for a living, Ragwasi had had a bee in his bonnet about shooting an elephant but I refused to countenance such a course. This was for several good business reasons. Firstly, there was not enough salt in Africa to make biltong out of an elephant. Secondly, the European diggers at Kimberley would only eat things that they knew, like beef and sheep and game and although we were able to smuggle a lot of things in under the title of 'game', elephant was not one of them. The African diggers did not want it either because it was tough as hell and had to be boiled three times over before you could even think about chewing it. Thirdly, although the ivory was valuable, it was valuable in Europe after you had paid all your profits away in transporting it to the Cape and being swindled there. Fourthly, elephants were big and dangerous and after our first encounter with one, I found out that a Martini-Henry bullet would not kill an elephant but would just make it very angry indeed. Four more bullets would not kill it either, but just made it four times as mad and from that point on I decided that if I could not kill an animal with two bullets maximum, then I would not waste my life trying. Why Ragwasi insisted on wanting to kill an elephant was a mystery to me.

'But think of it uPelly! Is this not what it means to live life audaciously?' he countered, holding the gun before him as though it were heaven sent. 'See! We put in a lot of black powder and tamp it down with this circular wad of paper. This will *double* the power of the powder - I know this because the man I bought it from told me. Then we put in the ball and put more wadding to hold it in too and so we have our chance to measure ourselves as *men* against the strongest animal in the world!'

'You are not making elephant biltong in my wagon,' insisted Boitumela, at volume. 'And do not think for an instant that I can be persuaded to skin and cook an elephant for you!'

Ragwasi would not be gainsaid, however, and a little over a week later, he and I set off on the spoor of an elephant, with Boitumela's threats ringing in our ears, Tepo's tears wet on my shoulder and Nathan Walker looking glum at being allowed to come with us as long as he stayed behind when the hunting started properly.

The best time to shoot an elephant is first thing in the morning because then you have all day to work on the carcass before every lion, crocodile or hyena within a hundred miles turns up for a share. However, elephants do not have pocket watches so you must just follow, do your stalk and hope for the best. When we found one, a particular type of elephant that Ragwasi insisted on, a big bull with tusks that were almost on the ground, I saw to my horror that it had the tell-tale 'tears' down either side of its head that showed it was in *must* and so doubly bad tempered. It was also an old bull, which meant that it had to fight harder to stay in the race and so was probably smart as well as mean.

We tracked it to a thorn thicket just beyond a small water hole surrounded by good green turf and leaving Walker with the horses, Ragwasi and I stalked forward and lay down behind a tree trunk to wait for it to come to drink. It was a hot day, nearly noon, the cicadas were ringing in my ears, the earth smelled like cinnamon, the frogs were jumping in the pond and there was a faint heat haze shimmering over the pool, which the elephant would not be able to resist. This was when Ragwasi planned to sneak up to within thirty yards of the beast and then hit him with his Zanzibar cannon smack on the forehead. I told him he was crazy and that there was supposed to be a soft spot on the side of an elephant's head, just to the rear and down from its eye where he should aim. He just looked at me with that upside down smile and said that it was vital that he kill it fair and square or it would not be acceptable payment.

'Payment?' I hissed. This was the first I had heard of money being involved. 'What payment?'

'I have not told you this before, uPelly, but perhaps it is time you knew about me and the *Mamlambo*,' he whispered. 'I made a bargain with her many years ago when times were hard, but I have not paid her in full for the good fortune she has granted me. She demands an elephant or she will take away my good fortune.'

'Mamlambo? Who the hell is she? You never mentioned her before.'

'It is a secret, uPelly, hidden from the white man and you must swear not to tell anyone.' He moved closer to me and went on in a low murmur. 'Shortly after Boitumela became my wife and we had our first child, we were almost starving to death because Kruger's Kommandos had driven all the people to the brink of destruction. I was desperate so I found a *Sangoma*, a spiritual healer, who knew where the Mamlambo could be found, and I paid to go into her lair and make my bargain.'

'What is a Mamlambo?' I asked, incredulously.

'She is a water serpent spirit,' he confided. 'This, the white man does not know about and the black man keeps it a secret from him, because she does not love white men, uPelly. Promise me, you will never go to her or tell anyone that I told you? Not even your wives?'

I had never, ever suspected that Ragwasi could fall for the gibberish that these Sangoma spouted. I had seen them many times in the Tswana villages and all over the farms in the Cape where they came along and told fortunes and scared gullible people out of their money. They were like the Gypsy women who tried to frighten the villagers at Dines Hall into buying lucky heather and, in my former unpleasant life, I had put the dogs on them more than once. This I never did regret for they were thieves and nothing more. Now I could picture in my mind's eye, a young Ragwasi, fearful in an uncertain future, living hand to mouth and wondering if his family were supported or wandering the veldt destitute. I could see the wheedling sangoma promising him his start in life, taking his hard earned cash and then giving him some *muti*, some opium maybe or *dagga* and then, when he was properly puggled, putting him into a cave where he would be open to any kind of trick. Poor Ragwasi – I realized then that I was not the only fool in our wagon, and I felt sorry for him. Africans lived in a world full of spirits back then.

'Ragwasi,' I said, appealing to his reason. 'Whatever this Mamlambo has done or said to you, you are not bound by it. It is just superstition and nonsense.'

'Not the Mamlambo,' he shot back, and I knew he was in earnest. '*She* keeps her promises. Everyone knows this because the price she charges is very high.'

'How much did you pay her?'

He dodged the question.

'Why do you think I am the prosperous and lucky man, I am now?' he pleaded. 'Why do you think my fortunes have changed?'

I gave him the obvious answer – hard work and a tight hand on his wallet – but he shook his head in refusal.

'She gave me riches in return for promising not to be sleeping with Boitumela ever again - and the sacrifice of an elephant.'

'You did what?' I pushed my hat back on my head and scratched. 'No wonder she is so bad tempered.'

'I let her take lovers and did not complain when they made her pregnant,' he replied. 'And I have always treated those children as the same as my own.'

I could not believe my ears.

'It was bad back then, uPelly, you must understand,' he continued. 'I was working on a farm trying to get cows and getting nowhere very fast. I had to do something.'

'Did you tell Boitumela what you did?'

'No, uPelly, I came home with a second wife and gave her *dagga*,' he confessed. 'It seemed the best thing to do. She does not know about the Mamlambo and you must swear never to tell her. So I must pay with the elephant or my good fortune will disappear and then I will have to tell her and she will nag me worse than before.'

'Ragwasi, you are quite mad,' I declared. I couldn't resist a smile either. I had been right about the *dagga* the first time I had asked him about his getting of a second wife.

'No, uPelly, African women expect this sort of thing,' he dissembled. 'They know that a bull must have many cows. They are not like white women who are unreasonable and expect their bull to stay with them only, even when they are pregnant or nursing a baby.'

I snorted, pulled my hat down and turned to see what the elephant was doing.

I got one hell of a shock. That old bull had stalked us while we were talking and it was no more than ten yards away, looking like Boitumela would if I told her about the Mamlambo.

'*Usizo!* Help!' whimpered Ragwasi, gripping my shoulder hard. 'She has come! The Mamlambo! She heard me tell you, a white man, about her and now she has come to take revenge on me!'

'It's a *fokken* elephant not a serpent,' I hissed as excitement flooded through me. 'And it is a bull, so shut up!'

'The Mamlambo can take any form – she has come out of the pool!' His hand gripped harder still as he started babbling in Zulu. '*Isikhuni sabuya nomkwezeli!* I have got my fingers burned through meddling with things that do not concern me!'

'*He* has come out of the thorn bushes and *he* will leave us alone if *we* shut up and stay still.' I could feel my voice quavering and I was swallowing hard to control it.

The elephant snorted. He was a big old fellow but I could see what Ragwasi meant about it possibly being female because it had long eye lashes and deep brown eyes. However, this was not an impression that lasted for long, because when he swung that massive head round and began flapping his ears and tossing his tusks at us, I knew he meant trouble. I put my rifle in my shoulder and rose to a crouching position and Ragwasi did the same.

'Ragwasi – the Indian gun. But slowly, eh?' I murmured. I felt his hand loosen from my shoulder and heard the rustle of his shirt as he bent to pick up his Zanzibari cannon. The elephant let out a huge bellow, like Joshua's trumpets before Jericho and I resolved at that moment to run for my life, but I knew a sudden movement would be the worst thing to do.

'I have it ready here, uPelly,' Ragwasi muttered back. 'I shall stand up and take the shot.'

I did not want him to do this because I was hoping that patience might see the elephant lose interest and move on. It was a slim hope, I admit, because those ears were now flapping and the grey mountain attached to them looked like it was going to come down on us like an avalanche any second.

'I am raising the gun now, and moving,' whispered Ragwasi. My instinct told me that he would have everything concentrated on the target now but how he came to miss the ball dropping out of the barrel I do not know. I felt it hit the back of my calf and I saw it roll in front of me and I realized in an instant that he had not put enough wadding in to hold that half pound of lead. All he had now was a barrel full of gun powder, but I was too late to stop him taking a step left and pulling the butt into his shoulder.

The elephant bellowed, put its head down and started at us. Ragwasi pulled the trigger. There was a huge bang, a massive cloud of dense white powder smoke ten feet in diameter erupted from the barrel, Ragwasi's hat flew off and the recoil knocked him backwards off his feet. I was deafened by the blast and my left ear was ringing and I knew I could not save Ragwasi from the charging bull so I threw myself to the right, over the log and scrambled away in panic. The elephant roared again, a strange sound to it, a mixture of panic and strangled triumph, and then there was a great rumble and the ground shook. Within a second, there was a strange slumping sound, like the sound of a full gunny sack sliding off a cart, which I took to be the elephant stomping the life out of Ragwasi. Then all was still.

I lay there hardly daring to breathe, feeling the heat of the sun on my back, waiting for the smoke and dust and heat haze to clear so that I could plan my next move. I expected that elephant over me at any moment, coming in to nudge me with its tusks and then kneeling on me, for that is how an elephant will kill a small thing like a man. I decided then, that I would make a run for it towards the pool, firing my Martini-Henry and then splashing as much as I could before heading into that thorn thicket. If I could distract it, it might leave me alone, I hoped. It was not a good plan, but it was the only one so I must make do with it.

Waiting for the snort that would announce the elephants presence, I swore I felt its trunk touch me, but I think it was just the sweat on my back making me imagine things. When I heard Ragwasi, I thought he was just making a last cry before he died, announcing to his ancestors that he was on his way and they should slaughter a cow and brew some millet beer ready.

'*Ithemba kalilbulala!*' he cried. 'Hope is not dead! I am alive and shall keep my fortune!'

This did not sound like the last words of a man dying under an elephant, nor was the triumphant way he was shouting these words typical of someone who was about to die under that same elephant.

I lifted my head to see him standing on top of the fallen elephant and brandishing the Zanzibar cannon over his head in a paroxysm of joy.

'We are the greatest hunters in the world!' he danced ecstatically, throwing the gun in the air and catching it. 'The Mamlambo is paid, uPelly, and we have lived our life *audaciously*!'

I got up cautiously. I was stunned. I could not understand what had happened. I had seen the bullet roll out in front of me. Ragwasi had an unloaded gun when he fired at the elephant. Even if he had been loaded, the momentum of the elephant would surely have carried it onto him. By any reckoning, he should be under the elephant, but he was on top of it and it was obviously as much dead as he was alive.

As I went over, he slid off the elephant and embraced me, thrice times over and then stopped.

'You promise you will not tell, *bru*? About the Mamlambo?'

'I will not, Ragwasi,' I replied, freeing myself. We English are not used to embraces, especially from men, and I always felt uncomfortable when it happened.

I went to look at the elephant's head to see if I had been wrong about the bullet. There should have been an indentation, circular, about the size of medium sized dinner plate and a fist deep where the bullet hit, but there was nothing. I looked at its chest and shoulders, but there was nothing and no blood either. I went over to the log where we had been hiding and I picked up the lead bullet where it had fallen. There could be only one explanation; the enormous crack and bang of Ragwasi's cannon had given the old bull elephant a heart attack. Ragwasi was so happy though, that I pocketed the bullet and kept my conclusions to myself. If he thought he had paid off the Mamlambo now, then who was I to ruin his picnic? I have the bullet still and look at it whenever Ragwasi starts boasting to his grandchildren about how he killed the elephant single-handedly while uPelly was cowering under a bush. If he tells that story one more time, I swear I will tell everyone the truth and he can be the butt of the joke for a change.

We took the tusks and cut some big squares of hide off the elephant which we could make into leather straps for all the parts of the wagon and traces that might need replacing, but the rest of the carcass was of no use to us. I hated the waste, but then reflected that there would be a lot of animals that would feed on it in the coming days, and the bull was near death anyway. Older elephants sometimes starve to death or die of thirst in the desert because the herd won't let them have a share of what is scarce, so at least it had a quick death. As it turned out, we were just about to leave when a wrinkled old Bushman trotted out of nowhere and asked us for a share of the kill. We were only too happy to oblige and watched as he slit open a square hatch in the elephant's side, dropped his bow and spears and bag on the grass and dived into its guts headfirst. I almost threw up at seeing this, which made Ragwasi laugh, but the Bushman was happier when he came out a minute later covered in black blood that made his skin gleam like an otter. He was clutching a big piece of the liver and grinning with joy. He popped it into his bag, thanked us in that clicking language that they speak, and trotted off as though he had just been to the store for a bag of mealies. By the time we had gone a mile, I saw that the first lion had arrived and the great wheel of life on the veldt had started to turn again. As a hunter, this made me feel a lot better about the elephant.

*

We spent nearly a year in the Namib and Kalahari, from 1877-78, and we had a fine time of it there. Apart from satisfying Ragwasi's desire for an elephant hunt, we trekked and explored westwards at our own pace and in our own time, shooting our meat, eating our mealies and generally doing whatever we wanted. We did have to do some work though and it was wise of Tom Cole to send Nathan Walker with us because otherwise Ragwasi would have been tempted to do not very much at all for the government's money. Walker had some surveying skills and he was able to fix latitudes and longitudes with a sextant and a pair of watches. He had also brought a theodolite and a two hundred yard chain so he pointed and measured and drew and sketched with the willing help of Dikeledi and Kagisso, whom he taught to speak English. Tepo liked to walk with him too when Boitumela got a bit much but I was never jealous because I could not afford to think like this as my calling would always mean I would have to be away often. He kept his measurements in a couple of big journals, one for rough and the other copied fair, and when he let me look at them I saw that he was meticulous with his recording. He also drew beautifully and even though he could not capture the special golden light of the desert or the perfect blue of the sky or the ochre and burnt umber of the earth or the yellow straw of the grass, it was only because he did not have paints. He got the shape and the feeling of the dunes and the mountains though, carving their sharp edges onto the paper with a sharp pencil and smoothing their softness with his thumb and a piece of charcoal. He captured the shapes of the gemsbok which are plentiful here and are the original unicorns, I am convinced, even though they have two horns rather than one. They look much more like horses in the way they stand and they often have socks and so are a better inspiration for being unicorns that rhinos, which I remember Mr. Bramston saying they were. They taste a bit like horses too.

We trekked from mountain to mountain across the Namib, sometimes making progress, sometimes doubling back and sometimes making risky gambles on the basis of an animal track or a smell of water. This was the main thing that the governor at the Cape would want to know because any gunrunner would need to follow water or move from water to water to cross the desert. There would always be grazing for animals because there were lots of succulent plants to be found around the mountains that cropped up like islands, but whether it was bush, desert or veldt, the key was a reliable supply of water. After several months of trying, we came to the conclusion that there was no way across the Namib from Walvis Bay because of this lack of water, but also because of the sand dunes that ran like a wall along the coast, forty miles inland. They were like mountains, I can tell you.

We tried several times to pass that barrier but the sand was too soft and too steep for the horses and there was no way at all that we would ever get our wagon up. The only way that a man could climb them was to get on to the edge of the ridges, which were sculpted to a knife point by the wind, and then toil up, stepping up one foot in front of the other like trudging up a narrow staircase. Walker was always trying to get to the top to do his surveying, but the sand was too soft to hold his theodolite and there was something in the sand that made his compass spin round and round so it was hard to do any surveying at all. Sometimes we caught a glimpse of mist in the distance, which we guessed must be the sea and we did toy with the idea of making the journey on foot. We decided against it though because we reasoned that as no animal could make it, neither could a gunrunner's convoy. Besides, distances are deceptive, the compass did not work and because one of your legs is naturally stronger than the other, it was possible to walk all day but find you had gone in a circle. This may sound crazy, but it is true and the Bushmen will confirm it if you ever ask them.

We decided to look further southwards and so we set off with the idea of finding a way to the sea which was not blocked. This was an arduous journey because there were long, waterless salt flats and stony stretches along the Tropic of Capricorn and then rocky canyons which sometimes took a long while to traverse or bypass. This was the time that Tepo chose to tell me she was pregnant, which set me in a rare panic because we were about five hundred miles as the crow flies from the nearest Cape Town doctor and you know how long that takes in an ox wagon. Luckily Boitumela took things in hand and when Charlotte was born, by the light of a hurricane lamp on the tailboard of the wagon, in a place that we had no name for, she came out quick and healthy and glowing. I had never seen a baby born before, although obviously I had seen animals give birth, and although it is very messy and painful for the women, it is also a happy occasion and this was no different. However, Charlotte was a very noisy baby and I was glad that I had work to do in finding a route for the wagon because it took me away for many hours at a stretch. Ragwasi said that this was a wise thing and commended me for my wisdom. He said I would soon be a proper African at this rate.

It was while we were looking for a route for the wagon through to the sea that we came across something so important that we swore to tell no-one about it. That is a contradiction, I know, but the Germans have since found out this secret so it does not matter that I tell it now, but at the time we really searched our hearts before we came to agreement. Perhaps we made a mistake; I have been over it in my mind many, many times since and I still cannot decide. What I do know is that I have never faced a bigger temptation, for the devil was in the Namib on the day we found the diamonds.

We had just made our camp for the night and Nathan Walker was stealing sugar from the barrel that Boitumela was keeping secret under a blanket in the back of the wagon. He often did this so that he could reward Dikeledi and Kagisso for helping him with his map making, but it was when Boitumela was giving him a ragged ear after she had caught him that he saw the first diamond. It was just by the cart wheel and it was about the size of a thumb nail. He did not know what it was right then but he put it in his pocket, once he had finished being scolded, and thought no more of it. We had a bad night then because there were leopards about and we dared not outspan the oxen in such dangerous surroundings and we had to let the children sleep in the wagon. Dikiledi had eaten something he shouldn't have and so had runny guts worse than baby Charlotte, while Kagisso had toothache from the sugar that Walker had given him. This made Boitumela even more cranky and even my sweet good natured Tepo had grown a little testy in such trying circumstances, and my offer of a swig of Cape Smoke was refused with menaces. No-one would have had much sleep anyway because there was also a pack of hyenas not far off in the bush making that horrible laughing noise and unsettling the oxen.

It was not until the next day when the sun came up therefore that anyone noticed a little dry river bed a short way into the bush that had a very unusual sparkle. Ragwasi and I went to investigate while Nathan Walker kicked over the coffee can again and spoilt our brew – man, that boy was clumsy – and what we saw took our breath away. In front of us in that sand were so many diamonds that I thought I must be dreaming. There were literally *thousands* of them scattered there, as though someone had emptied them from a pirate's chest and then spread them out with a rake. I scooped up a handful of the sand, shook it out and counted four yellowish pieces of crystal, each the size of a finger nail. Ragwasi did the same and got eight. I scooped a second and got one of those dull lumps of diamond that look like a silver sugar cube; it was bigger than the others. Ragwasi did the same and got a mixture of opaque and clear. We were standing on a fortune, enough to buy a kingdom, and we stared at the ground, the diamonds and each other with open mouths.

'Ragwasi,' I croaked. 'We have found a second Kimberley.'

'Is this a good thing?' he replied, uncertainly. 'I know it will make us very rich but one Kimberley is enough for the whole of Africa.'

Nathan Walker broke in on us. He was carrying three mugs of coffee and spilling most of it. When he saw our find, he spilled the rest of it. He knew what it meant too.

'I could buy Suffolk,' he said, quietly.

We went back to the camp fire and sat down, heavily. The children were still sleeping and so we called Boitumela and Tepo over and told them in low voices what we had found. Walker pulled out the gem from his pocket that he had found last night and showed it to them. It may seem strange to you that we were not jumping for joy at our new found wealth, but in truth we were all frightened because this wealth was so great that it had only danger attached to it. Until this time anyone likely to rob us would be a small person who we could deal with or if they were only a little bigger then we could lick our wounds and replace our losses. This wealth would attract very powerful robbers, however. It would attract proper desperadoes, freebooters, people who would make Logan's gang look like apple scrumpers. It would attract governments, for a find like this would be worth a war in the minds of politicians and their accountants.

It was Boitumela who said it first. She let go her usual frown for a moment and brushed a fly away from her face with her third and fourth fingers, before speaking to no-one in particular.

'We cannot take these diamonds. They can only bring trouble, for we cannot hide wealth like this and it will attract only bad things.'

She leaned over and threw some biltong into the mealiepap pot, warming away on the fire.

I looked at Tepo and could see that she was unsure why these diamonds were not a good thing, but Ragwasi, the same Ragwasi who was always so interested in business and making his wallet fatter, beat me to it.

'Once this place is known – and it will be, for if we come out of the Namib with pockets bulging with diamonds then everyone will want to know where they have come from – there will be another scramble like there was for Kimberley,' he said quietly, but with great authority. 'And it will be the Boers who will hear first and come here first. And to get here they will cross Tswana land and so will know it is good land. And if they know that Tswana land is good land they will want it. And if they want it they will take it. The Regt Dopper Kruger will start a war and his horses and guns will defeat those Tswana who he cannot buy with this wealth.'

I looked at him and I felt a treacherous thought enter into my head. I could take a bag, no! – a sack! - full of these diamonds and I could leave South Africa. I could go back to East Anglia, pay back my father, make restitution to the Stockwells – I would buy them their own farm ten times as big as anything they could ever have hoped for – buy a big estate, go around in a carriage and live the life of a wealthy gentleman forever. What was a second Kimberley to me, if I got my share – more than my share, even?

It was those words of my father's when the Stockwells must be evicted from the Yellow House that put this thought to shame: *do not accuse me of doing anything at all, for this is your work!* I thought about that hole at Kimberley and how its guns gave every ruffian a reason to rob, how its gin rotted out the Africans who drank it, how the need for meat gave the Boers an excuse to drive the Tswana off their lands and pay men like Logan to rob their cattle. Could I look at myself in the mirror after seeing another Kimberley explode and be happy for my father to say again, *this is all your work*? I could not.

'Why are white men so greedy for these things?' asked Tepo, holding up Walker's stone to the light. 'They are pretty but you cannot weave them into patterns like you can with beads.'

'They can be cut and polished to a great beauty,' I answered. 'They are precious in Europe as a love token and they are very rare. Other than Kimberley there is only one other place in the world where you can find them.'

'Golconda, in India,' volunteered Walker, and then put his head down, as if he had given a secret away. 'I have some family there, in India, I mean, not Golconda,' he stammered in explanation.

Boitumela fetched the plates and ladled out breakfast.

'The children must not know,' she commanded. 'We must not talk about this with them.'

We ate, each with our own thoughts, but it was Nathan Walker who gave us the solution we were seeking. I was surprised, but then he was full of surprises and I had guessed from his survey work that he had more education than I had and guessed from his blistered hands that he was more used to the pen than the plough. This I added to my conviction that his name was a fiction and that he must have some influential connection to be given that Constable's uniform when he was barely out of the nursery. I thought he must come from a political family, but I could not be sure then. It was the way he worked out a middle way that made me think of this.

'We cannot come out of the desert and become instantly wealthy as Ragwasi and Boitumela say,' he began. 'But we can take a number that we can let out onto the market little by little so we don't arouse suspicion or attract unwelcome attention by reckless spending. And I can make sure that no-one finds this place by marking its location in my journal wrongly.'

'What if someone else does find it?' asked Ragwasi.

'Someone *will* find it eventually,' replied Walker. 'But there is nothing we can do about that.'

Well, as we know now, some Germans did find it a few years back, but our silence and Walker's map kept it secret for thirty years and so I am pleased to say that I was not responsible for making a second Kimberley. They have not made one either, because of something else Ragwasi, Nathan Walker and I had a hand in and which I will come to in good time.

We made our agreement just as Nathan Walker suggested and the diamonds that we took provided security without attracting unwelcome attention, because our prosperity could always be ascribed to Ragwasi's business acumen or to my skill as a hunter. Actually, Ragwasi's business acumen did betray him sometimes; he invested in Rhodes' British South Africa Company when he stole Lobengula's country but has not seen a dividend yet because Rhodes and his sidekick Starr Jameson got it all wrong. He thinks I do not know of this investment but I found the share certificates when I was looking for Cape Smoke a couple of years ago. He keeps them in a secret compartment under his booze. I keep what's left of my diamonds in a vault in Cape Town. Nathan Walker's paid for a new church and a school in his home village in Suffolk, plus the stipend of two clever young men who attend Cambridge University each year.

We trekked on southwards and then a little eastwards because we had become convinced that there was no way across the Namib for gunrunners and we thought that we might start heading for home. It was still a tough journey though, with many wrong turnings, a broken wheel and the loss of three oxen to a disease that we could not identify. Walker suggested we should catch some zebra and put them in harness which showed his youth and inexperience because everyone knows that a zebra's back is not strong enough for work. You might as well try to put a snaffle on a giraffe. Tepo divided her time between the baby and making me some veldschoen out of the elephant skin while Boitumela calmed down a bit. Between you and me, I think Ragwasi was visiting her in the night and cheating on the Mamlambo but I never asked him about this. Actually it might have been Nathan Walker visiting her because he seemed to be yawning a lot and scratching like a tom on heat. I did not care. If it made her happy and stopped her nagging us all, I was happy too.

We were beginning to run short of things too after so much time and although we sometimes got vegetables and mealies from the Herero people, our supplies had now to be eked out more and more carefully. Nathan Walker could no longer steal sugar for the boys because there was none, nor could he kick over the coffee pot again because there was none of that either. We always had meat, of course, because we had guns and we were careful always to collect firewood to boil water. We had no Cape Smoke left though which was a tragedy, I can tell you.

We were about 250 miles northwest of Kuruman, following a series of flats where rain water gathered into shallow, brackish lakes when Nathan Walker stumbled on his second discovery. This time he did not just put it in his pocket and forget about it, but came running back to the camp without even his theodolite. I thought he was being chased by cheetahs, he came that fast, but there was a good reason for his haste for when he had called Ragwasi and I together he produced a brass cartridge case from his hand and let us look at it. It was not from a Martini-Henry, but it would fit one as we shoved it into the breech of mine to check this. Looking at the base, I blew on it to clear away the dust and saw there the maker's mark, *DWM* – the *Deutsche Waffen Munitionsfabriken*. This was a German bullet.

'Either someone has been hunting here where we thought only the Bushmen came,' said Ragwasi. 'Or someone has found a way through from the coast.'

'Einwald?' I looked at Nathan Walker. 'Lüderitz?'

Walker retrieved his journals from his box in the wagon, thumbed through them and then produced a much folded chart of the coastline. He smoothed it out on the tailboard and pointed to the blank space inland that he estimated was our position.

'Can we get back to Kuruman from here by following these pools?' he asked.

Ragwasi and I did not know for certain but we said that it was our guess that we could.

'Well, look *here*,' he pointed to an indentation on the coastline, where there seemed to be a headland curling around, like a miniature version of Table Bay. 'That looks like a place where a ship might anchor. So if there was a way from *there* to *here* then there is a way from the coast to Kimberley, if the gun runners were hardy enough.'

'They would need water and they would need to get over the dunes,' said Ragwasi. 'Show me where you found the cartridge.'

He led us to what looked like a dry river bed, but we could not be sure if it was a river bed because it was known that in this part of the world rivers sometimes are seasonal, sometimes have changed course and sometimes have not had water in them for years. This one had more sand than rocks in it and had good shade from some leadwood trees and a couple of kokerbooms, which made the searching easier. We split up, heading east and west, and then circled around looking for anything out of the ordinary. I found nothing, but Ragwasi came back with a bleached skull of his old rival, the mule.

'A mule can cover forty miles a day,' I reminded him. 'And they can carry a good load of guns and ammunition.'

'But there are no tracks here,' Ragwasi replied, thoughtfully.

This was not a conclusive answer to our puzzle so we decided we would take the horses and search in a wider circle. Sure enough, two or three miles further on, in a dry bed that ran parallel to the one where Walker found the cartridge, we came across the spoor of a mule train.

'But these are heading *west*, towards the coast,' said Ragwasi. 'And perhaps the cartridge also was going in that direction.'

Something fluttering white in the bush caught my eye. It was a square of newspaper stuck on a twig and when I dismounted, I saw that there was some more, screwed up under a rock, where a man had used it in answering a call of nature. The language was Afrikaans and it was a fragment describing the opening of a new shop in Pretoria and we were fortunate because it gave the date as 1878.

'This is still only half a story,' demurred Ragwasi. 'It only can tell us that a man from the Transvaal came here with a bullet and some mules in this year and took a *kak* in the bushes. It does not say that a man came across the Kalahari bringing Indian bullets and other things on mules to Pretoria.'

Later on as we searched further, we found more tracks, this time heading eastwards, but Ragwasi refused to be convinced without some better proof.

'This might be the same man who has got tired of looking or hunting and has turned about on himself, uPelly. It is not proof, and Cole uLootant will scoff at us if we bring him a tale like this and he will not pay all he owes us.'

We went on further and then repeated our search the next day and the day after, but turned up nothing at all, even after we put Boitumela on a horse to increase the number of eyes we had available. It was on the fourth day that we found tracks that went eastwards, a mule that had only recently died, an empty and discarded can of Hamburg sauerkraut, a piece of waxed paper stamped with a German eagle and the arms of the *Deutsche Waffen Munitionsfabriken*, plus a haze of dust on the horizon that told of a gunrunner's mule convoy going fast for the Transvaal.

'*That* is proof that Cole uLootant will pay for,' declared Ragwasi.

'That is proof that we will *all* pay for,' answered Boitumela.

'We have to get this news to the governor at the Cape,' insisted Nathan Walker. 'Right away.'

*

Chapter 6

The Governor's Promise.

Nathan Walker wanted to gallop off to the Cape straight away but Ragwasi and I would not allow this because he would probably get lost or trip over something and break his neck. With gunrunners about, we also had to get the women and children back safely, so we whipped up and went along as fast as we could following in the tracks of the mules. When we got back to Kuruman about two weeks later, everything was in uproar because while we were away there had been a big war down in the Cape between the government and the Xhosa warriors of the Transkei. Many of the Tswana chiefs were worried that Kruger and the *Regt Doppers* in the Transvaal would take advantage of this to rebel against the government too and so had gone to Kimberley to buy guns as a precaution. To their dismay, they found that Major Lanyon who was in charge there had banned the sale of guns to anyone without a permit and when one chief had tried to take them by force, had defeated him in battle. The Boers had started stealing more and more cattle too and they *did* have guns – lots of them and modern ones too, which they had already bought from Kimberley or were getting from the gunrunners. Everyone seemed to be getting very jumpy and as soon as we were back Ragwasi was summoned to a meeting with the chief of our area, Montshiwa.

Normally, Ragwasi would have run a mile before going to a meeting with a chief because he always feared that it would cost him at least one cow, but this time he went because Montshiwa had been told to gather his people together by *his* chief, who was called Khama and was supposed to be in charge of all the Tswana. I say 'supposed' because Tswana chiefs did not have any real power and could only order things that the people were willing to do anyway. The Boers however were a threat that could not be ignored and so from Khama through Montshiwa and down to Ragwasi all felt the need to do something. I did not go to the meeting, which made me feel uncomfortable because I thought they did not want me because I was a white man, but Ragwasi said I should not worry, but should escort Nathan Walker to Kimberley where he could make a report and we could get our money from Cole uLootant.

Tom Cole was away on the Xhosa frontier so we were directed to Major Lanyon's official residence which, like I have said before of things like this in South Africa, was a very grand title for a very little house. I have to say I was surprised when I met Major Lanyon, not because he was a tall Irishman, but because I thought he must be the son of either a black man or black woman. He was dark skinned like Charlotte, I guessed about Ragwasi's age and his accent was distinctly Irish but softer than Logan's.

'Be Jaysus,' he said, straight out when we came in. 'Ye look like ye've been dragged through a hedge backwards, so you do.'

To be honest, living out in the desert and veldt for the last year had made me forget my appearance and when I caught myself in the mirror, I admit I looked a bit of a sight. We had not been able to view ourselves these last six months and more because Walker had stepped on the mirror and broken it when he was trying to have a first shave. Actually I looked a bit frightening as my hair had grown into a proper lion's mane and I had not shaved because of the want of a mirror. Walker was not much better either, except that he had got a lot of spots recently. I resolved then that we must find a proper bath and a barber as soon as we had made our report.

'Gunrunners, ye say? And Germans too,' Lanyon shook his head in concern. 'That's all just what we don't need right now. And what would Kruger and the likes of him want with guns, when he has the protection of Her Majesty's sojers to keep him safe in his bed, to be sure? *Trouble*, that's for sure. It's more land and more cattle and more slaves, he'll be wanting.'

He poured us generous measures of Cape Smoke and then sat down behind his desk. It was one of those brass bound cherry wood affairs that military men are found of and about the only decent stick of furniture in the room. Taking Walker's journal, he flicked through a few pages and I could see he was impressed with the work that had gone into it. Then he offered us chairs and for a moment we looked at them without recognition; neither Walker nor I had sat on anything but a horse or heels for a year.

'Well,' he continued, when we had lowered ourselves carefully onto them. 'He shan't be having more slaves while Governor Frere has a say in it. You know that venerable gentleman freed all the slaves in Zanzibar a few years ago? While I was chasing slavers on the Gold Coast, he was putting paid to them up there, to be sure, so between us we've the whole of East and West Africa cleared up, so we have. Sure and we'll both be damned if we let the infernal old evil in through the back door into South Africa.'

'Will he protect the Tswana from the Boers?' I asked, for this was what Ragwasi, Montshiwa and Khama were most afraid of. 'Because if he will not, then we must have guns to protect ourselves.'

'*We*?' Lanyon looked closely at me. 'Now I wouldn't be mistaking you for a Tswana if I saw you walking through Phoenix Park on a Saturday. Well, that's your business not mine - the Boers think I'm a *kaffir*, so they do, and half of them with more than a touch of the tar brush in 'em, so they have. But if it's a promise of protection you're after, I can't give it. The Tswana are an independent nation and if it's foreign policy you're after, it's the Governor you'll need to be addressing, not a lowly soldier like me.'

'Will he see us?' I asked.

Lanyon looked at the Journal again and then shot a quick glance at Walker.

'Oh, I don't think there'll be too much difficulty on that score, do you Constable Walker?'

Nathan Walker did not reply and Lanyon moved on.

'His name is Sir Bartle Frere and I think you will have a fair chance of gaining his protection from enslavement,' he said quickly. 'But he does not love guns and his intention is to remove as many as he can from this country. And between you and me, while the man has no race hesitation, he *is* a Baronet, so you might strengthen your case with him if you take a man of rank with you. And you should go quickly because he will certainly want to see Constable Walker – I mean his Journal of course.'

We did not go quickly because Ragwasi and the Tswana chiefs spent a long time talking and I would not leave until I was sure that Tepo and Charlotte would be safe with her father's family. It was October before we finally set out, the three of us making a rendezvous just outside Kimberley and as we were agreed that we should go to see the Governor together and that seeing as a man of rank was needed, I promoted Ragwasi on the spot. That was how Ragwasi became *Prince* Ragwasi. He was carrying messages from Montshiwa and Khama anyway so I convinced him that this made him a Prince in everything but ermine – he did not take much convincing, I can tell you. Walker had his Journal to deliver and I went along because we would have to go through the Boer country to get to Pietermaritzburg in Natal Colony where the Governor was heading. I did not want Ragwasi to run into trouble with the Boers and could not place all my reliance on Nathan Walker's good sense in this respect. We could not go south about Basutoland either because the Xhosa country was only just pacified and we did not want to deal with the renegades, diehards, bandits and rogues that would be roaming there after the war. So in October 1878, we rode out to cross the Orange Free State to Natal thinking we would be gone a month at most. In fact we did not get back for almost seven. In fact we almost did not get back at all.

The reason for this was that when we got to the border between the Orange Free State and Natal Colony we were forbidden to go any further by the Free State army. They said that they had closed the border as a friendly precaution because there was trouble between the British and the Zulus and we must therefore go north into the Transvaal and round into Natal from there. I do not know if this was a true reason or if they were hiding something they did not want Nathan Walker to see because he was a Constable but we had no choice and it was not far anyway. However when we came down Laing's Nek off the escarpment and headed through the grasslands of the Lowveld to Newcastle we were forbidden to go any further again because there were rumours of Zulu and Swazi *impis* on the rampage along the borders. That is when we bumped into Tom Cole again and he drafted us.

'But I am Tswana! You cannot put me in your army Cole uLootant!' protested Ragwasi, when *Captain* Cole told us with his trademark grin that we were now in his troop of the Frontier Light Horse.

'Look on the bright side,' Cole replied, happily. 'You will be fed and clothed and paid at Her Majesty's expense for very little in return. And you get to live in this beautiful castle! What could be better?'

Cole's castle was called Fort Amiel, a white-washed square breastwork on a hill outside the town, with a lookout tower and a flag, built to house about a hundred men, of which thirty or forty were preparing to mount up at that moment.

'But I must report to the Governor at Pietermaritzburg, sir!' chimed in Walker.

'So you must, but until the Zulus calm down a bit, the road is closed,' answered Cole. 'King Cetshwayo has got 40,000 angry warriors and 20,000 guns down there and he says he will eat us all up any day now.'

'But we have no quarrel with the Zulus, do we?' I asked. 'I thought that they were friendly to England and Natal.'

'They are,' shrugged Cole. 'But now that we have taken over the Transvaal, Cetshwayo thinks we have joined with the Boers to steal the land across his borders. We haven't, of course, but he won't be convinced and so it looks like there will be a lot of trouble. As for the Boers, well they think we're siding with the Zulus and are threatening to rebel if we so much as boot a single Boer off a single acre of ground that they probably *have* stolen. So there will be trouble whatever we do. That's why we're getting every good Englishman and reliable African with a horse and gun together.'

What could we do? Walker had to do what he was told because he was a Constable and I had to join up because I was an Englishman. After thinking it over, Ragwasi agreed to join up because he thought this would gain him credit with the Governor when he finally got to see him. We sent word of our enlistment, along with some money, to Tepo and Boitumela and settled down to camp life as soldiers of the Queen. This was not hard as we had just had a year's practice at camp life. In fact it was a lot easier because the sergeant was not anywhere near a match for Boitumela when it came to nagging.

There is no doubt that we thought it was an inconvenience at the time, but actually the time we spent learning to be soldiers came in very handy later on. I was made a sort of corporal because of my experience as a hunter and so I learned how to control men in battle and how it was very important never to get excited, but to keep a cool head however difficult this might be. Ragwasi always claims he knew all this already, but he did not. It is just Cape Smoke and *dagga* talking because he was jealous of my promotion. I could see him thinking that it was only because I was white that I got the promotion, even after Tom Cole had pointed to the many black sergeants in our little army. If he had shut up about being a Tswana and not made an improper remark about Sergeant Makin's wife, he would have got a promotion too. We also learned just how deadly a horse and good rifle were when used in a proper combination and I tell you now we had the best teacher in Sir Redvers Buller. I know he did not do very well in the last war against the Boers here, but it is also fair to say that he did not want to be given the command either as he was twenty years past his prime. But Ragwasi and I served under him when he *was* in his prime, and we saw what a fighter he was when we got caught out on the Devil's Pass on Hlobane Mountain, which I will tell you about.

We met him first when we started patrolling up and down the border just after the Governor had sent in the ultimatum to the Zulus that they must disarm and that in return for that we would get the Boers out of their lands. Major Buller sent us to escort in a column of settlers who were to be evicted from the Luneburg district as part of this deal and he won our respect straight away because although he looked like a square-headed, stiff necked squire he showed he was not too proud to pick up a 100lb barrel of salt pork and throw it on the back of the wagon which it had just rolled off. He didn't scold the driver either, but slapped him on the back and asked if he needed any more help. This made us all laugh and direct our catcalls at the driver. We were a pretty rough lot and not used to military discipline but while Tom Cole and the sergeant had a hard time getting us to stand in a straight line, we would do anything for Buller because we knew that he could probably beat any of us at everything from arm-wrestling to horsemanship and shooting and that is saying something. Some of the real hooligans in our troop admitted that he was better at cattle-rustling than any of them too. He was a big man with a chest as big as that pork barrel and although his face had a naturally grumpy set to it - he had been kicked in the mouth by a horse – he was actually a cheerful sort of man.

This was a good quality to have in a leader because when the ultimatum expired and we began our invasion of Zululand to break the Zulu army and disarm it things did not go at all to plan. We did our part very well, of course, but further south the Central column got caught out and were defeated by the Zulus at a place called Isandlwana, while on the coast another column got itself besieged at Eshowe. While this was going on we had been skirmishing with some of the Zulus but when we heard the news of these defeats, Major Buller and his boss Colonel Wood decided we would not be defeated or besieged. They did not believe in it, or so Major Buller said, and said that if you wanted to win a war you had to attack, be aggressive and make your moves first. This was a valuable lesson which he taught us and so we made a camp at a place called Khambula and became aggressive. This was not very hard as Major Buller reckoned that the best way to get the Zulus to fight him was to steal their cattle and he had a lot of experts in our troop that he could call on in this respect. So we became cattle-rustlers for the three next three months while the main army in Natal licked its wounds and got ready for another try.

Our cattle-rustling came to an end on the 28th March 1879 when we went up Hlobane Mountain to sweep up the Zulu cattle that they were keeping up there. This area of Zululand is very hilly, like English moorland, and Hlobane was a big flat topped hill with steep sides, rocky *kranzes* and usually had a covering of mist on it because it was so high. We set off at 3.30 in the morning and went up the eastern side in a horrible, cold rainstorm that made all six hundred of us grumble and wish we were back in our beds with a warm woman. The plan was to get up to the top and then drive whatever Zulus and cattle were up there towards the west end where there was another force under Major Russell waiting to catch them and although we got a hotter fire from the Zulus up there than we expected, everything went according to the plan. That was until about ten o'clock in the morning when the mist lifted and Nathan Walker asked what that black mass was down on the plain. Ragwasi and I were trying to push the cattle down the hill through a place called the Devil's pass and making a hash of it but we followed his arm and saw 20,000 Zulu warriors jogging straight for us. For a moment I was back in the card room of the *Cross Keys* with that grinning monkey on my chest and staring at that Ace and wondering how I could have got myself into such a mess.

We were not the only ones to see it either and the Zulus that we were trying to push away from the sides of the pass took heart and started to give us what for properly. The Devil's Pass was not like a pass between two mountains, I should explain. Hlobane was like the shape of a tortoise with its head out, with us at the top of the shell wanting to get down across the neck and onto the head and it was the neck that we called the Pass. To get onto the neck you had to drop down about a precipitous fifty yards, difficult for the horses because it was full of rocks and bushes and so they had to be led or tugged, and if you cannot see this in your mind's eye how difficult this descent was then I will tell you that the people at the bottom of that pass were only the size of half a finger nail when viewed from the top of it and that is how steep it was; you would never get a wagon down it. And while you were trying to tug that horse down, the Zulus concealed themselves in these bushes and some krantzes on either side and shot bullets and ran forward to throw spears at us when they thought the gun smoke would give them cover. I tell you we were very lucky indeed that these were not the main Zulu *impi* or we would have been biltong that day, but it was still touch and go because these Zulus were brave men fighting for their cattle, just as Ragwasi and I had done.

Major Buller saw what was happening and gave orders to abandon the cattle and to get ready to defend the pass. He organized us so that we would push the Zulus away from the bushes and krantzes and allow us to get down the pass in an orderly manner, but then he saw that Major Russell was being pushed away from the bottom of the hill by the approach of the main Zulu army while a regiment had detached itself and was climbing the hill to cut us off. Most of us troopers could see what was happening too and we knew what would happen to us when we were surrounded, as we must be. One of them decided that hope was dead already and put his Martini-Henry in his mouth. I have to say, my heart went into my boots when I saw what was happening and I said a prayer and felt comfort that at least Tepo had the diamonds to keep her provided for. Ragwasi too was looking very serious but when he caught my eye he gave me that sideways upside down smile and I felt heartened by it.

'Look at that man uBuller,' he said. 'When *he* panics, so will I.'

I looked up and there he was holding a horse in one hand and scratching his arse with the other, while he talked with Tom Cole. He did not look like he was more worried than he would be if his cricket team had had a bad innings. Ragwasi nudged me and indicated a young Zulu preparing to throw a spear at us, and I potted him with the simplest of snap shots. It was my first kill of the day and I felt my instinct for preservation come back to me and resolved not to give in to fear, or panic. Instead I would keep a cool head and use my eyes and senses like a hunter.

'Everyone happy here?' asked Tom Cole as he scrambled over to where the thirty riders of our troop were. He had his usual grin on, but I could tell he was tense as he gave out his orders. 'Bit hot isn't it? Right – we are to get ourselves down across the *nek* and keep that lot coming up the hill from cutting us off. Think you can do it? I thought so too. So mount up and let's go. Sergeant Makin, lead the way. Cornet Walker, take your section next and I'll bring up the rear.'

The horse I had at that time was the stupidest beast that I had ever come across. If it could eat something that would give it colic, it would do so; if it could cast a shoe twenty miles from home, it would do so; if it could fart on parade when I was being inspected, it would do so. So as I mounted, I whispered in its ear that if it bore me out of trouble that day I would personally feed it sugar cane and carrots to its heart's content for a month of Sundays. She put her ears back, whinnied a bit and then flew down that rocky cliff like a mountain goat, with me leaning right back in the saddle as far as I could, and ignoring the sliding scree under her hooves and the shouts, cries and bangs of battle until we were on that flat *nek* and thanking our lucky stars that we still had *our* whole necks. Ahead of us, Sergeant Makin and his section had decided to take the safer way of going down on foot, but when I looked back I saw Tom Cole take the drop the same way that I had.

We didn't all make it. One horse fell and knocked another over and the two riders were killed under them, broken on the rocks, while a third was shot out of the saddle by a Zulu marksman. We had no time to mourn though because we were still in danger of being surrounded and so we dismounted and took up our firing positions and started knocking men down at 400 yards. I fired a lot of bullets that day, more than I did ever before or after, but I did keep a clear head and made as many count as I could. The Zulus did not press home their attack as hard as they should because I think they had experienced Martini-Henry bullets before. I was also surprised that they were very bad shots mostly and did not seem to understand the use of the sights. Most of their bullets cracked overhead or hit the ground well short.

Buller was a thing to see though. I would not have gone back up the Devil's Pass for all the diamonds in Kimberley; he went back up *five times*, each time to rescue a knot of men in trouble. He also kept his discipline and insisted we kept ours by not wasting ammunition by firing wild or too quickly. The only time I saw him angry was when he saw a boy come down the slope without his horse. *What are you going to do without a horse!* I heard him shout. *Get back up the hill and fetch it!* The boy did as he was told too. I watched him come down faster than I did when he had retrieved it. He was a brave boy, but I think his horse died later.

Finally, when we were all down, Buller led us back to the camp at Khambula, all the time keeping us well in hand, conserving the horses, dropping back to fire a few rounds with the rearguard and even sending off a troop to take some cattle. Ragwasi, Walker and I stuck hard by Tom Cole, who seemed to be iron bound, he held himself so tightly and it was only then that I realized that this was not his first time in battle because, of course, he had been fighting the Xhosa last year. Buller and he taught us how to stay alive during that long ride back; how to direct our fire so that dropping the right ten men would stop the whole hundred; how a bullet fired from a moving horse was wasted and how we had to keep cool, dismount, control ourselves and shoot carefully; how to move by sections so that we could always rely on our friends to cover us as we covered them; how to pick and force a way through a running fight. I think Ragwasi, Nathan Walker and I learned more about war on that day than we ever learned afterwards. Even when we had lost eight men and nine horses out of thirty, Buller kept up a sort of cheerful seriousness which I think did a lot to keep the shock off Nathan Walker. These examples of what a commander of men should be in battle deeply affected me and I took them to my heart when it became my turn to lead soldiers.

We only wanted to go to sleep when we made it back to Khambula, but this we were not allowed to do as Colonel Wood was expecting those 20,000 Zulus to attack him on the morrow. He was not wrong either but, to be honest with you, I was not afraid to be in this battle tomorrow because I reasoned that if the Zulus could not defeat us when we were ambushed, spread out and disorganized then they could not beat us when we were ready for them. Of course, they had given us a licking at Hlobane and between us and Major Russell, we had left two hundred bodies on that hill, but it was another lesson learned that a battle won is not a war won. I was also confident that if those Zulu warriors did not know the proper use of a Martini-Henry, the 1200 men in the camp at Khambula did, and an assegai and a shield was no defence against it. About one third of our force were men like Ragwasi and I, good with horse and gun if not battle hardened, while another third were Basutos, veterans of the Xhosa war or Boer volunteers who were experienced in war. The other third were British regulars, who we thought were a little wooden and inflexible, but I had no fear of them running at all. More than this though, once we had drawn our supplies, fed and watered the horses, and stuffed our pockets and pouches with ammunition, we were excited.

Buller sent out Raaf's Rangers, a bunch of Kimberley toughs which contained several of our business contacts and at least two of Ragwasi's cousins, to find the Zulus the next morning and extend an invitation to a battle, which was eagerly accepted. It took the Zulus until lunchtime to get into position and they were an impressive sight, for they had come in their leopard skins, monkey skins, big, white shields and headrings, each decorated in a different way according to their regiments and they moved and drilled in a very disciplined fashion. Colonel Wood let them do whatever they wanted to do unmolested because he had no fear of them. We had a good position, formed in a long square on a long ridge with good fields of fire out to more than a thousand yards all round and plenty of ammunition. Colonel Wood was that confident, even at odds of nearly 17:1, that I bet neither Forsythe, Salcombe nor any other Newmarket bookie would have taken his money. In fact, he got impatient with the time they were taking over it and sick of them boasting that they were *the Boys from Isandlwana and we have come to eat you up like pieces of meat!* So he sent us out to shoot them up and remind them that this was a battle not a bragging contest. They took the bait and came charging at the camp, shouting their war cries *Bayeete! Bayeete! uSuthu!* but it did them no good, because we just shot them down and shot them down and shot them down. It was easier than shooting Springbok during the migration and to be honest it made me angry because they were acting so stupidly. I had no personal quarrel with the Zulus, but I thought that they should have fought more intelligently and with guns. Every man in Africa had been to Kimberley to get a gun and here was an army that had left them behind at home. I shot and shot and shot and then at about 6 in the evening, they began to retire and we went out and pursued them without mercy, because Buller said to us that the only justification for fighting a battle was to win it and make sure it stayed won.

It stayed won. We killed maybe 2000 Zulus and probably wounded or winged twice that number. We would have killed more if we had not had to stop from time to time to let the smoke clear. We had only about twenty of our men killed in return. There were those who claimed that the Zulu King Cetshwayo was a martyr after the war, but all I can think of really is Cetshwayo sending his men to war to try their spears against guns when he sat at home with his wives and never went near a battle himself. Whatever the complexities of politics, this is something that I cannot forgive. I remember the bodies strewn about that hillside and the low murmur of wounded men crying in pain with the loathsome vultures circling above. Anyway, there was another big battle at Ulundi in July which ended the war with the Zulus, but Ragwasi, Walker and I did not see it because after Khambula, Colonel Wood finally gave us leave to go to see the Governor.

We caught up with him on the wide grasslands and long, steep ridges east of the Drakensberg after taking our leave of Captain Tom Cole who thanked us for our service and offered us our places in his troop whenever we wanted them back. We had gone to Fort Amiel to retrieve Walker's journals and we were very surprised to see that the Governor was travelling with just his secretaries, a small carriage no bigger than a cab and just a couple of small, round military tents. We were even more surprised to see that he was travelling through this dangerous country without a military escort and my first thought was that he was an ignorant civilian straight out from England.

'Don't believe it,' said Nathan Walker. 'He has fought in wars, founded cities, speaks many languages and although he can be testy, he is anything but ignorant and will follow his principles to the end.'

'Do you know him well?' probed Ragwasi.

'I was born in India and everyone in India knows him,' replied Walker, confidently.

'Will he listen to Ragwasi?' I asked.

'I think so,' he said, putting his spurs to his horse. 'And if he gives a promise, he will keep it. He has that reputation.'

We galloped down to the small camp and introduced ourselves to an Afrikander called Stegmannn who was a long nosed man with a long black coat and a big preacher's hat. He was nervous at first but when he found out that we were carrying news for the Governor he relaxed and filled us in on the situation while the Governor finished off a dispatch he was writing. They were on their way up to meet Kruger in the hope that now the Boers need not fear a threat from the Zulus, they might accept British rule and stay quiet. Stegmann told us that there were many Boers who did not share the views of the *Regt Doppers* and would be happy if they were just given some control over their own affairs and allowed to get on with farming. He also told us that Kruger had recently been to Germany;

we guessed that the reason for this was in Nathan Walker's journal and the tracks of the gunrunners that we had followed. 'Right now, Kruger has gathered many of his followers in a *laager* outside Pretoria and formed a Peoples Committee which has everyone talking about a full scale rebellion,' he said. 'We hope he will not be so foolish, but this hope hangs by a thin thread.'

'This makes me very nervous, uStegmann,' replied Ragwasi. 'For the Boer can be very hotheaded and grows braver the smaller his enemies get. And we have just made the Zulus very much smaller than they were.'

'Prince Ragwasi, a good day to you,' said the Governor sweeping back the flap of his white canvas tent and greeting us with a smile. 'Forgive my eavesdropping on your conversation but the walls of my palace here are rather thin.'

Sir Bartle Frère was an impressive looking man in his mid-sixties, slim, fit, balding a little, but his combed over grey hair still had some black in it. He had a grey moustache, a narrow nose over a prow of a chin and a bulbous forehead which must come about from having a large brain. His eyes were the thing that gripped me most because the pupil of his right eye seemed to be a little bigger than his left one. This gave him a look of seriousness, but also gave me the impression that he was a disappointed man, a man who had struggled too long against being ignored or passed over, who perhaps had seen too many compromises, too much mendacity but was determined to hold firm to what he believed to be right, just as Walker had said.

'And your companions are Constable Pelly and…Constable Nathan Walker, I understand.'

Nathan Walker looked down as he shook hands. 'Jolly pleased to meet you sir,' he said.

For a moment it seemed that the Governor was going to say more but instead he shook my hand, beckoned to a manservant to serve tea and then invited us all to sit on stools around a tiger skin rug laid out on the grass. Ragwasi looked at the skin and raised his eyebrows.

'What sort of animal is this that has the teeth of the lion but the skin of the zebra?' he asked. 'Is it an Indian thing?'

'It is indeed,' replied the Governor. 'I shot him myself outside Poona in '64 or thereabouts.'

'It's called a tiger,' I said, admiring the beast. 'I saw a picture of one once. Did you hunt it on an elephant?'

'You ride an elephant?' exclaimed Ragwasi.

'Indeed, Prince Ragwasi,' replied the Governor, inclining his head and taking tea. 'But an Indian elephant is not to be compared in size or temperament to an African elephant. The Indian elephant is so placid that we place a box on its back called a howdah which can hold two or three people. The mahout then sits astride the neck of the elephant and so we go through the bush until a tiger is discovered. Then we shoot it.'

'This is a marvelous Indian thing,' said Ragwasi, who was now the Governor's man to the end. 'Bayeete. I honour you for it.'

The governor took to Ragwasi too and addressing him always as *Prince,* showed a great deal of interest in the messages that he had brought from Montshiwa and Khama, chiefs who he had only distantly heard of. He nodded and accepted Ragwasi's complaints about the Boers but he would not commit himself to the aid and protection that the Tswana hoped for, but he did promise to give Ragwasi's complaints every consideration. He was also very interested indeed in our journeys through the Namib and admitted that he had never thought that there was anywhere other than Walvis Bay that would be suitable for use by smugglers.

'But I suppose there are any number of such bays and inlets, known only to guano captains and explorers and the like,' was his comment. 'I have known men who have explored the north and south poles who will tell you again and again that our maps are wrong. Indeed, when I was a young man, I sailed from Suez to India without benefit of any map bigger than a rough sketch and a pocket compass. It shows our want of knowledge and I shall, if I may, have your Journal copied and forwarded to the Royal Geographical Society in Kensington.'

This made us exchange some guilty looks because of our decision to hide those diamonds in the pages of the Journal. Nathan Walker told us that the Governor had been president of that learned society and now some of those pages would not add to their learning at all.

It was also curious to see how Nathan Walker and the Governor got on. Sir Bartle asked if he were at leisure to accompany him on his way up to Pretoria and when we agreed, they spent as much time as they could, riding or walking together on the veldt, and it seemed obvious to me that this was much more than a chance connection. Ragwasi thought that he might be an unacknowledged son, but there was no obvious physical resemblance that I could make out and however much we hinted, Walker gave us no firm answers. The only clue that I had at that time was in the Journal, where in a lot of his sketches of the desert Walker had added a small figure, like a child, always alone. When I asked him about this, he said it was just so that a person could get an idea of the scale, but I did not believe him. Anyway, he was entitled to his secrets, as I was.

We camped in a wide sward of good grass at the foot of a range of hills that ran like lions towards the hazy blue horizon, just a day short of the Boer laager, ready to make our final preparations but as we tended to our horses we were bothered by a party of forty or fifty mounted Boers who came up on us swearing fit to raise the devil himself. Ragwasi and I went for our guns but Stegmann forbade us and instead addressed the three who galloped up in their own language. They were big men, dark and full of fury and I guessed that they were proper Transvaal Boers from up in the north of the country because they seemed to have no English at all. This was often the case with those Boers who had trekked the furthest and longest and who never had desire or reason to go to Kimberley. Now, here they were, all tied up in buckskin, homespun, wide hats and spluttering anger. Stegmann stood up to them though and stuck his long nose out giving pound for pound, I reckoned. I had picked up a little Afrikaans in Kimberley but they spattered and growled and hissed at each other so fast and so bitterly that I could not follow. The Governor sat back on his horse pretending not to notice them – *refusing* to notice them – until they pushed past Stegmann and confronted him directly, their rage spittle flecked. For five full minutes they abused him to his face and even I could make out the foul language that they used and the epithets that they employed. Stegmannn protested of course and one of the Governor's secretaries attempted to protest likewise but in the end Sir Bartle just held his hand up, flashed an eagle eye and the Boers stopped shouting as though they had been slapped. I had never seen such a thing before and I have never seen it since, but in that moment he seemed to swell up with the courage that a man with an army at his back might enjoy and yet his whole army was two weedy secretaries, one Predikant, one Tswana and two Englishmen.

'I take no notice of you, Sir,' he said, holding the eye of the leader, his tone level but with the thrill of the coming storm in it. They didn't need to speak English to understand him. 'I take no *official* notice of you whatsoever. Go back to Mr. Kruger and tell him that I am coming. Go back, now! I command it.'

For a moment there was a crackle of fire between the two men like the lightning that strikes across the veldt in March, and then the Boers turned their horses, spat contemptuously, and rode back to their comrades.

'They want revenge for the death of Piet Uys,' said Stegmannn, as the thunder of hooves diminished. 'He was killed on Hlobane, it seems.'

'We were on Hlobane,' I began, but got no further before Ragwasi exploded.

'Piet Uys? The Piet Uys who crushed *our* soil with his wagons? The Piet Uys who burnt *our* homes, stole *our* cattle, destroyed *our* crops and all drove the Matabele off the Highveld and into subjugation?'

'His son, I think,' answered Stegmannn. 'Did you know him?'

'If I had known he was on Hlobane with us that day, I would have killed him myself,' said Ragwasi, taking hold of his horse's mane, as if to mount up.

I had forgotten that Ragwasi's father had been Matabele. He swung himself up into the saddle.

'Now I must forget my manners and put a hole into one fat, loud-mouthed Boer,' he said, angrily. 'Who are they that are so brave they come to threaten a small party like us when they were nowhere to be found when there was a real battle? *Voetsak hoerkind! Kakhuiskriek.*'

Predikant Stegmann stepped forward and grabbed Ragwasi's bridle before I could.

'Why do you want with these people in the English Empire, anyway?' Ragwasi shouted, trying to break our hold on the bridle. 'And what business is it of yours if I take my revenge on these barbarians?'

The Governor did not move through all this but rather was staring at the retreating figures, weighing them up, thinking, but then he turned his head ever so slightly and looked straight into Ragwasi's eyes too. I hoped that his talent for languages had not yet reached as far as swearing in Afrikaans.

'We have to have them in the Empire because it is the only way we can control them,' he said quietly. 'And if they are not in our Empire, they will be in the German Empire, and this will be much worse for Englishman and African alike.'

'Then let us attack them!' Ragwasi was still in a rage at those cowards and had not controlled himself. 'Let us bring your army up, join with the Zulus and Tswana and everyone else who hates these bastards and give them a hiding they won't forget.'

Sir Bartle looked at Ragwasi and then back towards the Boers who had paused on a low ridge by a spindly tree two hundred yards away. I could see that he was not dismissing the idea out of hand and I was surprised because Ragwasi and I had never talked with so powerful man a man before and did not really expect to be listened to.

'It is something that has been considered,' he said, after a while. 'But these men have friends and relatives in the Cape and if I attack them, *they* will rebel. Then in the confusion that such a war will involve, every freebooter with a horse and gun will prey on every African within reach and every chief with a grievance against a white man will take up his assegai and there will be nothing but war, fire, slaughter and every kind of cruelty on every side.'

He spoke firmly, calmly, like a man who had thought a lot about these things. He did not speak in haste and he did not talk down to us. He spoke to Ragwasi as if he wanted him to understand what he had done – and he had done a lot already, what with gun control, taking over the Transvaal, putting down a Xhosa rebellion last year and now fighting a Zulu war.

'If we rule with a firm, strong, fair hand, allowing all men their due consideration but forbidding absolutely the recourse to violence that is too common here, then I think this will appeal to the better nature of men. We will get the peace that most men desire – and this will be the best protection that I can give to the Tswana.'

'I think you are an idealist, uSir Bartle,' said Ragwasi. 'The Boers want this whole country for themselves. They think they have a right to any land they choose to take. Let us have a supply of Martini-Henrys and ammunition and the Tswana can have a guaranteed way to look after themselves.'

Again, he weighed up what Ragwasi had said before replying.

'I prefer to think of myself as a *realist*,' he replied with a wry smile. 'After all, I have done nothing here that I did not do in India. The Baloochis gave up their guns when they saw that trade and good, vigorous, settled government was more profitable than constant petty war and raiding. If we can take the guns out of South Africa and reconcile the Boers to our rule, then we will have peace.'

'You think Kruger and the *Regt Doppers* will listen to you?' I admit I sounded a bit impertinent, but the only good Boer I had ever come across was Mijnheer Cronjie. Also, many of those who claimed to be Boers were really just Irish or German renegades or Kimberley ruffians and they had only one idea of getting wealth and that was by stealing land from Zulus or Tswana or Basutos or Matabele or anyone and I said so.

'We shall see,' he said. 'Mr. Stegmann leads me to believe that the Boers are not as united as they seem. And you seem to agree with him. Perhaps we might apply a little *divide et imperia*?'

He was a cool one, I will say that. While Ragwasi and I spent the rest of that day scanning the horizon and patrolling around it, our guns never far from our hands, Sir Bartle acted as though he was having a holiday. He walked to and fro through the long silver grass, hands behind his back, sometimes smoking a cheroot, as though he was strolling about Wimbledon Common. He talked a lot with Nathan Walker too but neither gave us any hint of what they were talking about and even after supper, which we all ate together around the camp fire like old friends, Sir Bartle acted as though he was as happy as if he was in the bar of the Royal Geographical Society. At breakfast the next morning, I made a half-hearted attempt to dissuade him from going to the Boer camp but he shook me off with a shake of his head and, taking his morning chai, went away for one last solitary walk on the veldt. Only then did my doubts really rise up. He looked to me like a hanged man walking.

The Boers had assembled at a place called Erasmuspruit, a flat, yellow piece of veldt cut through by narrow streams, good for horses and cattle with firewood nearby. There were a lot of them too, maybe three or four hundred families and they were already beginning to stink the place out because the Boers have no camp discipline when they get together in big groups. You should know that a Boer is a very independent sort of person and he will say that his neighbours are too close if he can see a smudge of smoke from their hearth on the horizon. I was already amazed that Kruger had got so many of them to agree even to meet together in one place and at one time, because they were quarrelsome, independent folk who would argue over anything. There they were, though. Five hundred wagons, their hooped covers like billowing clouds drawn up in two great concentric circles, with a third one to act as a kraal for the thousands of oxen, horses and cattle that they had brought with them. There were lots of people down there too; men attending to the stock or inspecting a wheel; woman in their white caps, blue gowns and white aprons spreading washing on lines strung between the wagons and baking up mealie flour for pot bread; and children, shrieking in fun, carrying water or hanging around the heels of the adults. There were guns there too in plenty and I heard later that in one of the wagons there was even a cannon concealed. It was testament to Kruger's leadership that he had got them to draw up their laager so that there was a long avenue through the middle of them which led up to a big tent where he intended to give Sir Bartle Frere his marching orders.

When we approached to within a mile of them, reining in at the top of a small rise in the blue mid-morning, they caught sight of us and the word of our approach ran through those lines like a rumour of war. A bell rang its iron alarm and men began tumbling out of wagons, mounting up and reaching for their guns. Already there was a Kommando of forty or fifty men riding from the cattle kraal towards the main laager amid a lot of angry shouting and booing and whistling, which made the secretaries nervous and the horses jittery. Walker, Ragwasi and I also exchanged nervous glances and made sure that our ammunition was to hand and our spurs ready. We could run but we could not fight and we were not brave or foolish enough to try.

'Sir Bartle, surely we must withdraw and wait for an escort,' said the Predikant Stegmann. 'I had not expected such a hostile reception as this.'

Sir Bartle Frere sat on his horse and looked straight ahead. He was as cool as a cucumber. He didn't even fiddle with his tie.

'You are all to wait here,' he said, simply. 'And no one is to shoot whatever happens.'

I looked at Ragwasi, but he just shrugged back and before I could ask what was up, the Governor clicked his tongue and began to walk his horse forward, down the hill towards the laager. Walker gasped and spurred up, but the Governor snapped up a hand to stop him. I looked at the secretaries and then the Predikant in a silent appeal for them to stop this madness, but they would not meet my eye, so *I* spurred up, intending to stop it myself. This time it was Ragwasi who intervened though.

'*Isala kutshelwa sobona ngomopo,*' he murmured, insistently. 'The wrong-headed fool who refuses advice will come to grief. If he wishes to die, uPelly, then he has chosen this moment and there is no reason for us, who have survived so much already, to die with him.'

Ragwasi was right of course, so I sat and watched, fixed with a morbid fascination as this man walked his horse forward to certain death. I could see bullets being thumbed into Martini-Henrys, belts being hitched up, angry men nodding and gesturing, pistols being cocked and women pulling children back into the wagons. From out of the laager, a crowd began to spread out to right and left, just as that Zulu impi had done at Khambula, so that the Governor would soon be beyond any help that ten times our number could give. The Boers jostled each other, man and horse, as though each rifleman wanted space to get a better shot in, and within a few moments there must have been two or three hundred weapons cocked and ready at the shoulder, every one aimed at Frere's head. But he did not vary his pace and as he kept coming the noise died away until the Boers faced him in grim and bitter silence. He kept that horse walking slowly, steadily, towards the centre of that line, his grey trousers and grey hair standing out against his black coat and black horse, and against the straw yellow of the veldt and the white of the wagon covers.

When he came to within seven or eight yards from the line of guns bristling out from the beards and homespun of a hundred years of hatred and hostility, he stopped and in that moment I truly believed I was looking at a dead man. All it would take was one slight pressure from one itchy trigger finger and the whole line would blaze out at him.

Nobody moved. For a moment I thought the wind itself had stopped and the crickets themselves were holding their breath. The Governor waited for a count of ten, as still as a statue while the horse fidgeted, and then he walked the horse straight forward again.

'My God!' hissed the Predikant. 'It is Daniel who enters the lion's den!'

The Boers did not shoot. Instead, slowly, hesitantly, then all at once the crowd parted, backing away to let him through, the nearest putting up their guns but not retracting their fangs. Their movement revealed that long avenue between the wagons, each with men and guns on the boxes, like the throat of a beast lined with teeth. To me, Frere looked like a cow being paraded before the slaughtermen at the Bury market.

'Walker! uPelly!' urged Ragwasi. 'This man is going to die. We must leave if we are to save ourselves. These are *Boers* and you know they are no better than wild animals!'

Sir Bartle kept his horse moving down the throat and the jaws closed behind him and the avenue filled up with people following him, spilling out of the wagons like mealies from a sack until we could just make out him out, still mounted, in a clear space before the big tent. A man with a beard and a stove pipe hat appeared, like a troll from a cave, and the Governor dismounted and went in to the tent. There was a moment's silence and then pandemonium broke out as all the Boers started talking at once and then the man in the stove-pipe hat came out, shouted something which I did not catch and then the Boers turned around, went back to their wagons or stood around in small parties. I let out a whistle of relief when I saw arms being shouldered, weapons being un-cocked and pipes and Cape Smoke bottles coming out instead.

Ten minutes later, a rider came out of the laager and called for the Predikant, who duly rode forward with the two nervous secretaries, leaving Ragwasi, Nathan Walker and I alone on the veldt.

'Do not be fooled, uPelly,' said Ragwasi, still expecting the worse. 'This is how the Zulu Dingaane killed the Boers when they first came into his land. He invited them to a feast and then killed them all while they were eating. Kruger knows this because he was a small boy then and will not have forgotten.'

Nathan Walker dismounted and loosened the girth on his saddle.

'If they were going to kill him, they would already have done it,' he said, phlegmatically, pulling out biltong and army biscuit. 'And now the Governor will win their trust. Wait and see. Luncheon anyone?'

I agreed with Walker and dismounted too.

'A man *that* brave deserves to get away with anything.'

'He is a mad man,' declared Ragwasi, sliding off his horse. 'Like uBuller, but his bravery is colder.' He thought for a moment. 'Perhaps he will not die today,' he conceded.

We sat and ate, but we did not relax. We kept the reins through our arms and our Martini-Henrys close and although Ragwasi laid on his back in the sun for a while he did not sleep. Every once in a while we would scan that encampment for some sign of movement, but all seemed still, waiting, listening for word. We could see the Boers with their big beards and bigger bellies chomping on clay pipes, checking their weapons and wondering if there would be war and from time to time we would see them peer out at us from behind their hedge of wagons. The flies buzzed and the crickets chirruped and the horses champed for hour after hour of hot sun and shimmering grass. The lowing of the cattle spoke of peace and the lazy days under willows by a good stream that we longed for then but in the pits of our stomachs there was a gnawing anxiety that we would soon be leaping for our horses and riding as hard as we could for home. We were wide awake and ready when we saw the Predikant emerge from the big tent in the late afternoon, and our girths were tightened and we were mounted by the time he came galloping up the hill.

'He has done it!' Stegmannn shouted joyfully, his eyes alight as though he had been given a new gospel personally by the Lord himself. 'There will be peace! Kruger has agreed! The Boers are to have self-government as long as they stay within their borders and there will be a British Administrator and troops to see that they do! They will live as peacefully as the Afrikanders at the Cape. Rejoice! Sir Bartle Frere has done it!'

I could see that Ragwasi was still wary, but when he saw the Governor come out of the tent, shake hands with Kruger - the man in the stove-pipe hat, we now realized – get on his horse and come riding back to us, his scepticism collapsed. We rode forward to greet him and his smiling secretaries but before we could congratulate him, he spoke directly to Ragwasi. I could see he was happy because I knew better than anyone what a gambler feels like when he wins at long odds.

'I believe Montshiwa, Khama and the Tswana may rest a little easier in the possession of their lands,' he said, cheerfully. 'We have the heads of an agreement with Mr. Kruger and I have appointed Major Lanyon, who I believe is friendly to your cause, to be the Administrator at Pretoria. I believe that the whole of South Africa will now be unified under the British flag and we may look forward to an era of peace.'

'You will guarantee us protection against the Boers?' replied Ragwasi, who had never taken his eye off the main point of his mission from Khama and Montshiwa.

Sir Bartle paused, thought for a moment and then nodded his head several times in succession.

'You have my personal guarantee that as long as I have power and influence in this country, the Tswana will have my aid against the Boers should they need it.'

'In return for?' Ragwasi was too good a businessman to know that nothing is for free.

'In return for leaving the Boers in peace within the borders of the Transvaal,' answered the Governor.

Ragwasi almost snatched the Governor's hand off.

'We have a deal,' declared Ragwasi, with a big smile. 'And you can count on the Tswana to keep this bargain.'

'Mr. Pelly,' said Sir Bartle turning to me. 'It is also my intention to appoint you as Agent to the Tswana, so that you may represent the views of the Cape government to them, bear messages between us and to help ensure that the Boers keep to their side of the bargain too. You will be my eyes and ears, if you are willing?'

I was very willing to do this and asked if I could have Nathan Walker to help me. This was also agreed and so the next day we set off for home as happy as ever we could be while Sir Bartle stayed behind to negotiate all the details of the settlement with Kruger. We were whistling and singing all the way because we had survived being drafted into the army and killed by the Zulus, gained valuable experience in that war and we had the Governor's promise that we would be safe from the Boers. We were aware that he had not allowed us to buy guns to defend ourselves, but this we balanced with the knowledge that Major Lanyon would not allow the Boers to buy them either. No deal is perfect but we were happy with this one.

And this was how it should have all ended, with an Act of Union in 1879, with all the peoples of South Africa, English, Boer, Zulu, Xhosa, Tswana, native, settler, miner, farmer, hunter, trekker or transport rider negotiating deals and making business. If it had ended here we would not have had three years of war between the British and the Boers, Bambatha's rebellion among the Zulus, the Germans would have been kept out of the Namib and the Herrero would not have been massacred by them. The Zulus would not have had that big civil war either and lost all their lands and we Tswana would have kept ours too.

But we know now that we did not get our Union and what a vale of tears our country became. Perhaps now, in 1911, there will be healing. We can only hope.

Why did we not get our Act of Union in 1879, I hear you cry? What went wrong? I will tell you. It was because the week after he had done the deal with Kruger, Sir Bartle Frere was sacked by politicians in London eager to save their skins from getting the blame for the loss of those soldiers at Isandlwana, even if it meant sacrificing ours. Bah! Now I must stop and get some of Ragwasi's Cape Smoke because just thinking about this makes me so angry I will end up stamping on my hat.

Actually, I will tell you one more thing quickly before I open this bottle, because it is important and it did ruin my happiness that day. Our road back to Kuruman meant that we must pass the Boer laager and just at the tail end of it I caught sight of a person, two people, who I had never expected to see again. They were sitting on the tailgate of a wagon and I am pleased to say that they did not notice us and that Ragwasi did not notice them either or he would have got us into a fight with the whole Boer army. One of them was that Fenian bastard Logan who I thought I had killed with my Martini-Henry. Now you will ask why *I* did not start a war with the whole Boer army either. The reason is that the other person sitting on the tailgate of that wagon was Daisy Stockwell.

*

Chapter7

The Republic of Stellaland

It is a good job that Ragwasi is not close with the Cape Smoke because it is his brandy that I am drinking. He is at this moment watching his many children and grandchildren playing rugby football. I think it is rugby football but it might just be a riot. Anyway, he likes it better than listening to his new wife whining. Why he took her in, I don't know. He is old enough to be her grandfather, but he says that people keep sending him wives all the time and he cannot turn them away because they might be offended. This new one is always after money. The last new one was happy with beads, but this one wants money. I don't blame her for trying, but she has not got much hope because getting money out of Ragwasi has got harder and harder over the years. He is happy to share Cape Smoke but not money. I think it is because of those share certificates that he bought in Rhodes' company. Actually, I should not be so hard on him about these certificates because he bought them thinking that Rhodes was going to rob the Boers and he liked that idea a lot. I think he felt he might get something back, because they had robbed him all his life.

Tepo and Boitumelo have gone to church to light a candle and to sing. Neither of them are Christians but they like to do this because they can wear European hats. Tswana women do not usually wear these types of hats, but Tepo and Boitumela have got it into their heads that these hats are a good thing and who am I to gainsay them? They went through a phase of wearing those big funnel type hats that the Dutch hausfraus wear but then they decided they were *common*, whatever that means. I do not keep up with modern fashions. I am happy with clean drawers and veldtschoen and will wear anything as long as it does not include a tie. People did not wear ties when I was young; my father wore a stock to keep his neck warm sometimes and this was sensible because it was like a scarf. I do not understand why I should be expected to strangle myself with one now and if I was a bit slimmer, I would use the one that Tepo bought for me as a belt instead. Actually, it is folded up in a drawer.

Where was I? Yes, Daisy Stockwell. You will want to know about her because you will see how old injuries can come back to haunt you when you least expect it. And I have to admit that although I had thought about the Stockwells with shame many times, I never, ever, expected to see Daisy sitting on the tailboard of a Boer wagon in Erasmusspruit with a ruffian like Logan. When I saw her, I pulled my hat down a bit further and galloped on, hoping that I had not drawn attention to myself. At that moment my heart leaped into my mouth, that monkey was back on my chest and, to be honest, I felt sick. Ragwasi and Walker wanted to know what was the matter but I just shook my head and picked up the pace a bit and hoped that I could outrun her.

I was wrong about that. The world is a small place and I found this out a couple of days later when we stopped at a farm just along the Vaal River called Viljoensrust. Nathan Walker always seemed to be eating then and he had bought some Boerewors from a *padstall,* but it had disagreed with him. Actually, it could have been the Colman's Mustard that he had bought because he had not had it in years and missed the taste of home, but either way, something had put a road through him and we could not *schlep* our way all the way home like this. It was also very cold at night and there was frost on the ground in the morning, so this was also a reason for us to lie up in Viljoensrust for a day or two, while Nathan Walker sorted his bowels out.

It was on the second day, while Ragwasi and I were eating good beef and bread provided by the Boer and his frau that we saw the wagon pull up before the stoep and Daisy leap down off it. She had not changed much in the six or seven years since I had seen her – I lose count because I always go by the number of summers and if you come from the northern hemisphere to the south you will either have two consecutive summers or two consecutive winters if you are unfortunate. Anyway, she had not changed much. She was still good looking and as I ignored my foreboding and surveyed her, I thought she had got prettier still, the way some women do when they stop being girls and fill out a bit. Her features were finer and her skin was better for a bit of a tan. Her black hair was swept back a bit too, which showed a neck as graceful as a swan's and I confess I did think a thought which Tepo would not have been happy with. She was driving the wagon on her own as she had done back at Dines Hall, except this time she had mules rather than horses, and she handled them with the confidence and skill that I remembered her for. She even checked hooves before she tied the reins to the post and came onto the stoep to knock.

I did have the urge to head out the back but the frau answered the door while my mouth was full of beef so there was no escape. She came in with a smile, turned her head and her face fell like a boulder off a cliff.

'Oh my God, it's Nicholas Pelly,' she said and the disdain dripped out of that voice as though I had evicted her yesterday. 'So this is where you've been skulking, you vermin.'

She could not say more because there is a law about hospitality in Africa and it is a fool who breaks it, so after we had made polite introductions, Daisy and I carried on a tersely civil conversation at the frau's table while she gave us *rooibos* tea. Ragwasi went quiet. After so much time, I was still ashamed of my actions but I had tried to learn to not think about it and pay off the score to fate by living generously and fully – living audaciously, as I phrased it. However, here my fate was, sitting in front of me, Fortuna who I had worshipped at the stables and the tables, come back to pay me out in the shape of Daisy Stockwell.

'What brings you to South Africa?' I asked, tentatively, wondering if she was going to throw the hot tea in my face.

'Eviction,' she said. 'Perhaps you recall it?'

'Daisy, I am sorry for what happened and I will make amends if I can,' I replied, quietly, but she was not having any of it. I noticed that Ragwasi was keeping his eyes on his beef and was chewing very slowly.

'Oh, I think I told you then that I want nothing from you, *Master* Pelly,' she replied, with an acid smile. 'Now that Mother and Father are on the Parish, they are *well* provided for. And my brothers have capital enough for us to start farming again, here, soon.'

'On the Parish?' My heart sank at the thought of Ezekiel and Judith confined to the poorhouse.

'But don't worry,' said Daisy, brightly. 'I dare say your family will be next, the way prices are in the market. You do know your younger sister is like to be an old maid, don't you? Now there's no dowry left? Not with her looks, anyway.'

These were sharp barbs, and all the more painful because I did not know if they were true or not. Of course, we all knew that farms in England had been having a tough time, but I had not had word from or sent word to my family in these six years. I had resolved that I would not contact them until they contacted me because I did not want to give them more pain by reminding them of what a poor son and brother they had. All I had allowed was Mijnheer Cronjie to let them know that I was alive and well if they asked. This you will think stupid and stubborn and you would be right, but my father was an unforgiving man and I could not slink back to him unless I went back as something decent enough to forgive. I had not reached this point then, in my own estimation.

Daisy took great pleasure in telling how her parents, Ezekiel and Judith, had found another small holding down in Suffolk, but it had failed because the days of smallholders were coming to an end in East Anglia. The competition from American wheat and Danish pork was too great and they had run up some debts before being forced on the Parish, and Daisy had gone to find her brothers in London. Tom and Luke had done well and thought they could do better still, if only they could get a bit of land where they could farm for themselves. They heard of South Africa and ended up in the Transvaal where they had heard that they could get good land for a song and were welcomed, even though they were English and not *Regt Doppers*. So Daisy Stockwell and her brothers had become Boers and they were now looking for a piece of land.

'And where will you get this land now that Mr. Kruger has just agreed with Governor Frere not to steal any more of it?' interrupted Ragwasi. 'You do not look to me like a thief.'

'You think that is what Mr. Kruger has agreed to, do you?' Daisy replied archly, looking at Ragwasi with a contempt that I thought she had reserved specially for me. 'And why should he listen to the false words of a *landlord*? My good friend Mr. Logan reckons that the English government will never keep its word – especially as there is an election to parliament due soon.'

'You know Logan?' said Ragwasi, looking at me uncertainly. 'But he is a dead man!'

I shook my head.

'He is very much alive and well,' said Daisy, looking at Ragwasi. 'It wouldn't be you who put a bullet in him for poaching a bit of springbok while he was out with my brothers would it?'

'Is that what he told you?' I replied, wrinkling my nose in disgust and cursing myself for not tracking Logan down that day outside Kuruman and finishing him off. 'I would stay away from him, if I were you.'

'It's the likes of you, I should have stayed away from, Pelly,' she snapped back. 'Logan's well in with Mr. Kruger and he will give us a *big* farm in his country, unlike the land of my birth which will have me evicted from a miserable *smallholding* to pay off the debts of a wastrel.'

She stood up to leave, all spitfire again, while the hausfrau fluttered around, distressed that even strangers should fall out in her house. She stomped out onto the stoep, lifted the reins from the pole and was onto the box and whipping up at the moment when Nathan Walker came around the house.

'Well if this isn't a complete nest of vipers, I don't know what is,' she shouted in exasperation. 'Nicholas Pelly, his pet *kaffir* and Jonty Manchester, whose father also threw my parents off their land for no more debt than they would spend in a week on ribbons. A pox on all of you! Hey! Walk on!'

Ragwasi and I had followed her onto the stoep and so had heard her curse as she whipped up and rattled off down the red road that lay like a dried blood stain across the green veldt. When she had gone, we could not help our eyes sliding towards our compatriot.

'My name is Nathan Walker,' he said, putting his head down and walking back around the house.

'It seems that I am not the only one who was secrets from his youth,' Ragwasi smiled, as we were left alone with our thoughts. 'Ragwasi and the Mamlambo; uPelly and uDaisy Stockwell; Nathan Walker and uJonty uManchester. *Akulanga lashona lingendaba* - no sun sets without its story, uPelly.'

*

From the time that we delivered the Governor's promise to Montshiwa and Khama, we had eighteen months of peace; that was all. Daisy Stockwell and Logan were right. The English government did not keep its word. I have told you that the government sacked Sir Bartle Frere already, but then they changed their mind and kept him on, but only in charge of half of South Africa, and placed someone else in charge of the other half, who was then replaced with General Colley, and then they sacked Sir Bartle Frere again and replaced him with someone who was only temporarily in charge, so no-one knew what was what or who was in charge of wherever in South Africa. On top of this, there was an election in England in 1880 and a politician called Mr. Gladstone promised Mr. Kruger that he would give back the Transvaal to the Boers if he was elected as Prime Minister –'retrocede' was the fancy word he used, but it didn't matter what word he used because Mr. Gladstone never kept his word and went back on it as soon as he was elected. He said that 'retrocede' did not mean 'give back' really. Mr. Kruger never believed an Englishman again and from the middle of

1880, everyone knew that the Boers were preparing for a rebellion. And I mean *everyone* because Mijnheer Cronjie told me in a letter, warning me that all the Afrikanders in the Cape – men and families who had been loyal to England since the British had first come in 1815 - would prefer Mr. Kruger to Mr. Gladstone because everyone knew where they stood with Kruger. They said that if there was to be a Union then it should be under the Transvaal flag not the Union Jack, but the English government did not want that either and so the Act of Union that Frere wanted disappeared and with it our hopes of peace.

If you think this is complicated, you should know that it has taken me thirty years to get this far! Imagine how I felt about it then, when I was ignorant of politics! Now you know why I stamp on my hat and have to drink more of Ragwasi's Cape Smoke. I remember Nathan Walker and I trying to explain it at the time to Ragwasi, Tepo and Boitumela, one night after I had got an official letter from someone called Mr. Strachan, who I had never heard of, telling me that Sir Bartle Frere had definitely been sacked completely and for the last time. It was the middle of 1880, and we were huddled up by the fire against the cold.

'So is the Transvaal British territory still?' asked Boitumela, toasting a bit of meat.

'It is, as far as I can see,' I replied, rustling through some letters. I had got a lot of letters since becoming Agent to the Tswana. I had not had a single letter in seven years, barring a couple of notes from Mijnheer Cronjie telling me my financial affairs, and now I had four all at once. 'But there will not be a Union. And the Zulus are to be given their land back.'

'But I thought you had gone to make the Zulus be part of the Union by taking their guns away?' asked Tepo.

'We did, but there has been a change of plan,' I answered as best I could. 'But I don't know what the new plan is.'

'Who is this Mister Glad uStone? Is he your new chief? What happened to the Queen?' asked Ragwasi.

'Gladstone is the Queen's chief counselor,' explained Nathan Walker, helpfully. 'He does not think we should have an empire and should give it back. The Queen does not agree with him though.'

'Why does she not put him to death then?' Ragwasi queried, throwing another log on the fire and drawing his blanket tighter. 'That is what a strong chief would do if a counselor tried to give his lands away – especially, if he wanted to give away lands to the Boers.'

Nathan Walker and I realized that explaining the British Constitution could take all night, even if we *could* explain it, and so didn't try.

'The important thing is that the Boers do not succeed in their rebellion,' I said. 'For if there is a war, then many of them will take advantage of it to start stealing Tswana land, even when they ought to be joining Kruger's army.'

Boitumela agreed.

'The Boer is like a toad, hopping and hopping when your back is turned. If you do not pay attention, he will hop right into your hut and steal the milk.'

'I do not think we should worry too much, uPelly,' Ragwasi said complacently. 'We have seen uBuller and Colonel Wood fighting and I do not think that Kruger will be a match for them. We can sleep easy in our huts if we do not allow the Boers to sneak up when we are not looking. And we still have the Governor's promise and he will not abandon us.'

'Do not be too sure about the promise,' warned Nathan Walker. He was ashamed to be English there, that night in the firelight, and so was I. 'Mr. Gladstone and Sir Bartle Frere are old enemies and if Gladstone will not regard his own promises as binding, he will not respect anyone else's.'

If we were ashamed to be English that night, I can tell you we ate ashes when Kruger did raise his *Vierkleur* flag on 16th December 1880, shot down Colonel Ansthruther and his men when they were marching up to Pretoria eating peaches, and blockaded Major Lanyon in the town itself. We covered our heads in humiliation when General Colley was defeated and killed at Majuba Hill by Kruger's men on 27th February 1881, the same hill just by Laing's Nek where we had ridden up from Fort Amiel to meet Governor Frere. It got worse and, I swear, Walker and I could not find the courage to look anyone in the eye when we heard that Mr. Gladstone had changed his mind again and given in to Kruger. On 27th March, the Transvaal became independent again and Kruger crowed so loud you could hear him in Kuruman. The ink was not dry on that disgraceful surrender document, the Pretoria Convention, signed on 3rd August 1881, on the orders of

Mr. Gladstone personally, before our troubles began. I have checked the dates to make sure. I have tears now, you see, because Mr. Gladstone, sitting in his study far away in London thought the Pretoria Convention was just a piece of paper. For us it was damn near a death warrant.

And now I must break off to go and wipe away these tears because Tepo and Boitumela will be back from church soon and the rugby match is coming to an end and I do not want everyone to see me so sad. I will get some more Cape Smoke and go for a walk with the cattle and control myself.

*

We had all been visiting with a Chief called Mankurwane, a cousin of Tepo's, about a hundred miles away, up near Mafikeng when the whirlwind came. When I say 'all', I mean Tepo, little Charlotte and myself, Ragwasi and Nathan Walker because Boitumela had stayed behind in Kuruman with Dikiledi and Kagisso to look after the cattle. We had drunk beer with Mankurwane, a stout old gentleman who had that habit of looking at something very close and then moving it away to look at it again at arm's length, and we were preparing to leave when there was a commotion in the *lolwapa*. A family had come in and they were in a great taking because their village had been attacked and their cattle taken. This was a matter of concern, of course, but hardly something that Mankurwane was not used to and we expected to be asked to join with the other Tswana men and go run off the cattle rustlers before they got away.

'*Setilo se ke, Mma. War eng?*' said Mankurwane to the eldest woman. 'Take a seat and tell me what is the matter.'

Of course the whole village was crowding around to hear and the woman was crying and shouting and putting dust on her head, so we knew something very bad had happened.

'Nthuse! Nthuse!' she wept, the tears making streaks in the dust on her face as she begged for help. 'The Boers! They are sweeping up everything that is bigger than a chicken! They have taken our children and our cattle and they have burned our crops. They are coming! They are coming!'

This set up a great buzzing among the people gathered and as our little party exchanged anxious looks a great shout went up.

'They are coming! They are coming! Aiee! Aiee! *Kotse! Kotse!* Danger!'

On the horizon was a finger of smoke – no, two – then, three – snaking up from the bush, the unmistakable spoor of a burning village. Ragwasi, Walker and I were on our horses and riding out to see what was up before you could say *Jack Flash* and it did not take us long to discover the cause of that burning. About three miles away across the flat veldt, horsemen were riding towards us. Lots of them, probably a hundred, well mounted, with good guns slung across their backs, dressed in homespun and full of threatening purpose.

'These are not cattle rustlers,' said Ragwasi, angrily. 'This is a *Commando* come to drive us off the land. We must get our people away!'

Over to the left, a little knot of refugees broke cover from a patch of bush and began to run in our direction. They were spotted and an order was given, arms waved and a troop of Boers broke away from the main body. The horsemen galloped up behind the running people and began shooting indiscriminately at them. We saw a woman fall, spilling her sleeping mat and her pots and then her child in front of her and then a man hit the ground heavily as he went to help her.

'There is no time!' cried Walker, appalled at what he was seeing. 'We must fight. The people cannot run from horses.'

'You are right,' answered Ragwasi. 'But this battle we cannot win and so we must retreat. Turn your horse and go back to Mankurwane.'

Walker looked at Ragwasi and then at the advancing Boers and I could see that his hot head would get the better of him, so I shouted at him too.

'Go back! Get Tepo and Charlotte and tell Mankurwane to get away and call his warriors together!'

He still hesitated, so I commanded him.

'I am your officer! I am the British Agent and you will obey me!'

For a moment I thought he would defy both of us and I do not know what I would have done next, for a man can only be led, not driven in these situations.

'I don't like running,' he protested. 'Those people need help!'

'You are not running!' shouted Ragwasi, still more angrily. 'Did we not retreat at Hlobane, so that we could win the next day at Khambula? Think with your head, Nathan Walker, and ride fast!'

He obeyed at last, though loathe, spurred up and galloped off and I prepared to follow him, but Ragwasi was dismounting.

'What are you doing now?' I cried.

'I want to let them know we are here,' he said, grimly, pulling out his Martini-Henry. 'And I want the people to know that someone will fight for them.'

I agreed with him, so I slid off my horse, took his reins and tethered both to a tree. We ran forward to a little pile of rocks and took aim. The Boers were getting closer and we could see their gun smoke as they hunted those poor people down like animals. Ragwasi put his sights up high because he thought he might try a long shot but I shook my head – half a mile is way too far for a shot at a moving target on a horse. We were too late to save the people who could not save themselves by hiding, and we could see small children being roped like new calves and dragged across saddlebows, but at four hundred yards we put our skills as hunters to use. Ragwasi hit one of the Boer's horses and it threw the rider, while I thought I had knocked another out of the saddle but could not be sure because of Ragwasi's smoke.

'One more shot,' muttered Ragwasi and I nodded, because after this they would see our smoke and would be on us.

We fired simultaneously and this time I was sure I got a kill, but we did not wait and were back on our horses looking for another place to shoot from. This was how Buller and Tom Cole had taught us to delay the Zulus when they chased us from Hlobane, because a man will not advance blindly if he does not know where his attacker is. Instead he will lie down and look for his adversary and this is what we counted on, for it takes time to find a man who has moved, hey?

These Boers were good horsemen and they had some experienced riders with them, so they did not wait as long as we would wish before they came after us. However, our shooting made them cautious and made many of them hang back because they were robbers who wanted to enjoy their spoils, not soldiers who were doing their duty. I think we killed two more and hit at least one more horse before we decided we had done enough and raced down to Mankurwane's lolwapa. When we got there we were pleased to see that he had had more sense than Nathan Walker and had got his people out rather than stay to fight unprepared. It was no problem for us to follow their tracks into the bush, down a watercourse to some caves where they could shelter for the night. I was glad to see Tepo and little Charlotte safe there but we still had a lot to do to make sure that all our people were safe from these wolves. There were not very many Tswana men here because most were spread out with the cattle or working in Kimberley but we could expect reinforcement through the night and so felt a little safer than before. After we had organized the weaving together of strong thorn bushes and then building a small wall from rocks for us to lie behind, we lay down and waited to see if the Boers would attack us.

They did not attack because they were too busy stealing everything and burning everything and had no need to attack us because we could not stop them. In the morning, as Mankurwane's men started to come in from their own lolwapas, a short reconnaissance showed us the black scars of burnt homes still smouldering, grain pits ripped open and plundered, pots and sleeping mats strewn about and no cattle left at all. When he saw the damage Mankurwane began to rage and declared that he would fight the Boer to the death and that we should prepare ourselves accordingly.

'How many guns do you have?' asked Ragwasi, looking at the Tswana men gathering round, brandishing their spears and beginning to make big boasts about what great warriors they were.

'We have our *muti*,' answered Mankurwane loudly, to the cheers of his warriors. 'It will protect us from the bullets of the Boer and then we will close with him and kill him with our spears.'

'*Muti*?' said Ragwasi, quietly into his ear. 'Please tell me that you are not relying on magic alone to defeat the Boer.'

'What else do we have?' stormed Mankurwane, dropping his voice so that the warriors would not hear. 'We cannot buy guns from Kimberley and when our people have gone there with guns, they have had to give them up in return for a piece of paper.'

'Gun control?' Ragwasi turned to me. 'This is not what was intended by the English government surely?'

'I do not know.' I hung my head in shame and frustration again at the workings of my government. They had intended to take the guns out of South Africa, but had not taken them out of the Transvaal. 'I do not think they know either.'

'We will fight! How can we be men if we do not fight?' Mankurwane was shouting again, as much in accusation at Walker and myself as Englishmen, as he was to encourage his warriors. 'How can we live if we have no cattle and no grain in our pits?'

The Tswana warriors cheered again and Mankurwane gave orders to his sangomas to prepare the *muti*, told his warriors to sharpen their spears, dust off their shields and put on their leopard skins ready for war.

'Are we to stay and fight alongside them?' asked Nathan Walker.

Well, we did stay and fight but it did us no good. We fought for the rest of that year and into the next and we lost every time. Without guns we could not fight the Boers. Without horses we could not match their speed even when we outnumbered them and ambushed them. They simply rode away a little and then shot us down. Our *muti* was of no use and our spears were never washed. Our cattle was taken, our pits opened, our lolwapas burnt, our men culled, our children enslaved, our land torn from our bleeding hands and those who were left melted in tears into the desert. We lost three of Tepo's cousins and four children from her family were apprenticed to the Boers; 'apprenticed' is what they called making someone a slave. Mankurwane's people were pushed to the brink of extinction by the Boer *kommandos* and then were divided against themselves with bribes of gin and promises of a scrap of scrub veldt to survive on if they signed everything else away. Further north, Khama's people were also attacked but the land up there was not as good as it was further south and so they survived better. I saw Logan and the Stockwell boys riding in those *kommandos*, though I never got a chance to get any of them in my sights.

I sent message after message to Kimberley and the Cape pleading for help, pleading for the government to honour the Governor's promise, or at least allow us to get guns out of Kimberley but we got nothing back. I was told that because Sir Bartle Frere's promise was not written down and formally ratified, it did not exist so Mankurwane's people died abandoned. Finally, Mankurwane himself gave up, and settled for what he could get to save what was left of his people. I do not blame him. He did his best but even a strong lion will be killed by hyenas if there are enough of them and he has no help. And there were many Boers and no help ever came.

In the winter of 1882, we left poor, broken, humbled Mankurwane and went to answer Montshiwa's call for aid and as we three rode south to Kuruman we began to understand why he needed it. About a hundred miles east of Kuruman at a place that we called Huhudi but which the Boers called Rooigrond because of its good, red earth, right on the border between the Transvaal and Montshiwa's land, a whole town had grown up. This was a town like any other, with shops and stores, a church, a barber shop, gunsmiths, blacksmiths, a gin shop and even a doctor's surgery, except that every last part of it was on wheels. There were 20,000 people there and every one of them was in a wagon. I tell you, when I first saw it I thought the clouds had fallen to earth, or someone had invented a way to grow cotton in big bunches, or it was a giant's washing day, there were so many wagon covers. They had organized themselves into a big square for defence, but also they had a regular grid of wide streets inside the encampment so that people, horses, mules and cattle could get around. This was important because the water they needed came from the plentiful springs and shallow lakes that lay dotted around in the veldt and each day the animals needed to be taken out of the laager to drink, graze and then be brought back in at night. I guessed that there must be at least 3,000 wagons and carts collected together there and 30,000 beasts at least and when the dust rose as those fine cattle moved against the sunset they set the whole sky ablaze, copper, bronze, ochre, umber, molasses and gold.

'*Hau*!' exclaimed Ragwasi, as we looked down on it from a knoll. 'Where has this *lolwapa* come from, uPelly?'

'There are more arriving still,' said Nathan Walker pointing, and I picked out a well-handled mule team throwing up a cloud of dust not two miles away, driven by a black haired woman that I knew could only be Daisy Stockwell. 'And it looks more like a Roman army on the march than a village, to me at least.'

'Is this Transvaal land or Montshiwa's?' asked Ragwasi. 'Can you tell?'

I reached into my saddle bag and pulled out the letters that I had been sent from the Cape. One of them had a map contained, but examining it carefully gave me no answer. I handed it to Nathan Walker, who knew more about maps than me, and he looked too.

'I cannot be sure without my theodolite and an accurate timepiece,' he said, dismounting, turning the map this way and that and holding it up against the sunset. 'But I would say that only *half* of it is on Transvaal territory. The near part is definitely on Tswana land.'

'How can a *lolwapa* be in two different places, uWalker?'

'It cannot, but this is important because it means it is disputed territory,' he replied, taking a few paces towards the encampment and looking thoughtfully at it.

'Mankurwane's territory was disputed but the Boers have taken it anyway,' I growled. 'What difference does it make?'

Walker thought a little more, then scratched his head and then smiled a triumphant smile and held his arms out wide.

'It makes a difference because the borders further north were not defined by the Pretoria Convention,' he shrilled happily, spinning around in joy. 'This border *was*! That means that the English government will *have* to take notice of us now because they have *guaranteed* this border. If they do not enforce this border, then no border *anywhere* in the world is valid.'

'We have seen what an English government guarantee is worth, uWalker,' said Ragwasi. 'You have been drinking Cape Smoke and Square Face mixed up, this is very obvious.'

'No, no! You don't follow me. When the Boers attacked Mankurwane, the government refused us because the promise was not written down and they pretended there was no promise,' cried Walker, jubilantly.

'You are right,' said Ragwasi, growing impatient. 'Their promises are worthless. It is proved. And it is certain that the Boers will attack us. This is their purpose.'

Walker threw his hat in the air with glee and put his hands to his head as though he was about to shout *Eureka!*

'But if *we* attack the Boers first,' he picked up his hat and threw it in the air again. 'Then the English government will have to come here because they will have to defend the Boers. *They are required to defend this border by the Pretoria Convention.*'

'You are mad!' shouted Ragwasi. 'You are inviting the English government to come and save the Boers *from* the Tswana. Will they not send uBuller to attack us then?'

'No! No! No! A thousand times - No!' Walker was absolutely dancing with delight by now. 'When they get here and see this is disputed territory they will do what they always do. They will set up a Boundary Commission and they will draw a proper line on the map, which the Boers will have to agree to. And even Mr. Gladstone will not allow the Boers to cross that line, because it will be drawn up by lawyers and he believes in law as the basis of civilized politics.'

'Mister Glad uStone does not keep his promises!' shouted Ragwasi again, louder. 'You have told me that and I have seen it with my own eyes in your shameful face too, each time we have sent a letter for help for the Tswana!'

The picture became clear in my mind and although I did not know if Nathan Walker was right, I did think that we were a lot closer to Kimberley than Mankurwane was. The English government did not like trouble on its borders and our friend Captain Tom G. Cole was stationed down at Kimberley. If he could be persuaded to come north, even if it was only with a couple of troopers and a flag, surely the Boers would not dare attack again? At least not before there would be talking – and talking can take a long time.

'Ragwasi, I think that he may be right, even if he may be wrong,' I said. 'But if lawyers are involved then I will tell you that time can be gained, because lawyers get paid for talking and they can talk for a long time.'

'The pen is mightier than the sword!' cried Walker happily.

'Do not talk like a calf,' barked Ragwasi at Nathan Walker. *'Uhlakanipha nganhlanye njengomese!* You are a knife only sharp on one side and so are not as clever as you think you are.'

'Nathan Walker,' I ordered. 'Get on your horse and ride for Tom Cole at Kimberley. 'Tell him that Montshiwa is going to attack Rooigrond and that he must get his troopers up here quickly if he is to avoid a massacre. Tell him that there are *British* subjects in Rooigrond who will be killed if Montshiwa attacks – that's right; Daisy Stockwell and her brothers. That should get him moving.'

'Absolutely right away! Hooray the Tswana are saved!' he beamed, running for his horse.

'Then when you have seen him go to the telegraph and send the same message to Mijnheer Cronjie, the Governor and then to the editors of the *Cape Argus*, the *Grahamstown Post* and the London *Times*, and the London Missionary Society.' With a flourish of pure inspiration, I remembered 'Jonty Manchester' and my conviction that Nathan walker came from a political family and so added, 'And anyone else important that you can think of.'

'Yes Sir!' he cried, as he saluted and dug in his spurs. 'We shall appeal to the beast that haunts Mr. Gladstone's waking dreams and nightmares – public opinion itself!'

'Is this an Indian thing that you are doing, uPelly?' complained Ragwasi, appealing to me with wide eyes as Nathan Walker flew off like an arrow. 'I do not understand. Talking never stopped a Boer when he is stealing!'

'This time, things may be different,' I said, turning my horse. 'But we must tell Montshiwa to get as many men together as we can. And we *must* have guns this time. We must use some of our diamonds to buy them, Ragwasi.'

'Where can we buy guns? Kimberley will not sell guns to us,' he protested.

'We'll buy them from the gunrunners, of course,' I replied.

*

To our great relief, Tom Cole appeared a week later at the head of a troop of Mounted Rifles, dusty, tough, red crossbelts across their blue tunics and a match for any Boer *Kommando* on the veldt. As they rode into Rooigrond, a hush fell on the town and the inhabitants stared guiltily out of their wagons, like felons whose conspiracy has been unmasked before it could be put in motion. I rode down with him, through the lines of the wagons, observing the sullen faces of the Boers, the disappointment of the adventurers, the fury of the freebooters cheated of their prey and the sheer hatred of Logan and Daisy Stockwell who did not keep quiet but abused us openly and without restraint.

The town, still growing, had now acquired a *Llandrost* and *Heemraden*, in the persons of Jacobus van Niekerk, Nicolaas van Pittius, and Piet Bezoidenhuit, as unsavoury a gang of *Regt Doppers* as you could ever hope to meet. Each of them had the characteristic, patriarchal straggling beard, commanded on them by God or Moses or some such prophet, and dressed in plain homespun, with plain buttons, plain collars and plain little black ties. Each of them oozed suspicion from under heavy brows and their disgust at having to breathe the same air as an Englishman was almost palpable. Piet Bezoidenhuit, had a permanent sneer, and kept fingering a bible that he carried in his hand, as though it were a charm against the corruption of *kaffirs* and Englishmen. We might have been vampires. Jacobus van Niekerk, looked at us as though he would dispute our membership of the human race, but then I remembered that the version of Christianity that the *Regt Doppers* followed still divided men into the *Elect* who had been chosen by God – them, obviously – and the rest us, who counted for nothing. Nicolas van Pittius kept playing with a bullet all the time we were speaking – and I could see it was a German bullet.

'What do you want here, English?' hissed van Niekerk when Cole offered to shake his hand.

Cole bristled. Like the rest of the British army, he was looking for any excuse to wipe out the stain of the defeat at Majuba and this one would do.

'I'm here to tell you to move your town three miles east and back inside the Transvaal,' he stated, flatly. 'As per the relevant clauses in the Pretoria Convention. You remember? The ones about staying on your side of the border?'

'The *Pretoria Convention* is it?' scoffed Bezoidenhuit. 'The Pretoria Convention that we don't recognize and you cowardly English won't enforce?'

'That's the one,' said Cole, plastering on a smile. I never saw him find it so difficult to find one before. 'So get in your wagons and move. Don't be a difficult little *bore*, what?'

Van Neikerk lifted an eyebrow.

'Is your hearing gone, *rooinek*? Didn't you hear me tell you there is no Pretoria Convention here?'

'Oh don't be such an ass,' replied Cole. 'I know that communications in the backward little hovels that you call towns are not brilliant, but surely you have heard of a thing called the telegraph? We have one in Kimberley. I'm sure your

President Kruger would have told you of the Pretoria Convention by now, even if he doubted your ability to read it for yourself. I could have one of my *black* troopers help you with any words that you don't understand, if you wish. Especially the ones that say *Get your town back three miles east.*'

'For your information, you *rooinek hoerkind*,' Bezoidenhout taunted. 'You are not in the Transvaal. This is the *independent* Republic of Stellaland, so both you and your precious Convention can *voetsak*. There is no treaty in existence that can stop us taking what is rightfully ours from the *kaffirs* and you English have no authority here, Captain.'

'Can this be true, Tom?' I blurted out. 'Is it possible to just set up a separate country like that?'

'You have heard of the United States of America, I take it?' said Van Niekerk, chuckling at his own joke.

'We shall have to see, won't we?' observed Tom Cole. He had been caught out by this unexpected manoeuvre, there was no doubt, but he was determined to have his way. 'But in the meantime – *move the Independent Republic of Stellaland three miles east!*'

'And if we don't, *rooinek*?' threatened Beziodenhuit, sticking his bull head forward. 'What will you do, with your handful of kaffirs and troopers that we would have killed at Majuba if they had not run so fast? What will you do, eh?'

I thought that Tom Cole was going to kill him on the spot but I put my hand on his arm and he gave one of his big smiles, right in these animals' faces. One that said *I am smiling now, but not as much as I will smile when I put my bayonet in your guts, suck your last breath in, and spit it back in your face so that you can pay the Devil with it when you meet him.*

We beat a retreat. What could we do? This was a whole new kettle of fish and neither of us had any knowledge or experience of whether a new country could just turn up and establish itself in the veldt like this. Tom Cole, was completely at a loss, but left us a couple of troopers to keep an eye on things before he went straight back to Kimberley to report. Only Nathan Walker was delighted when I explained what had happened.

'A new country magicked out of thin air!' he proclaimed, delightedly. 'Who would have thought of it? This means a lot more lawyers will do a lot more talking and that means we have a lot more time for Ragwasi to buy guns for Montshiwa's men.'

He was right too and although the cattle lifting started almost straight away, the biggest difference I saw was in the number of letters that started coming in from the Cape, from politicians, journalists and all sorts of officials wanting reports on the situation. We also noticed that the number of messengers running back and forth to Pretoria increased too. Soon enough, visitors, secretaries, and all and sundry started to turn up, asking questions, taking notes, pointing theodolites, writing down statements from anyone with a statement to make and making arrangements for meetings to arrange meetings for preliminary talks for more meetings. The lawyers had started doing their business. Nathan Walker was as happy as Larry.

And boy did they talk! They talked all through 1882 and then into 1883 and I thought they would talk all the way into 1884 too and every day that town on wheels grew until it had doubled in size and the wheels had put roots down into the soil. Tepo and I had time to have another baby in the time they talked! I have never heard such talking and I did not understand very much of it because lawyers talk in their own language and they have very complicated rules about talking which they must all talk about before agreeing to talk about the thing they came to talk about in the first place. They talked until my head hurt and I left this job to Nathan Walker because although he was young, he seemed to understand legal things and politics more than I. As I say, I have always thought lawyers were swindlers in another guise and I was growing more convinced by the day that he was from a political family. It seemed to be working too, because although the town was growing and individual Boers still tried to steal our cattle and our land, hopping and hopping a little closer here, taking a little more there - there was no *Kommando*.

There was a comet then too, which appeared in the sky during the day and hung there all summer and which the Boers took as a sign from God that *Stellaland* had his divine blessing. I called my firstborn son 'Joseph' because it reminded me of the Bethlehem star and he was born at Christmas time. Nathan Walker said very sourly that the last time there had been a comet, England had been conquered by Duke William and if Mr. Gladstone stayed in power much longer, it was likely to happen again. Ragwasi agreed with him and said that this was an unnatural spirit

– he did not mention the Mamlambo by name – who would not bring good things.

We were able to stop the Boers taking too much for other reasons too. The first of these reasons was that Ragwasi and his son Seretse took some Tswana and intercepted a gunrunner's convoy in the Kalahari. Seeing that they were Boers and that they were a long way from anywhere, he decided to keep our diamonds in his pocket and take their guns by force. He killed all of them, sold the mules in Kimberley and bought horses and handed out the guns – German made – to the Tswana. This meant that Montshiwa's army was stronger and the sight of armed and mounted Tswana confronting a Boer and telling him to turn his wagon round or else, became common and one that brought gladness to our hearts. The second reason was that we took some of those diamonds and sold them quietly in Kimberley. We had to sell them very quietly because the law had been tightened up and selling any stones that did not come out of De Beers or the Kimberley Central mines was heavily punished. This was another reason for why I hated Kimberley; the mine owners had grown so greedy and powerful that they turned the law on its head so that if you were caught you were guilty until proved innocent. I have never heard this principle applied in any but a tyranny and it has since been used as a precedent for all sorts of bad treatment. Anyhow, I used the money to enroll men of good character, Englishmen who had no race hesitation, in my own private constabulary for service with the Tswana. Nathan Walker said this was probably not legal, but I did not have much confidence in any law beyond the assegai and the gun. Tom Cole helped by looking the other way and this made us stronger still.

Then in August 1883 two things happened which made us realise that talking would never solve our problems. The first of these things was told to us by Ragwasi who had gone back into the Kalahari to try to find another gunrunner's convoy but ended up tailing a strong party of Boer horsemen who he suspected were being sent to escort those convoys. He followed them all the way to the coast, to a place that was called Angra Pequena then, where he found a German ship unloading guns in the bay, a stockaded warehouse with outbuildings on the shore and a flag flying on a pole. He sent Seretse down pretending to be just a curious local to see and hear what he could, but they were not speaking in a language he could understand. He was able to find out, however, that the boss was called Adolf Lüderitz, there was a German flag on that pole and that the area was now to be known as German South West Africa.

'Are you absolutely sure about this?' Nathan Walker was aghast, when Ragwasi brought the news back to Rooigrond.

Ragwasi affirmed that he was and pointed to the flag of the Republic of Stellaland hanging outside the tent where the talking was taking place.

'It is the same colours as on this flag, red, white and black, except it does not have this green band,' replied Ragwasi.

'Then it is a German flag and our worst fears have come true,' he concluded. 'Kruger has got his German alliance and intends to link up with their new colony at Angra Pequena so that he can guarantee his independence with German guns and German troops. That means he will attack the Tswana whatever happens in these talks. The prize is too great for him to resist. Our only hope now is to make a direct appeal for help to public opinion in London. We must leave immediately and get the next available boat from Cape Town.'

And that was how the second thing happened to make us realize that talking would do us no good, because someone near that tent, someone from the Republic of Stellaland, someone called Daisy Stockwell, overheard us talking and told someone who decided that we would have to be stopped from going to London.

I knew it was her. Nathan Walker had told me that she was often hanging around the talks, chatting here and there, as she sold cakes and biscuits to the lawyers and visitors and commissioners and what have you. We suspected that she was gathering gossip for the Boers and Nathan Walker had told whoever he could to be wary of her, but whether anyone heard him or not, I do not know. She was careful not to step out of the disputed area into Tswana land, however, and we had seen her deep in conversation with Logan and Van Niekerk many times. She did not avoid me as much as I tried to avoid her, however, and this was why I was very suspicious of her. She had no reason to talk to me that I could think of, except that I still had the title of British Agent to the Tswana. I cannot think that she would take any pleasure out of such contact unless it was in pursuit of revenge. And that is a dish best served cold, as we know. I knew it was her because when we had agreed that Nathan Walker should go to London, I walked around the corner of the tent and I saw her hurrying away and although I did not pay heed to it at the time, she was not stopping to sell her cakes to anyone. I should have paid more heed and I have regretted that I did not many, many times over the years.

We decided that we would go south to Kimberley where we could enquire about the cost of tickets for the ship and then telegraph ahead so that the tickets would be waiting for Nathan Walker at Cape Town. I would accompany him, leaving Ragwasi in charge of my constabulary, which was another thing I regret but I did not think it would be unsafe for us. We had been back and forward to Kimberley routinely and thought no more of it than you would think of wandering to the end of your stoep and back. We rode with haste and expected that we could make it in a little over two days if we pushed the horses hard, but when we got to Mokgareng, a little place by the Harts River, just short of half way, the hair on the back of my neck stood up and my skin got goose pimples.

I knew we were being followed. I could hear the sound of hooves on the turf in my head even though there was no sound on the wind. I could smell the scent of horseflesh and leather even though there was no sign of a rider to nick the wide horizon. It was the hunter's instinct and I did not like it. So then, as it got towards evening, I told Nathan Walker that we would pretend to make a camp in some trees by a little kopje, light a fire and then when it was fully dark, go round the back of the kopje and wait. If we were being followed, then a campfire on the veldt was spoor that no-one could resist and we might see our pursuers by the light of the fire. Just before last night we came upon a suitable place, close under a little table topped mountain with good water and two or three stands of bluegums nearby to give us cover. I lit a small fire and then led Nathan and the horses into a place where we could see without being seen, just behind the shoulder of the ridge screened off by trees.

Sure enough, about an hour after last light we heard the sound of drumming hooves and then the cautious approach of riders who were wary of what they might find around such a fire. It was too dark to see how many were there exactly, but I thought there were a dozen or so by their sounds. One of them had Logan's accent, but two other voices were definitely English and there was a Boer there too. The fire did not fool them long, for no-one leaves a fire unattended on the veldt and as soon as they realized that it was a stratagem, they cursed and kicked and stamped it out. I heard the sound of weapons being drawn and cocked too but the night was dark and our cover was good and I was confident that they would not discover us.

At that moment the mare that I was riding chose to let out a great whinny and from that point on all we could do was ride like hell and hope the blasted horse did not put its foot in an ant-bear or honey-badger hole and break our necks with the fall. We rode at right angles to the direction of Kimberley for an hour or so in the hope of throwing our pursuers off the scent, but they knew where we were going and when we ventured south east to resume our course the next morning, we found that they had spread their net right across the veldt. As the sun came up, we saw them sitting on their horses, silhouetted, waiting for us, each man half a mile from his neighbour but able to signal with his gun when he saw us. Our horses were tired and almost blown but we had no choice but to race for a gap in their picket line in the hope of bursting through before they could concentrate their forces on us.

'We'll never make it,' said Walker, looking left and right and calculating the distance.

'Ride straight at that man directly in front,' I replied, pulling out my Martini-Henry. 'He won't stand if we fire at him from close up and his mates will either stay clear or stop to pick him up if we drop him.'

'Fortune favours the brave, eh?'

I wished he had not said that because it reminded me of my gambling days. If only he had said 'Live life audaciously' things might have turned out better.

We dug our spurs in and went like the wind, with me holding the reins in one hand and balancing the rifle across my saddlebow with the other. I looked across at Nathan Walker beside me and I saw the light of the rising sun turn him to gold. He had grown and filled out and become a man since Ragwasi and I had first set our eyes on him. He was no longer the awkward boy in a constable's uniform that only fit where it touched and who handled a gun no better than a cow with a musket. His ears no longer stuck out, and his beard had grown and ladies had begun to take a strong interest in him for his fair hair and grey eyes. It was easy to see why, for he was a man of bravery and learning and intelligence and he would be sure to make his fortune even if he did not have a lot of diamonds already. As we galloped across the bright veldt, into the sun with our eyes peeled for the inevitable moment that we would be spotted, knowing that there was danger ahead and there would be danger behind too, we exchanged a glance and a smile that made us brothers. He was my *bru*.

But Fortuna is a woman and she was tired of being beaten by Nicholas Pelly. The rider in front spotted us going full tilt at him, gave a great shout and fired his gun at us. By any fair gamble, he should not have hit us at that range or at the speed we were going but he did and my horse went down with a hole in its neck. Walker pulled up for a moment but I told him to go on and he put his spurs in again, the horses ears went flat and he leaped forward as I struggled free. I looked to my left, saw three riders were converging on me, so I took my rifle and my bandolier and ran for the cover of some nearby rocks, just as my horse struggled up screaming and headed off in a crazed gallop towards the sun. Nathan Walker, I could see, was riding better than he had ever ridden before, like a centaur in that golden light, and I was sure he was going to make it through and away for Kimberley and the Cape. I willed him on with all my heart and mind and stomach, more than I had ever willed on a Newmarket favourite in the last furlong to riches, then lost him in the red haze as the dust came up and he headed into dead ground. He was gone.

A bullet cracked from my left and I saw it dig a chunk of earth out of the ground by my foot and so I put my head down too and tumbled breathlessly into the shelter of the boulders. A couple of other shots cracked by me, striking chips off the rocks and then the riders were past, heading off after Nathan Walker. I fired back but they were moving too fast, I couldn't calm my breathing enough to be accurate and I had grit in my eyes from the ricochets. There was nothing then except the receding rumble of hooves and I hoped that my *bru* had got clear and that he would carry our hopes to safety.

But five or ten minutes after, there was a rattle of shots from ahead, followed by some shouted orders and then, to my surprise and horror, the riders turned about, split left and right and began riding hard to get around me and cut off any thought of flight. I thumbed another round into the chamber and waited. I would not waste another shot by trying to hit a moving target because that whole *Kommando* was coming towards me now and they had Nathan Walker running behind on a rein. His hat was gone and he looked bloody, and I could see he was limping as they half whipped, half dragged him back. They had shot him off his horse, it was plain to see.

They came in to fifty yards of where I was hidden.

'Come on out Pelly, you bloody bastard!' It was Luke Stockwell. Just behind him stood his brother, Tom, both of them tall, dark and as stupid as Daisy's mules. I remembered them from the village school at Dines Hall where they had their own dunce's caps and corners to themselves. Big George used to say that it would be a wealthy man who could find a use for those two boys and no one had been surprised when they had gone off to London. They would employ anyone in London, then; but now they were here and they had murder written all over them.

'Think you can cross the Stockwell family whenever you please, Pelly?' shouted Tom Stockwell, loosing off a bullet at the rock I was hiding behind. 'We've got this Jonty Manchester bastard and I've got it in mind to poach a brace of evicting landlord bastards this morning. It'd make Mr. Logan right pleased.'

'Then after that we'll kill all your nigger friends like we did before,' taunted Luke. 'And after that we'll see who's got a taste for evictions done the Boer way!'

There was a loud crackle of rifle fire and a berg adder shot out from my hiding place, making itself scarce while the slugs banged off the rocks and sent fat sparks into the morning.

'Come on, Pelly! Or we'll shoot this Manchester bastard for the landlord's abortion that he is.'

Nathan Walker was slumped on the ground and I could see that one side of his head was swelling up like a balloon and that he was bleeding out onto the sand from his mouth and nose.

'It'll be better for you. Mr. Logan is on his way,' called Tom. 'He'll be here in a minute and you can guess how he'll feel about an English landlord who don't come quietly.'

I thought about it. I might even have given myself up, but there was another crackle of shots, this time from the direction of Kimberley and although I could not know who was firing them, I reckoned that there were more guns there than were accounted for by this little gang. This meant that perhaps the people who were doing the shooting were not Boers and at that moment I would count anyone who was not a Boer a friend indeed. The best thing, I decided, was to play for time by doing what everyone up at Rooigrond was doing.

'Look Stockwell, this all happened a long time ago,' I drawled, trying to sound reasonable and open up a negotiation. 'If its compensation you want then we can discuss this like businessmen.'

'You think you have money enough for what you did to my parents?' shrieked Luke Stockwell, banging another bullet into the rock. 'I'm going to hang you like a dog.'

There was more shooting from away to the right, this time a little closer, I thought. Whoever was doing it was probably doing it to the rest of this gang and if they were shooting at Logan, on that basis they would definitely be my friends for life.

'You don't want to negotiate?' I shouted, trying to keep the tremble out of my voice as I slid my rifle forward. 'Fine. Come and get me.'

I popped up and took a snap shot, which I knew went home, because there was a howl of pain, a flurry of answering shots and the sound of horses' hooves moving left and right. I heard Nathan Walker cry out in pain as they jerked him to his feet and dragged him off. He was babbling something, but I couldn't make out his words.

A few moments later and the shots started coming in to my little sandstone sanger from all directions. They were well aimed, deliberate shots and I knew I was done for. Sooner or later, someone would get the angle and trajectory right and I had nowhere to run to. All I could hope for was that whoever was shooting in the distance would get here soon for here there was no twist that would not bust. I poked my head out from a low corner of the rock to see what I could see and nearly got a bullet in my head for my pains, but in that second I saw a knot of riders coming hard towards this battle, and I was certain that Logan was in the van of it.

Less than a minute later, my guess was confirmed right because I heard his Irish accent shouting to my attackers to get on their mounts and get moving because the devil himself was on their tails. Looking out again, I saw that the devil in question was a troop of horsemen and I knew enough about the way they rode and the way that their leader held his arm just *so* to tell that it was Captain Tom G. Cole and his men. My God, I was relieved. We would be saved. I looked for Nathan Walker and saw him go swinging in an arc like a pendulum from right to left, losing his balance as his captor swung his horse and jerked the rein that held him. I put up my rifle and I shot that bastard out of his saddle and saw Nathan Walker collapse on the ground just as Logan rode up.

'Pelly!' Logan's voice rang out through that morning like a hymn to Satan. 'You'll be living to see another sunrise, so you will. Make the most of it. But this landlord's bastard Manchester will do no more evicting here in South Africa, nor in England or in Ireland neither.'

And with that he shot Nathan Walker dead.

I felt that bullet go to my heart and I lay transfixed with horror. I had seen men die in battle many times, but it had never occurred to me that Nathan Walker would ever be one of them. He was too good, too straight, too clever, too honest, too brave to die.

Logan, the Stockwell boys and the rest of them rode off without a backward glance and I did not have the wit to put as many bullets into their stinking backs as I was capable of because my whole heart had filled up with grief. My hands were shaking uncontrollably and my knees turned to water when I tried to stand up. From somewhere within me a howl emerged, like the sound of a lost soul, and I felt my hands begin to pull and tear at my face. When finally I was able to command my legs to obey me, I staggered over to where my friend and my brother lay, but there was no hope. Logan's bullet had smashed his head open and there was just a mess of blood and bones and yellow brains and I dropped to my knees and cried out again in despair, cursing God, Gladstone and the government for bringing Nathan Walker to his death. I did not know such an intensity of grief was possible and when I was brought back to my senses by the approach of Tom Cole, I felt that my old enemy the grinning monkey had stamped on my chest and beaten me into a dull insensibility. How many times had I had that bastard Logan in my sights? Why had I not tracked him down and killed him for what he did to little Sipo? These are questions that only Cape Smoke can settle but I know that the bullet that killed Nathan Walker blew a hole in my life that has never closed to this day.

'This is Jonty Manchester? Are you sure?' I heard Tom speaking to someone, but as though he was a long way away, as though I was at the bottom of a well even, and I could not see clearly because my eyes were so full of tears that I thought that God was drowning me in sorrow.

'That's him. Illegitimate son of Lord Hartington and the Duchess of Manchester,' said the other voice. I recognized it from somewhere but I could not have cared less if it was the Angel Gabriel calling me at that moment.

'*The* Lord Hartington?' replied Cole, incredulously.

'Oh, there is only one Lord Hartington, Captain Cole,' said the voice, complacently. 'He is the Secretary of State for War in Mr. Gladstone's government – and he hates Mr. Gladstone with a passion.'

I recognized the voice from that day in Kimberley when it had saved me from Logan and taken five bob off me for the privilege.

It belonged to Cecil Rhodes.

*

Chapter 8

The Burning of Rooigrond

We buried Nathan Walker in a place of honour, covered with a shield under the cattle kraal at Ragwasi's lolwapa. I put the guns of those we had killed on that last ride together at his feet, like a Viking warrior would have done because he was from East Anglia after all and this was his heritage. We got a missionary called Mackenzie, who was friendly to the Tswana, to say some words too because he was a Christian, I guessed. Montshiwa who had come with his people and had brought many cows to be slaughtered, called on us all to praise this man who had come from across the sea to fight for the Tswana against the Boer and swore that when the mourning was over, there would be no more talking about Rooigrond. He had heard too many words already. Then Ragwasi started to sing a lament and the Tswana joined in with their magnificent voices and I swear the choir at Westminster Abbey could have done no better or given more honour to a man. They called on their gods and ancestral spirits, Modimo and Badimo, to guide him into his new life and save him from becoming *dipoko*, tied to the earth through grief and left to haunt the living. Tom Cole brought his troopers and they joined with my constables to fire a salute over his grave so that we propitiated every nationality, religion or profession. I could hardly master my own grief through that time and as I lowered him into the grave we had dug for him, it was as though his spirit was slipping through my fingers. Afterwards, when I went through his belongings, each time I touched something that had belonged to him, I felt that pain as though it was new.

We sent his share of the diamonds to Mijnheer Cronjie to pass on to his family and I sent whatever was left of his papers along with them. There were a lot of sketches of churches and other things, so I added a note stating my belief that he had wanted to be an architect or perhaps a scholar before whatever had happened to him had happened and he had come into our hands. Sometime later, I got a letter back saying that his diamonds had been used to build a church and endow two scholarships to Cambridge University so perhaps my guess was right. The letter was signed 'H' which I took to be Lord Hartington's signature. So, Nathan Walker's spirit slipped away but his heart remained in Africa with us and he is with us still and always will be. I am contradicting myself again, but this is how I think. Ragwasi and I have agreed that when our time comes, we will go under the kraal with Nathan Walker and go hunting and looking for diamonds again in the desert together again. And now I must break off from this story and go and drink Cape Smoke because I cannot bear the pain still.

*

So now it is the next morning and I have a heavy head and a parched mouth and I am trying to wish that I had never started on this story, so much grief it has in it. I cannot give up though. Africans do not have the choice of giving up because although this is a wonderful and bounteous land it only gives up its wealth to those who watch the land or who have mined deep in the earth and to make a success of either of these things it is necessary to keep going through fire, wind, storm and rain. Even when the weather is good, the toil is still hard and to be an African is to recognize this without complaint. It is only in a man's family that he can enjoy his riches and a family is necessary for an old man because the toil wears him out eventually and the weight of the past bears down on him more surely than the heaviest yoke. It is a burden that cannot be avoided, only set aside from time to time, laid down, as it were, by the side of the oak that I take shade under now.

My granddaughter is bringing out a can of coffee for me. Tepo is pretending to be angry with me for drinking too much but I know that she does not mind me drinking a lot as long as I don't drink alone. Last night Ragwasi joined me and we drank far too much and remembered Nathan Walker and the old times and became foolish and Boitumela gave him such a scolding. This does not matter very much because being the old fools that we are we are not affected much by being told off by our wives. I think they know this and they put up with us because better the devil you know, hey? So here is the coffee and it has extra sugar in it and I feel better already so I must begin again. I am writing all this down partly because of my granddaughters so that they can know how it was before and how it came to this. How they will cope in this new world after this Act of Union which, as I have said, seems to me to give away far too much to the Boers, is beyond me. But young people are strong and no-one can tell where they will end up by looking at where they started from. Look at me. Look at Rhodes. Which brings me neatly back to the days after we buried Nathan Walker and I must swallow the lump in my throat that has come back.

*

When the three days of mourning were almost over Cecil Rhodes turned up to talk politics with Montshiwa and as we, Tom Cole, Ragwasi and I, shared millet beer and beef, he told us of how Mr. Gladstone was becoming more and more unpopular in England and that it was expected that Lord Hartington might soon take over the government from him. Rhodes had changed as much as I had since I had last seen him. He was richer, stouter, had been to Oxford to get a degree and had got himself elected as an MP to the Cape Parliament to boot. But he had not changed in the way his eyes remained lidded and calculating and I made up my mind then and there not to accept any deal that he was proposing. And I knew he was going to be proposing a deal because it was written all over him. If a swindler's deal was an animal it would look like Cecil John Rhodes, I can tell you.

'The death of Jonathan Manchester here, regrettable though it is,' he said, wiping beer from his mouth with the back of his hand. 'Will certainly strengthen Lord Hartington's determination to honour the promise that Governor Frère made to the Tswana.'

Ragwasi spat into the fire in disgust and muttered something in Tswana that I missed.

Montshiwa nodded in agreement. This was really the first opportunity that I had had to take in Montshiwa because Ragwasi was my chief and Montshiwa was a stickler for the proper forms so I had had no direct dealings with him. He was a taciturn man, with heavy brows and snow in his beard, but there was an air of determination about him that Mankurwane had not possessed. Looking back now and making the comparison, I would say that Mankurwane was brave but without hope, while Montshiwa was cautious and was resolved that when he made his stroke, it would be strong, decisive and effective. Now he was listening carefully to what Rhodes was saying about politics in England, but I could tell that he was not convinced.

'Mister Rhodes,' he pronounced it *Rodoss*. 'We have waited a long time for the English government to make up a mind that seems to be a very confused mind. We have waited so long that Khama is weak, Mankurwane is poor and Stellaland has grown from a calf into a bull. We have waited so long that our God, Modimo, has had time to put another star in the sky and then take it away and put it back in his hut. We have waited so long that the Germans have now come into the Kalahari so that Kruger is now at our back as well as at our front. We have waited so long that the son of the English chief Nathan Walker is dead and we are shamed in front of his father. We have waited long enough.'

'That's just it though,' replied Rhodes. 'The wheel is turning faster now. And if you want a sign to prove that Hartington is coming, I will tell you that the comet you saw over Stellaland appeared at the same time that Lord Hartington's brother was murdered – in Phoenix Park, Dublin, where Gladstone had sent him.'

Ragwasi's eyes widened at this. 'Can this be true?' he asked me. 'Is it a sign from your Gods too?'

'It is a coincidence,' I replied. 'It is no proof.'

Rhodes shrugged. 'Maybe,' he conceded. 'But fate and fortune rule the affairs of men as much as anything else. And it was Hartington who forced Gladstone to send the army to conquer Egypt two years ago.'

'Where is Egypt?' asked Ragwasi and I confess my ignorance that I did not know that there had even been a war, let alone that Egypt was now in the British Empire.

'A long way north of Lobengula's country,' replied Rhodes. 'And this is why you can count on Hartington. One day there will be a railway line that goes all the way from the Cape to Cairo; and it will come through here. Yes! Here, Rooigrond! Because this is the road to the north. Hartington will come because he will not allow Kruger and the Germans to link up and cut this road. All you have to do is hold off, give a little land away for a railway station and line and in return you'll get the protection of the British government.'

'This is true, I think,' added Tom Cole. 'There are rumours in my regiment that commanders have been chosen and troops are already being made ready in England. They could be here anytime.'

'So you would counsel me to wait even longer,' said Montshiwa, sizing up Rhodes. 'You would counsel me to wait for a promise to be kept that has not been kept and an army to come which might not come? You would counsel me to give away more land for a railway that might come one day in the future? *Rodoss*, we are counting the *Kommandos* that are gathering in Stellaland *now*. These *Kommandos* are certain things, things that we know are in existence. If we wait any longer they will become like a crocodile that can eat the sun itself.'

'It'll be better for you in the long run,' asserted Rhodes, rooting in his pockets. 'I'd advise you to wait for a few months more at least.'

Montshiwa shook his head. 'We can wait no longer. We will strike soon and strike hard.'

'I would have to advise you not to attack Stellaland too,' interjected Tom Cole, looking distinctly uncomfortable. 'My orders are to preserve the peace and that means preserving it for both sides while the talks are going on. I'm sorry, but this would put me and my troopers in the awkward position of having to prevent you attacking the Boers.'

'What?' I exclaimed, incredulously. 'Let me get this straight; you are telling me that Lord Hartington is sending English troops to evict the Boers from Stellaland, but if we, the *rightful owners* do it, then you and your English troops will stop us? This is insane!'

'Just wait a few months more,' pleaded Tom.

Montshiwa stood up and repeated: 'We can wait no longer. We will strike soon and strike hard.'

'And I shall strike with him,' I said. 'Tom, there is too much politics and not enough honesty in all this. Mr. Rhodes, I am sorry, but I don't believe that this Lord Hartington will come. He has had plenty of opportunity to come already. All I have heard from the government is double talk. We were given a promise. It was not kept and Nathan Walker is dead. That's it.'

Rhodes and Tom Cole stood up simultaneously and Ragwasi and I did likewise.

'I would strongly advise you not to attack Stellaland,' insisted Rhodes. 'I speak with the authority of the Cape government on this. And I *will* order Captain Cole to resist if you do.'

Montshiwa drew himself up before calmly replying: 'We can wait no longer. We will strike soon and strike hard. *Rodoss* – you have *no* authority here, because this is *Tswana* land. Captain Cole, you are a friend to the Tswana and I do not think you will do this thing that *Rodoss* threatens.'

'I must. I have no choice,' answered Cole, bleakly.

'Then I shall order my warriors to look out for your men and not to kill them. Make sure that they wear a red band so that we may tell them from the Boers,' he said, finally. 'For in one month from now, we *will* kill the Boers.'

*

I do not blame Tom Cole for warning the Boers that we were coming. He was duty bound to do it, and anyway, when armies gather it is impossible to keep it a secret that war is coming. Rhodes went to Van Niekirk and the other Boers and tried to cut a deal with them to move back three miles temporarily but they were too pig-headed to take heed. The inhabitants of Stellaland got wind of what was afoot somehow and even before we arrived to evict them, for a good three weeks the veldt was full of cattle and wagons and families and horsemen heading eastwards. Tom Cole did his duty and put his troopers in a picket line across the veldt to stop the approach of our army, but when he saw the *kommandos* forming up in Stellaland to resist us, he saw it was useless and withdrew. He rounded up all the commissioners and lawyers and visitors and, along with Cecil Rhodes, escorted them back to Kimberley.

We had gathered about five or six thousand warriors, of whom about a thousand, including my forty constables, were mounted and armed with good rifles and so for once we outnumbered if not outgunned the Boers. I guessed that they had about two thousand men; they should have had more, but as I have said before, many of the Boers were really just robbers like Logan or land hungry settlers like the Stockwells, who had every intention of enjoying the fruits of victory without risking their skins like soldiers in a fair fight.

So when night fell, and Montshiwa ordered the advance, we went forward in darkness so that the Boers would not have light to shoot by. When the only light came from the lamps on the Stellaland wagons and the stars above, we gave a great shout and rushed forward together in one mass, trampling through the Boer line, which seemed to melt in front of us and served our notice of eviction in the most forceful way possible. The lamps of the wagons became our tools of destruction as we smashed them on the wagon covers and sent one after the other up in a great blaze of scarlet and orange. There was very little actual fighting, because many Boers were too cunning to fight when they could not win and so went to ground or headed out into the safety of the darkness and the veldt. One or two diehards and hot heads cried out to the Lord for divine assistance but the Tswana warriors slit them open in no time at all and their cries were drowned by the roar of the flames that swept through the Republic of Stellaland and returned it to its original Tswana name, Huhudi.

The horses did not like the flames, but the light from the burning wagons was enough for me to lead my constables around to the back of the town where we intended to lie up and be ready for the morning when I feared the Boers would counterattack. Ragwasi led a troop of mounted Tswana around from the other direction too so that we would meet up in a pincer. It was also our task to stop any more wagons from leaving and this we wanted to do very keenly because without his wagon a Boer cannot settle on other people's lands. I ordered my men to let anyone who wished to leave, do so peaceably but they could take neither horse, nor gun nor wagon with them. Anyone who resisted was to be killed because to show mercy in a battle is the shortest way to make sure you do not survive it. This also we had learned from Buller and Tom Cole and we had plenty of our own experience to have learned its wisdom completely by now.

Most of the Boers were so frightened of the cries of the Tswana and the flames that were spreading among the wagons rapidly now that they obeyed without question. Many times that night, I had to harden my heart when I saw women and small children climbing down off horses and wagons, carrying only what they could out onto the veldt, in tears and grey with fear and worry for the future. It had been the same for the Mankurwane's people though, except that we did not take their children from them and so could not be called inhuman completely.

Sometime in the night, while I was ordering an elderly Boer off his wagon a shout of alarm came from Ragwasi's end of the line, followed by a lot of shooting, the rumble of wagon wheels and the braying of hard driven mules. Someone was trying to shoot their way clear and I knew in my heart that Logan and the Stockwells would be in the centre of this trouble. When I ran over to see what was happening I found out that my guess was right. One of my constables had a broken arm where they had driven their wagon straight at him and Logan's voice, full of curse and urgency could still be heard shouting at Daisy to whip up and whip up hard. There was still light enough from the fires to shoot by and so I brought my Martini-Henry to my shoulder and fired a bullet through the wagon cover and then another one at the flash of the muzzle as someone in that wagon fired back. I could see Daisy Stockwell's silhouette visible by the lamp on the wagon's box and I had put my foresight onto the nape of her neck before I realized what I was doing and caught myself. There was another muzzle flash from the wagon, so I fired at that instead and received two more shots in return before I could not fire again without risk of hitting her.

I was not going to let Logan escape again though and calling to Ragwasi to tell him of my intention I set off to hunt the Stockwell wagon through the night. This was not difficult. Actually, it was harder to keep myself concealed than it was to track them, because they kept the lamp lit and a wagon makes a lot of noise anyway. They stopped after a couple of hours and I was able to watch them from the cover of some dead ground as they looked back at the burning of Rooigrond. The wagons had gone up like tinder, throwing up orange flames that filled the night sky like the sword of an archangel, and I was tempted to shoot the whole gang on the spot, as they witnessed the end of the Republic of Stellaland and the end of their present hopes of stealing Tswana land. It was a pleasant feeling; although I was ashamed of having been the reason for evicting Daisy Stockwell from the Yellow House at Dines Hall, I was not sorry to be completing this eviction. I had sympathy for her, but not for her brothers because they had had a living in London and had decided to get a better one by sailing all the way to South Africa to become thieves. And Logan, I wanted dead for the murder of Nathan Walker and little Sipo's broken head and I was not going to let this opportunity pass by. He had survived too long already had that man and now I was going to kill him. You will say that I had no right to take the law into my own hands and kill this man for revenge, and you would be right. But there is a difference between justice and the law and I had seen enough of lawyers to know that there would be no justice for Nathan Walker if the lawyers got involved and started demanding signed pieces of paper and statements and so on. Cecil Rhodes was a lawyer, and I rest my case on that. I had made up my mind that Logan was going to die by my gun and that was proper veldt justice.

At least one of my bullets had gone home already because I could see them going backwards and forward to tend someone inside the wagon, but I could not tell who it was. I knew it was not Daisy because I could see her shape by the wagon lamp when she passed it and as the hours passed and the morning started to arrive, I could see it was not Logan either. This was because I saw him start to outspan one of the mules and then heard him declare his intention of riding on alone.

'Sure an' you'll be fine,' he said, climbing onto the mule's back and tugging at its bit. 'I'll be back with help, so I will.'

'You mean you're abandoning us!' shrilled Daisy in reply. 'There's no help between here and Pretoria, you bastard! We need all the mules if we are to get away.'

'Bastard is it?' he replied icily. 'Sure an' you've a way with words, so you have, you English bitch.'

I watched as he tugged out a pistol, put it to the head of the second mule in the team and shot it. The mule collapsed in a tangle of harness while the others tried to bolt, but the wheelbrake being fixed on, they simply tangled themselves up further. Daisy tore at her hair and screamed maniacally in rage.

'Logan! Don't leave us!' she bawled, to no effect.

The light was coming up rapidly now and so I was able to take a proper aim at Logan - a proper hunter's aim this time. I put the foresight on his temple and at thirty yards, held my breathing under control, allowed myself to imagine the flight of the bullet and visualize how it would strike home, then squeezed gently, evenly, knowing he was already dead. I was concentrating so hard that I did not hear the report of the gun but I did see the red spray that told me I had made the perfect headshot. Nathan Walker had got justice.

If I did not hear the report of my Martini-Henry, Daisy Stockwell did for she leaped for the wagon like a springbok and before I could get another round in the chamber she was hauling a rifle out and waving it around in search of a target.

'Put the gun down Daisy!' I shouted. 'It's me, Nicholas Pelly, and I will not harm you. Put the gun down.'

'You expect me to trust you?' she spat back, looking for me. 'After what you and your mercenaries have done to us?'

I choked on that word because *mercenary* is a dirty word to describe my constables.

'You have one shot in the rifle, Daisy,' I commanded. 'Use it or put it down. For God's sake, I am not going to hurt you.'

She turned to speak to someone in the wagon and I wondered if it was one of her brothers. It was only a brief consultation and then she held the gun high in her right hand.

'Nicholas Pelly, we are British subjects and we demand your protection!'

I told her to put the gun down and then I went forward cautiously. She hopped down from the wagon and followed me as I went to the tailgate and let it swing down. Luke Stockwell lay there, clutching a bloody shirt across a bad stomach wound. It looked like one of my rounds had found him and when I looked at that wound closely, I knew he could not recover from it.

'Is your brother Tom here?' I asked quietly.

She shook her head. Her face was drawn and pale and she knew as well as I did that Luke was done for.

'We lost him in the panic,' she said. 'And Logan would not wait for him.'

I held out a hand to her, but she took a determined step back. 'I am your prisoner, Pelly, but it doesn't mean I want anything from you.'

'Daisy,' I appealed to her quietly, holding my hand out again. 'Is there nothing I can do so that we may put this behind us?'

For a split second I thought she was going to melt, but then the sound of horses rumbling across the veldt distracted us both and the moment was gone. The sounds were coming from both directions and I saw quickly that Ragwasi was heading one troop from the west while from the east, I could see a *Kommando* racing towards us.

'Daisy,' I said. 'I can give you your farm back in England…'

'Damn your eyes!' she exploded and threw my words back in my teeth. 'I'll take what I can get with the help of people who I can trust. I am a Boer now!'

Her rejection of my hand cut me because I had diamonds enough to heal all the material wrongs I had inflicted on her and to recompense her parents too. How could I ever make restitution if she would not accept it? And how could I make restitution to her parents, for first evicting them, then killing their son? I had set Daisy on this course by my gambling and she had tangled herself up with thieves and robbers. I could not say that it was my responsibility that Luke Stockwell lay bleeding to death in that wagon but I was responsible for Daisy's position. I wanted to make restitution to her and her parents so I could be free of my shame and look my father in the eye again. I had been away from Dines Hall for ten years now and I knew I was not a wastrel anymore, but his own opinion is nothing in a man's estimation of himself unless he receives forgiveness from those he has injured and makes restitution.

She began to holler and wave at the approaching *Kommando* and so I had no choice but to make myself scarce. I ran back to my horse, mounted and within a minute was riding hard for Ragwasi and his men knowing that I had lost all hope of reconciliation with Daisy.

We outpaced the *Kommando* almost straight away because they stopped to help Daisy and so we got back to Rooigrond as daylight came up, which was as desolate a sight as I ever wish to see. The veldt was scorched black around each burned out wagon as though giants had been cooking and there were sparks and bits of flame here and there with ash in the wind like snow. What had not been burned had been looted and so there were household goods, trunks, clothes and split open sacks strewn about like discarded socks. There were bodies here and there too - Tswana, Boer, English - but the loss of life was not to be compared with what we had witnessed at Hlobane and Khambula and if I was to be brutally honest, I would say the Boers had got off lightly. As I have said before, the only justification for winning a battle is to make sure it stays won and to my eyes, this was a battle won that would not stay won for very long because Montshiwa had not struck hard enough to be decisive. As we went back to the Tswana army, I could see that many of the Tswana were happy and had helped themselves to Cape Smoke and Square Face. They were boasting and had lost their discipline and across the veldt stretching away from Rooigrond or Huhudi or whatever we would call it now, there was a line of Tswana men heading for home with loads on their heads.

'Where are they going, Ragwasi? We have to get them back,' I was horrified. 'Kruger will not take this lying down. This is the beginning of the war not the end.'

'You are right, uPelly,' he replied grimly. 'Look!'

From north through east to south there were horsemen on the horizon. Kruger had come with the Boer army and it looked like the whole Transvaal had been emptied to provide it. The horizon began to fill up as more and more arrived until I guessed there were more than ten thousand horseman lining up there. Looking back, I saw Montshiwa riding here and there trying to get his army back into some sort of order, but many took flight at this terrible sight, hoping that their legs would carry them faster than the horses of the Boers. We put spurs to our horses to join him, but by the time we had formed a ragged line in amongst the charred ruins of Stellaland, we were no more than two thousand – a third of our original number - and I could see the Boer leaders counting, taking their time, preparing to make sure that when they won this battle it would stay won forever in their favour.

I shook hands with Ragwasi, because I knew that our time was up. I would not run. I could not because this was now the only way that I could make a proper restitution for my sins. If I did run, it would mean that I was happy to allow the eviction of the whole Tswana people from their farms and I could not be haunted by the spectre of the Yellow House for the rest of my life. I told off the youngest of my constables to take my hastily scribbled note to Tom Cole, charging him to look after Tepo and little Charlotte and Joseph and saying that Mijnheer Cronjie knew how to manage my affairs. Ragwasi sent his son Seretse back to Kuruman on a good horse to tell Boitumela and the other women and children to hide in the bush or go to the Reverend Mackenzie for safety. Together, we told Seretse that he must make sure our families were safe and that he must take them to the Cape. Like the good son he was, he demanded to stay and fight alongside us, but like the good fathers that we were, we told him that he must run to live to fight another day.

'There is nothing left but to fight,' said Ragwasi. 'Now I must pay the Mamlambo in full and you will pay Daisy uStockwell in full too. We will go back to the desert with Nathan Walker and there we will hunt and live a good life as spirits. *Sobola Manyosi* - the honey always comes to an end. Perhaps it will not be so bad.'

I put a bullet in my Martini-Henry. '*Bayeete*, Ragwasi,' I said, giving him the Zulu salute. 'Go well, my *bru*.'

We had come to the end of our story and we were prepared to die well at the end of it in the hope that a better story would be written after we had gone. I closed my eyes and waited for the rumble of hooves that would herald the final advance of the Boers.

And then Tom Cole appeared. I did not see him approach but suddenly, he was there, appearing out of a cloud of hooves, dust and horse flies from behind a line of burned out wagons, with that big grin spread over his face, just like the first time I had seen it on the ship ten years ago.

'What's all this then?' he called out, cheerfully. 'Got ourselves into a bit of a pickle have we? Whatever would Lord Hartington say?'

He pointed to the south west where we could see another army approaching, an army that was neither Tswana nor Boer.

'With Lord Hartington's complements,' chuckled Tom Cole. 'The First Mounted Rifles, all volunteers come all the way to uphold England's honour whatever Mr. Gladstone says.'

He pointed to the south.

'And over there are Carrington's Horse – Basutos and Xhosa mainly. Ruffians the lot of 'em, but a match for any Boer, I'll warrant,' he proclaimed. 'Ought to all be locked up in jail if you ask me.'

We must have looked like fish, the way we stared, open mouthed in disbelief. Montshiwa rode up and nodded to Captain Cole, before looking at the advancing army with equal puzzlement.

'Who are those riders in the red jackets?' he asked. 'Are they come to fight for us or against us?'

'Those would be the Inniskilling Dragoons,' replied Tom knowledgeably, giving Montshiwa a salute. 'And if you look a little further you will see Mr. Rhodes' contribution, the Diamond Fields horse, but don't look too closely, eh? That lot really *should* be in jail.'

A troop of horse artillery galloped out onto the veldt, unlimbered and banged off a shell to land squarely in front of the Boer lines.

'*Hau!*' shouted Ragwasi. 'That is bigger than an elephant gun!'

'That,' said Tom Cole. 'Is the official announcement that the Governor's promise is to be honoured after all.'

He turned to me and Ragwasi and said quietly.

'Well done, old man. If it wasn't for you and Ragwasi, I fear there would be no Tswana left.'

*

Chapter 9

The Deal

Ragwasi and I drank too much Cape Smoke last night again and so I write this down today with a very shaky hand but I am not as unlucky as him because at least I am not being shouted at by Boitumela. It is a very hard thing to be told off very loudly in the morning by a wife with a sharp tongue for such a little thing as drinking too much brandy. At least it was not gin.

We drank too much again because we were remembering the day that Tom Cole turned up with that army and saved us from being killed. We were very happy and it does not seem quite fair to me that Boitumela should object to Ragwasi drinking too much to celebrate such a day because if that day had not happened then Boitumela would have no-one to shout at and then she would be very unhappy indeed. Tepo is very tolerant in this respect, which is a blessing, I can tell you. She has taken the noisiest of the children away with her to church too, which is a double blessing. Boitumela will also go to church soon and then Ragwasi will have his peace and quiet, so there are three things now to be thankful for.

Anyway, now I must tell you what happened when that army arrived and went face to face with the Boers and what happened afterwards. It is fitting that I have a hangover while I write this part because what happened at Vierzehnfontein was the headache that came after the champagne of Tom Cole's arrival at Rooigrond.

There was to be a meeting at Vierzehnfontein, a place we did not know the name of because it had no name until the Boers had given it one. Even Tom Cole did not know it was called this. Later, when Ragwasi went there he did not know it was called Fourteen Springs either and wondered why it was called this because there were only eight as far as he could tell. Anyway, such things happen. We must just leave it at that. At this meeting everything was to be decided and we had very high hopes of this meeting because the army that had come from the England and the Cape was led by Sir Charles Warren who was a tough fighter and knew about South Africa and about Kimberley and everything that went with it. He became famous later for being the policeman who was not being able to catch Jack the Ripper, but then and there he was famous enough for us. About fifty years old with a big fuzzy moustache and the look of a gamekeeper rather than a soldier, he was made out of horsehide and old leather and Ragwasi claimed that when he walked he could hear him creaking and that anyone who tried to make biltong out of him would have a very hard time and regret it. We had confidence in him because he was not afraid of Kruger and the Boers and we thought he would get a good deal.

However, it was not Sir Charles Warren who was to do the real talking in this meeting. He was there to look tough and stare into Kruger's eyes and make him blink. This he did very well because he took detachments from each of his English and African regiments to show that there were plenty of Englishmen willing to fight alongside Basutos, Xhosa and Tswana to stop the Boers making everyone into slaves. And he was successful too because Kruger let those lidded eyes slide down and told all his crew that there was to be no war now and that they must just be grateful for this thing because if they fought they would lose everything. He hated saying this of course, but although Kruger was a bad man he was not a stupid one.

That's when the real talking started and it was Cecil Rhodes who spoke the most words. He was what people call a 'pragmatist' which means that he had no principles but that he knew how to make everyone else forget their principles and make a deal that they could live with even if they didn't like it. Ragwasi says Rhodes' grandparents must have been a balance sheet, a pocket book, a gun and a forked tongue because he could always come up with a deal. I agree with him except that he must have had a fifth grandparent who was a pirate and a sixth one who was a robber baron. Did you know his father was a vicar? No, neither did I. It is hard to believe. Perhaps these traits in a man's character jump a generation. Ragwasi says because he was born in Bishop's Stortford then he must have done a deal with an English Mamlambo who lived in the river there and who gave him a favourable deal because the Mamlambo there was obviously an ex-vicar who looked kindly on a vicar's son. He might be right.

So Rhodes did a deal which allowed the Boers to keep the farms that they had taken as long as they promised not to take any more.

'What?' gasped Ragwasi, when Tom Cole gave us the news. 'The Boers have lost this war and yet they have won our lands? Have you been drinking Cape Smoke and taking *dagga*?'

Cole shuffled a bit. 'It was the best that could be done,' he said, tossing a pebble into the camp fire. The sky was clear above and the clouding stars of the January night promised a crackle of thunder in the morning. 'Rhodes insisted that the settlers were too desperate to be denied farms and that they would keep no law until they had them.'

'Can they not go back to where they came from over the sea?'

'They cannot,' answered Cole. 'They *will* not. But this way, they may be satisfied and the Tswana may keep what they have left.'

'How do we know the agreement will be kept?' I asked, passing him the bottle. I felt sorry for Tom G. Cole. He was always the bearer of bad news.

He shrugged and took a pull on the bottle. 'It will be kept because this is now Her Majesty's Bechuanaland Protectorate.'

'Where?' asked Ragwasi. 'I have been a Zulu, a Matabele, a Basuto and now I am Tswana. What is a Bechuana? Is it like a baTswana?'

'Something like that,' answered Tom. 'But it means the Queen will protect you from the Boers.'

'Give us lots of guns and the Tswana will protect ourselves.'

'It is the Queen's view that the fewer guns there are in South Africa, the better.'

'Does *Rhodoss* think this too?' said Ragwasi. 'Who will work in his mines in Kimberley if he does not give them guns?'

Tom Cole had no answer to this because there was no answer. Rhodes had done a deal and although it was not a fair deal, it was a deal that we had to live with. In fact, nobody thought it was a good deal, but perhaps it was a good deal because the Boers did keep to it. Even Kruger kept to it because Rhodes had bribed many of the Boers – who were not really Boers but people like Daisy Stockwell – to accept the deal, get a farm and become British and Kruger did not wish any more of his people to be bribed and stop being Boers. The war was over and now we had to get on with our lives. We had a hangover, it is true, but you can live through a hangover. You probably know this. So we did not save the Tswana as Tom Cole declared. Well, perhaps some of them. It might have been worse; we could have been Zulus. They lost everything when the Boers invaded their country.

So now it was 1885 and I had been away from Dines Hall, East Anglia and England for twelve years. *Het!* That is a long time, but I had come a long way in that time and I had had a lot of forward motion and now I could look myself in the mirror when I shaved. I was a wealthy man; a married man with children; I was a hunter and trader and modestly successful in my profession; I had fought in wars and had faced death; I had also meted out justice to Logan. There were only two things to do now to complete the restoration of myself to the full civilisation and decency of a man's place. I must make restitution to Judith and Ezekiel Stockwell, if Daisy would not allow me to make restitution to her; and I must seek the forgiveness of my father. It was time to go home.

I took my leave of Tepo, mounted my good chestnut mare and rode down to the Cape under the hot summer sun intending to be gone no longer than six months depending on wind and weather. There I took ship for England and sailed up the African coast on one of Currie's Union line steamers in a state as apprehensive in its own way as when I had last sailed this route. I had changed, but I did not know if my father had and this long question troubled me through the roll and pitch of Biscay, a storm that swept up the English Channel and then the icy Northern gale that drove us up the Thames towards the forest of shipping in the pool of London and past the Tower Bridge then under construction. It troubled me as I wandered around the new buildings of Whitehall while I gathered my courage to take the train and it made my hands tremble when I finally bought my second class ticket from the new station at Liverpool Street to take me to Dines Hall.

What would he say? Would he recognise me? I was different now, as much in appearance as in character and the desert had laid its marks on me in tanned skin and parchment crow's feet. My hair was not so much blonde now as bleached and there was silver in there too and my hands had grown big, my wrists thickened and I was all whipcord and tendon and rawhide. Looking about me, I saw that even my clothes were different. My *veldtschoen* slipped on the wet pavements, reminding me that they were designed for drier places than England and although the cut of my jacket was not obviously different to me, I could tell from the way people smiled a little that I was not in the main flow of fashion. I saw also that my carriage was different; here people walked hunched up against the rain and fog, but I walked tall, not out of proudness or arrogance but because I had grown used to walking with my head up and my eyes on the horizon rather than the pavement. This was probably why I kept slipping on those pavements, hey?

As the train took me through the spring countryside, along Blackthorn hedges so full of blossom that I thought there had been a heavy frost, another question, one that I had long suppressed, began to nag with an insistence that I could no longer ignore. What would I do if my father did not care to see me? I had asked Mijnheer Cronjie to telegraph ahead for me and he had done so; but there had been no reply. I had thought for so long that I needed his forgiveness so that I might have my own self-respect back but now, as the possibility of having it refused - as Daisy had refused it – began to weigh on me, I wondered if I needed it at all. These were all doubts and uncertainties jogged to the surface by the movement of the carriages on the rails and they did not abate as I came nearer to my destination. Instead they jumbled themselves up and interlocked with each other like the horns of the rutting springboks and I decided then and there that I must not go straight to Dines Hall but must lie up in an hotel and bide my time a little and allow my thoughts time to clear. I got off the train in Sudbury and took a room at the Black Boy. I had been there many times in my previous life and wondered if I would be recognised.

It was market day in the town and the sounding of lowing cattle took me back to my own *lolwapa* which now seemed so far away. At the same time, each piece of truckle cheddar that I put into my mouth and each swallow of the good, wholesome beer that the Black Boy provided took me back to my shame at Dines Hall all those years ago and I pondered on whether time or sea miles made up the greater distance between my old life and my new. The beef was very good, well hung so that it fell apart at the touch of a knife and so different from my own

Tswana beef which, though tasty enough, could never be this tender because we had no cool houses to hang it in. This was why we made biltong of it, but I found myself thinking that I preferred my own beef nevertheless and preferred the millet beer and Cape Smoke that Ragwasi and I drank, in preference to the bitter and cognac that was available here. When I ate the potatoes, my mouth watered for mealipap, even though they were good and new and full of flavour. The noise of the vendors and the hurly-burly of the market also intruded on my thoughts because although Sudbury was not a very big town like London or Cape Town or, God forgive me, Kimberley, it was too big for me and I found the loom of the buildings over my head oppressive, as though someone was reading something personal to me by leaning over my shoulder. In the same way, I felt that the windows did not let enough light in and the cries of the traders and stall holders did not let enough silence in so that I could not hear in my head to think and I missed the blue sky, the sough of the wind in the acacias, the cicadas and the cinnamon scent of the earth. I was missing my home; and I realised then that Dines Hall was *not* my home. In truth, I had become an African.

Not African enough to stop the flick of the eye from under that mop of craggy black hair recognising me. There was a momentary surprise quickly veiled and then a wry movement of the gap toothed smile. Big George; fourteen shillings a week Big George; leading a heifer to market and looking in at the pubs for his preferred bidders. Big George; the last person I had seen at Dines Hall and now the first to see that I had returned. Big George; the man who had earned the respect that he was held in. Big George who had said I ought to be served out in the same way that Ezekiel and Judith Stockwell had been served out. Big George, carrying out the sentence my father had handed down to me. Big George who had said that I was on my own, outcast. Big George, who thought slowly, calmly, carefully and was very nearly always right. He saw me through the window and pinned me with eyes that looked all the way back to that time and calculated whether the intervening years had improved me.

Certain that those years had improved me, I made as if to stand but before my knees had time to buckle under the weight of his judgement, he shook his head a little and turned away, tugging at the heifer. I sank back into my seat and watched as he made his way towards the church end of the market, turned off into Gaol lane and disappeared. I was discovered and the word that I was within a march of Dines Hall would be known everywhere by the end of the day because the wagging of tongues carries news in the English countryside every bit as fast as it does on the veldt or in the bush. Tomorrow, someone would come for me. My time for reflection was up.

*

I was up early and hired the Black Boy's cob to take me up to Dines Hall. I reasoned that if my father sent a messenger then I would meet him on the road and, true to my belief that it was always better to have forward motion than to wait for one's fate to arrive hotfoot and with all the advantages, I set out. Ragwasi would have said that I was living life audaciously, I am sure, but I was not sure about this course of action because I had hunted many animals through the bush and had come close enough to lion, leopard and Cape Buffalo often enough to know the importance of caution as a counterbalance to audacity. As I went forward on the Dines Hall road, the sky grey, my heart pewter and the sound of the horse's hooves leaden, I realised that I was in unknown territory however familiar the hedgerows and houses were to my eyes.

Things had changed very little in a physical sense. The trees that I had climbed as a boy were still trees that were climbed by other boys and the springing crops that spread a softening green across the brown loam were the same springing crops that I had helped plant and harvest before. The wind was the same, in the west at this time of year, laden with the scent of coming rain that made the cob pick up its pace as if eager to have this day's work over and be back in her warm stable before the clouds sent down their drenching drizzle. And yet I was older and I saw these things through different eyes. They seemed part of a landscape that I was no longer part of; the desert sand had reached into my bones and rebelled. It was coming on to rain too.

Up ahead on the horizon, about a mile away where the road met a cart track and made a nick in the hill, I caught sight of Big George, his hair and gait unmistakable even in this charcoal light. He was coming towards me on his own cob, unhurried, allowing her to clop along at her own pace, her pendulum hooves marking her own time, like a pencil tapped on a desk by a pensive mind. I halted and let him come to me. I wanted to give him the time he wanted.

'Master Nicholas,' he said, his accent strong, wide mouthed like Ragwasi's, but higher in pitch. 'We 'eard you was comin'.'

'Hello George. How are things?'

'Same old, same old, I would say,' he replied, as his eyes travelled over me, weighing me up. 'Planting, harvesting, hedging, ditching. Life goes on, as they say.'

'How is my father?'

'Best you make that judgement for yourself,' he replied.

'Will he see me? I have had no reply to my communications.'

'Best you find that out for yourself too. But he sent me to make sure it was you I saw in the Black Boy yesterday. And it seems it was.'

'My Mother? Sisters?'

'You must ask your father.'

'The farm?'

'Still working. Your father knows how to manage his business.'

'Is there news of the Stockwells?'

'Not much that is good. We heard they gone foreign.'

'Judith and Ezekiel?'

'Your father found them. They have not prospered. Why have you come back?'

'To make restitution.'

'It may be too late after all this time.'

'Lead on, George,' I said. 'Perhaps something may be done.'

We went past the neat cottages and I saw that there was new thatch on some of them, and clean smocks on the children running in and out of them. The army stud seemed to be prospering too, the field full of shiny chestnut mares, springing turf and bouncing foals. Only the Yellow House stood out from the general wellbeing; its brick chimney stack was twisted and broken, the lime-wash peeled away and the thatch burnt from the centre of the roof, exposing a forlorn set of broken toothed timbers to the sky. George did not look at it, but rode on facing directly forward. This was not something I could rightly countenance though.

'George,' I said, reining in and pulling out a leather pouch from my inside pocket. 'I have money now and however things go with my father, I would see that Judith and Ezekiel were provided for.'

'They are provided for,' he replied, without looking back. 'Money is not everything.'

What was I to do in the face of this stone wall? I pursed my lips, straightened myself in the saddle and went on through the drizzle.

As we came closer to Dines Hall, so the number of familiar faces increased and I noted how so many of my father's retainers had found useful work to do in places where they might gain the best advantage of view. No doubt the house would be full of servants polishing above stairs and neglecting the laundry and kitchen duties too. I was not wrong as I came into the quad through the soughing elms and saw every window filled with faces peering out from under caps, from behind hands held to mouths and through the twitching lace, each eager to see the return of the prodigal son. There was no sound beyond the wind and the reluctant hooves of the horses; the chickens had stopped pecking in the cobbles, the dogs cowered in the corner and even the geese were silent.

My father stood framed by the doorway, wearing his black coat and white stock, white breeches and black boots, his hands behind his back. He had not changed much. He still carried the weight of silence about him and his eyes were as coal black as ever; perhaps he had a little less hair and was carrying a little more weight, but not much. I dismounted.

'Father,' I said.

'Nicholas,' he replied. 'You have been in the newspapers.'

This was something of a surprise to me but I suppose the correspondents who came out with the army must have written down my name in their dispatches; I did not know; I did not read the newspapers.

'Is Mother here?'

'You have not heard?'

I shook my head.

'Two years ago. Consumption. I wrote to tell you.'

It was then that I knew it was too late for me to cross the gap that lay between us. This was not because of anything that my father had said, but simply because of lack of use, lack of contact, lack of conversation, lack of common interest, lack of all the daily rubs and grinds and jokes that bind men together. We had nothing in common anymore. I had broken the connection all those years ago with my stupidity and it was too late for it to be repaired. The scars had healed over and the weals had faded until they were scarcely remembered.

He invited me in, of course, but the subsequent interview in his study merely confirmed me in my first impression. The silence was still there, the same familiar smell of beeswax and tobacco, the same motes in the light, the same tapping of the copper beech against the windows and the same pile of account books, ledgers and business correspondence. Even the ship model was there, unchanged, still sailing, never docking at a home port.

We talked of family, the farm and business more than my African adventures. The estate had weathered many challenges since my departure and had come through them, though not unchanged; the village had shrunk in population as the attractions of full time employment in the towns had drawn the young people away, but there were still enough of the old retainers to make the place look recognizable to the farm I left. My sisters, I was pleased to hear, were married and settled, though neither of them in the neighbourhood. The youngest, Hattie, had been enamoured of a scheme to go to America for a while, I learned later over the coldest dinner I had ever endured, but she had then given it up in favour of a railway engineer from Bath in the West Country. Victoria had married a Norfolk parson; both had many children and had embraced the ordinary life that I had so feared. My father gave no indication as to whether he was pleased or not, though I suspect he was not disappointed. Towards me, he exhibited a wariness as though weighing me up once more and wondering if the rightness of the decision he had made to exile me had been vindicated by the product of that decision now sitting at his table. He was interested in my hunting experiences and interested too in my meetings with Sir Bartle Frere who he considered to be a good man much wronged and he was pleased that I was married and had children of my own; he shared my lack of race hesitation, having been in India, and professed a desire to meet Tepo, Charlotte and Joseph and that they could all be found places at Dines Hall should I so wish it. I smiled at this thought; I could not describe to him what Africa really meant to me and how I had become part of it and how it would be unthinkable to come to England without bringing half of Tepo's clan with me. He was torn, I think, in trying to reconcile the Nicholas Pelly who he had read about in the newspapers – and when I read them, I was not surprised that he was confused because I did not recognize myself in those reports – and the boy he had put aboard the SS African Star. That I had changed in station and appearance was obvious, what he wanted to know was whether I had changed in character and the only way I could answer that question was through my actions; he would never accept words. So the next morning I began to take action. I would acquire forward motion. I took my leave and went back to London.

There are people who say money cannot buy happiness but I have never met one who could convince Ragwasi of that remarkable statement. Reverend Mackenzie once tried to persuade him over a can of coffee and a camp fire but without much success.

'I have been so poor that I have had to sell my soul to a devil,' he had replied, which made the Reverend start, I can tell you. 'And on balance, I prefer to be rich. And if that money is making you unhappy, I shall be pleased to take it off your hands and spend it on buying the thing that you think cannot be bought.' Usually, if Ragwasi thought a proposition was utterly ridiculous, he would underline his rejection of it with a thunderous fart, but because the Reverend was a sangoma, he generally refrained from behaving so badly in his presence.

I was firmly on Ragwasi's side of the argument too; money is a choice and if you have no money, you have no choices and choices are really what freedom is about; and if you have freedom to make a choice then you can choose the ones that make you happiest; and of course, the more money you have, the more choices you are allowed to make. And I *had* money. I had masses of it and because I was a long way from Cecil Rhodes and his diamond monopoly, I could easily sell the diamonds I had found in the Namib without attracting very much undue attention.

A couple of small ice-blue stones were enough to buy back the Yellow house and get it repaired; the biggest problem in buying it back was in finding out who owned it because Salcombe was gone, swallowed up by bigger thieves I heard, and it took a while to find out who the legal owners were. After that, the problem lay in handing it over to Judith and Ezekiel Stockwell without allowing my hand in their restitution to it becoming known because of course, all things are instantly known in a village. In this, I was fortunate to have the help of Mijnheer Cronjie, who recommended a firm of London lawyers so discrete that I had a great deal of trouble finding their offices, but who were able to do things at a distance which were efficacious to the task. Really, I will never understand how legal people can move a piece of paper and the world turns over with it. Knowing also how small villages can harbor big jealousies when good fortune comes to some but not others, I also undertook to have built a village hall which might be used as a clubhouse, pavilion meeting room or school as the Trustees appointed to look after it saw fit, so that the good fortune might be spread more evenly.

I could not, of course, conceal my presence entirely; all the servants knew that I had returned and their gossip – never mind what the newspapers had written about me – would have kept the washerwomen and worthies beating their gums together for a month of Sundays and the gaps in their knowledge that facts had left undiscovered were filled in by rumour and wild speculation. I did not mind, but kept my counsel to myself and my visits to Dines Hall short.

As the time came closer when it would no longer be possible to conceal further my plan to bring restitution to the Stockwells, I began to have second thoughts. Would they welcome my involvement? Would I be able to hand them the keys to the Yellow House without referring to my involvement? Did they know that I was responsible for the death of their son, Luke? Had they received letters to this effect from Daisy? If they did, would not my presence among them cause great distress, even to the point of bringing on a brain fever or some other melancholia? If they did not, would it be right of me to tell them and so break their hearts yet again? All these questions buzzed around and around in my head like hornets when the honey-badgers were breaking into their nests and I confess it was a real moral dilemma to which I had no clear answer. One day, I would steel myself to tell them everything and hope for forgiveness and then the next I would favour the approach of a thief in the night and the more I thought about it, the less sense I could make of it. Under normal circumstances I would have talked it over at long length with Ragwasi as he chewed his biltong but this was not like being out under the desert stars where time is so plentiful it has hardly any meaning at all. I could not stay in England for much longer and I began to feel the approach of that deadline like a hangman's noose dangling around my neck.

The answer came to me as I paced up and down in the very same paddock behind Dines Hall where I had waited to receive news of my fate all those years before. As I watched the green line of the trees sway in the distance, I realised that I was looking at the problem from the wrong way up; the true way of looking at things was really that it did not matter how I felt about the Stockwells' situation but rather how the Stockwells themselves felt about it. Coming all the way here to seek forgiveness from them was really a very selfish thing to do for I would not be healing their old wounds but exposing them again so that I could feel better. By the same measure, giving them the Yellow house would not be making restitution but placing them under a debt of obligation to me that would rankle with them every time they opened their front door. This was not the way a man ought to behave and this meant that the only way I could make proper restitution at all was not to seek forgiveness from them but to recompense them in a way that they could not possibly know that it was I who was making the recompense. My hand could not be exposed.

To this end I conceived a plan which would, I hoped, achieve my aims by a roundabout way and so instructed my lawyers to turn over the newly restored Yellow house to my father in payment for my debt to him. After that, I established a stipend for Judith and Ezekiel Stockwell that purported to come from the estate of a now deceased Boer farmer to whom it was claimed Daisy had once been kind. It was a flimsy façade but one which I knew my discrete lawyers could maintain for as long as Judith and Ezekiel might live and though they did not move back to Dines Hall, they were able to maintain themselves well in the almshouse that my lawyers were also able to arrange for; they would not die in the Poorhouse now but would enjoy a measure of security and independence at least for their remaining years. The arrangement worked well enough and though I did not get the great satisfaction of forgiveness, I could at least live with myself and look in the shaving mirror with a quieter conscience.

So now, the last thing that I must accomplish before returning to South Africa and taking up my African life was to settle things with my father. This I knew would be a difficult undertaking because as I have mentioned already, he was an unforgiving man and I had done much in my youth that required forgiving and I had used up all his stock. In this case, I doubted that all the diamonds in Africa could replenish that stock either and it never even crossed my mind to think that even a mountain of wealth would be of any use at all. It was with a very heavy heart therefore that I set out one last time for Dines Hall; it did not feel very much like forward motion; it felt like wading through a strong flowing drift when you can't see the bottom and the water is up to your neck; but sometimes there is nothing for it; you must just plunge straight in.

Up the drive, under the translucent emerald of the elms and through the barley that swung and shook like the tawny hide of racing lions, the Black Boy's cob plodding and clopping along the familiar way until I was within a hundred yards of Dines Hall and, though I am not a very great smoker, I felt the need to stop and smoke a cheroot; I wished that I had Cape Smoke with me, though it would have been a bad thing to arrive for my interview with my breath afire with Dutch courage, and when I struck a match, I saw that my hands were trembling in a way that they had not done so since the Devil's Pass.

Into the courtyard, where once more my coming had been anticipated and every mullioned window had its servant's cap peering from behind it. I put the horse into the yard, feeling the wings of the house encircle me like that Zulu impi on Hlobane and then, taking my courage in my hands, pulled up and stared straight into my father's face as he waited by the door on the topmost step.

'You have come to take your leave?' he said. It was more of a statement than a question. 'I had anticipated it.'

'Father,' I said, without dismounting from my horse. 'I did what I did and am heartily sorry for it. I cannot undo these things but I have made what amends and recompense I can, little enough and late though it is. Now I would ask that you hear my apology and grant me your forgiveness, though I do not deserve it.'

He looked straight back at me, his black eye as piercing as ever it was, as hard as obsidian and as clear as a diamond.

'I shall not hide from you my disappointment at the way you grew up,' he said, firmly and clearly. 'And I will not blame myself or your mother for the way you turned out. There was a willfulness in you from the beginning, Nicholas, and that willfulness I marked as the harbinger of your downfall earlier in your career than you will have known. I knew that the day must come when you must be taught a hard lesson and I do not regret the lesson that I taught you.'

He looked down at his boots for a moment and then snapped his head back up again.

'But the lesson appears to have been well learned. You are a different man as well you might be. Indeed, you appear to be the man I hoped for, rather than the wastrel I got and I honour you for it, my son. You have my forgiveness, for what it is worth.'

I was ready to leap off that horse and run to him, to shake his hand in pure joy, but he had not finished and stopped me with that imperious hand of his.

'You have seen war and foreign lands; you have wealth, position and a family of your own; so go back to Africa and fulfil your duty to them, for I count your duties here and to me complete. I wish you well, Nicholas. Give my regards to your family. Now be on your way.'

Aye, he could be a cold, old bastard. In that moment I might have turned my back on him forever if this was the best he could do, but he made a quick movement forward and held up a hand to me. I went to shake it before I realized that there was a small package in it.

'Open it,' he commanded.

I did so. Inside was a ring, with a Golconda pear diamond mounted on an Arabian red gold band; my mother's pride and joy; the ring that my father had given her upon their engagement and which she had worn every day of her life.

'Perhaps there is room for one more diamond in Africa,' he said. 'Though it seems to have an embarrassment of them.'

*

And that, I suppose, is that, and this bit of the story of my life has come full circle and can now come to rest like the good brown cattle coming home across the good green veldt and the good red earth of Africa when the setting sun turns all things to cinnamon and umber and that last puff of warm wind comes off the desert to the north. Here now, sitting on my own stoep, on my own farm, with my own wife and children and probably soon some grandchildren too, I am content as far as a man can be content in the troubled times of his life. My father is long gone, of course, and though I saw him again on my odd trips to England I cannot say that we ever made up properly and as fully as a man and his father should do. Certainly I think that the wounds I inflicted upon him as a young man were not so great as the ones he inflicted on himself by tearing me away from the family and sending me into this fortunate exile. Perhaps it is true that the punishment inflicted on a miscreant hurts the person doing the punishing more than it hurts the miscreant. Perhaps; but this philosophising is beyond me, I think and so will leave the last word to Ragwasi, who is the very soul of philosophy once he has a full glass of Cape Smoke and a cheroot.

'This diamond is an *Indian* thing, uPelly?' he said, when I showed him my mother's ring. He was silent for a little while, smoking and drinking, his thoughts running across his brow. 'An Indian diamond from England in Africa. This world is shrinking, uPelly, and I do not know whether this is a good thing or a bad thing.' I waited for I knew he had not finished. 'And all that we have been through is because you gambled your father's cattle away when you were a foolish young man.'

There was still more to come, I knew.

'*Eesh!*' he said, finally. 'And I thought I was foolish to visit the Mamlambo.'

Printed in Poland
by Amazon Fulfillment
Poland Sp. z o.o., Wrocław